DARWIN'S
DECEIT

(✱) **green**hill
https://greenhillpublishing.com.au/

Mulcahy, Liam (author)
Darwin's Deciet
ISBN 978-1-923088-59-7
FICTION

Cover Image by Adobe Stock
Cover Illustration by Liam Mulcahy
Typesetting Calluna Regular 10.5/16
Cover and book design by Green Hill Publishing

In the shadows of history lies a secret
waiting to be uncovered.

DARWIN'S DECEIT

LIAM MULCAHY

"We stopped looking for monsters under our bed when we realised that they were inside us."

CHARLES DARWIN

THE CATHEDRAL

Taranaki Cathedral, New Zealand. 11:45 pm.

THE CATHEDRAL DOMINATED VIVIAN Street, its imposing medieval architecture a stark contrast to the sleek, ultramodern buildings lining the tarred road. Locals whispered that the unassuming sanctuary concealed a treasure trove of secrets and stories, enough to span generations. Yet the cathedral remained silent, its memories only stirred on Sundays when the choir's harmonies and the organ's melancholic wail spilled onto the street.

Throughout the years, numerous vicars had contributed to the cathedral's modernisation. The grounds were now carpeted with manicured grass, framed by trees and lampposts, while the interior boasted updated furnishings. Despite these improvements, the cathedral's ancient roots were undeniable.

Under the cloak of darkness, the streetlamp's glow reflected off the car's polished surface. The vehicle crept along the street, and the tinted driver's side window lowered. A rugged, blonde man with a weathered visage peered out, scrutinising the houses as they inched by. An ugly scar marred his right cheek, and the upper portion of his right ear was missing.

He scowled, expectorated, and spat out into the street. Light spilled from numerous windows—too many for his liking. The neighbourhood was still stirring.

"Hey, Mikey, it seems they're takin' longer than usual to go to sleep," remarked the man sitting beside him.

Mikey sighed and turned his gaze toward the approaching cathedral.

"What are we going to do now?"

"Stick to the plan," he replied nonchalantly, with a noticeably thick Australian accent. "If we're quiet enough, no one will ever know we were here."

Mikey steered the car off the road, stopping mere inches from the cathedral's fence. He checked his wristwatch, exhaled deeply, and sank into his seat.

"What do we do now?"

"Now, we wait, Gareth" Mikey answered calmly.

Mikey carefully studied the illuminated cathedral. It appeared serene and motionless from his vantage point. Gareth reached into his breast pocket, extracting a wrapped sweet. As he unwrapped and popped it into his mouth, he began to make loud chewing sounds which irritated Mikey.

"Shut up!" Mikey angrily demanded.

Gareth appeared to freeze and slowly swallowed the half-chewed sweet.

Moments later, Mikey spotted him—a bald man in a long black cassock exiting the western door. The men observed as he locked the entrance and tested its resistance. Satisfied, the vicar strode away, descending the pedestrian stairway.

Mikey's eyes narrowed as the vicar climbed into a small blue

Toyota. The car's headlights flicked on, illuminating the street as it drove past. He followed its progress in the side mirror until it rounded the bend they'd come from and vanished.

A second later, his phone rang. He picked it up from the dashboard and put it to his ear.

"Hello," he rasped. "Yes. I just saw him get in his car and drive off." He paused.

"Are we good to go?" he asked after a beat.

Another pause.

"Very well then. We'll be joining you shortly."

With that, he ended the call and slipped the phone into his pocket.

"Quick," he whispered urgently to Gareth. "Our window of opportunity is here."

Exiting the car, they closed the doors softly behind them. Mikey scanned the length of the street. Aside from the lights within the houses, no other signs of life were apparent. It was one of those tranquil nights. Finally, after a rough start, things were going in their favour.

"Let's get out of here," he instructed Gareth.

The pair entered the compound via the pedestrian stairway and approached the single door ahead. As they passed through a pool of light, their full profiles were revealed. Gareth, thin with a receding hairline, wore baggy clothes, while Mikey stood tall and muscular in his black denim pants, shirt, and matching boots.

Upon reaching the door, it swung open, disclosing another man. He appeared to be the youngest of the three, but the differences didn't end there. He was also the shortest and had an innocent-looking face.

"Did you take care of everything, Pete?" Mikey inquired.

"Yes." Pete nodded. "The vicar was the last person to leave. I stayed in one of the rooms until he left. There's a bit of a problem, though."

"What is it?"

Pete sighed. "I think it's best if I just showed you."

He led them down a corridor and into the vestry. A pile of clothes lay in the corner. Pete lifted the garments, revealing a body underneath.

From the corner of Mikey's eyes, he could see Gareth's eyes widened in horror as he hastily made the sign of the cross. Mikey's face, however, remained impassive. He stared at the pallid corpse of the elderly man and glanced at Pete.

"What happened here?" he demanded.

"I had no choice. He walked in here while I was hiding. I thought everyone was gone when the vicar locked the door. I was wrong. This guy was doing the final check of the place, I guess, and he found me. He threatened to call the police. I couldn't let that happen."

Mikey shut his eyes and bit the corner of his lip. He preferred for things to go smoothly, without any casualties. But there was nothing they could do at this stage. His eyes snapped open.

"You idiot," he said. "Cover up the body and start searching. We need to find it and get out of here as fast as possible."

Years of experience had taught him to avoid entanglements with the authorities, regardless of the crime's severity. The police were a hard line, and he had no intention of crossing it now.

"We need to make this quick," he told the men.

"Gareth, you're going to walk down the aisle with me."

Gareth gulped in fear but stiffened at the sight of Mikey's glare.

They left Pete to deal with the body and entered the cathedral, awestruck by the stained-glass windows and the one-sided row of wood-covered columns reaching up into the vault above. Against the stone walls, the dark brown vaults and columns harmonised with the overall aesthetic.

"Goodness me," Gareth exclaimed. "It's even more impressive inside."

"Sure," Mikey replied. "But we're not here to discuss architecture and design. Get to work. Start searching at the baptismal font, then move to the left columns." He pointed at the pews on the left. "I'll handle the right. Don't forget to report your findings."

"Aye, aye, boss," Gareth acknowledged.

Gareth nodded again and headed toward the baptismal font. There was a flash of hesitation on Mikey's face.

"Hold on," he called Gareth back. "You know what we're looking for, right?"

"Yes." Gareth nodded. "A cross."

"Great. You'll know it when you see it. It's nothing like the ones you've seen before. It should have that symbol I showed you earlier."

Gareth nodded and headed towards the baptismal font.

Mikey sighed. A fortnight of relentless searching had led him to this point. Before this, he had alternated between various cathedrals, each time starting full of expectations only to end in bitter disappointment. Throughout his hunting career, he had never encountered a search that left him as frustrated as this one.

Maybe he would have been better off pursuing the Javen rhinos that his last employer had been targeting; at least that venture guaranteed a payday. Before this new venture came along, he had carved out a fairly stable existence through such pursuits. Being a man who thrived on opportunities, he had mastered the art of grabbing them as they came and holding on tight. His relentless commitment to seeing things to completion had kept him in the game when others might have abandoned ship.

He had even searched graveyards, having some graves dug up on multiple occasions. This was his third cathedral visit this week.

Typically, it would be just another disappointment. But the intel for this location was different. The previous sites were identified by tracking the cross's historical footprints. They had done the same for Taranaki Cathedral, the last known location of the cross with the engraved symbol. An eyewitness account claiming the cross was still in the cathedral raised their hopes of finally finding it.

Nonetheless, Mikey wasn't one to indulge in notions of hope or optimism. Things either happened or they didn't.

He walked slowly, searching both through and under the pews. He scoured the windows and the walls and ran his fingers over the walls as he did so. There was always the possibility of secret rooms or cabinets behind the walls. This was a medieval building, after all. He kept his hearing sharp as well, not just for when the other men came calling, but for other sounds that could occur during the search.

Nearly an hour had passed, and Mikey was beginning to feel the frustration mounting within him.

So, this is yet another failure.

The muscles in his jaw tensed as he gritted his teeth. He noticed movement in the periphery of his vision.

He spun around immediately, reaching for the back of his waistline, as if to grab his gun. He paused. It was only Pete. Mikey felt the tension ebb from his muscles and withdrew his hand from his weapon.

"What are you doing here?" Mikey asked, a hint of annoyance in his voice.

"I've searched everywhere," Pete replied, "but there is no sign of the cross."

"Join Gareth over there. Let's make this quick and thorough.

We've already been here past the hour."

The trio scoured the entire nave until they ended up at the altar.

Gareth made a hasty religious gesture across his chest.

Mikey glanced at him from the corner of his eye.

Your prayers won't solve this, he thought. *No amount of prayers will help us get what we want.*

He studied the altar. It was more ornately designed than the rest of the nave. Its tall, arched windows towered over them, stretching from the floor to the ceiling. Mikey examined the paintings on the windows when he caught sight of something fixed at the centre of the tabernacle.

He squinted at the object and pushed open the barricade cordoning the altar from the rest of the cathedral. As he walked inside and moved closer, the object became clearer. It was a cross and not just any cross. The cross was ornate and thick, with its horizontal bar closer to the top. More importantly, it bore the symbol Mikey was seeking—the Koru, embedded at its base.

Mikey reached out and tried to pick it up. It wouldn't budge. *Of course, it wasn't going to be that easy,* he thought to himself. He took a step back to look for other clues. On either end of the tabernacle, there were two smaller crosses, neither bearing the symbol.

"Did you find it boss?" Gareth asked as he approached the altar.

"Yes, it's here. But there's something missing."

Mikey walked over to one of the side crosses and tried to pick it up. Unexpectedly, he noticed a mechanism at the base of the cross that allowed it to rotate.

"Check the cross at the other end. Can it rotate?" Mikey called out; his voice echoing across the cathedral.

Gareth walked over. Soon after, Pete joined the two at the altar.

"It's rotating too," Gareth said, with a hint of excitement in his voice.

Mikey pondered his next move for a moment. The plan was to find a cross with the Koru symbol on it. *I've done that. What now?* Then he remembered. He was told if he was stuck, he needed to recall a clue written on the suicide letter.

"Remember me when you come into your kingdom," Mikey recalled.

"What?" Pete looked at him with confusion smudged across his face.

"Do any of you know what that means? Remember me when you come into your kingdom."

"Isn't that what the Good Thief said on the cross next to Jesus?" Gareth chimed in.

"The Good Thief?" Pete asked.

"Yeah. The Good Thief. There were two thieves next to Jesus when he was crucified. The Good Thief asked for forgiveness. The other thief, The Impenitent Thief, didn't care about his fate," Gareth explained.

Mikey walked swiftly back to the centre cross. An idea had struck him. "You two, stand by the crosses at the sides. Gareth, which side of Jesus' cross was the Good Thief on?

"Um, the right side I think," Gareth responded.

"Ok, I want you to turn the right side cross towards the centre.

The left side needs to be turned to face away from the centre. Is that clear?"

The two men nodded and did as Mikey had instructed. Within a few seconds, a 'click' was heard. Instinctively, Mikey pulled the centre cross towards him, exposing it to the full glare of the lights from above.

Suddenly, a grinding sound was heard from beneath the altar as it dragged slowly across the ground. A draft could be felt, rising from the ground. There was a hollow opening underneath the ground, hiding a small chamber. Its entrance was dark and decorated with decades of cobwebs. Mikey stepped into the chamber and turned the torch on his phone for guidance. His men followed behind.

A huge grin blossomed on Mikey's face. But it wasn't the hidden chamber that created fluttering butterflies in his stomach. It was the vial that sat on the floor of the chamber, untouched. Mikey reached down and picked it up.

Finally.

He turned and stared at two of his confrères, his eyes cold and calculating. The vial was held out in his open palm. A clear liquid swished around the vial. He held it up to his eye, examining its contents. Then he beckoned to Pete, the one guilty of murder.

"Come," he said, his voice devoid of emotion.

Pete hesitated but obeyed, his eyes darting between Mikey and the vial. Without warning, Mikey whipped out a jack-knife and slashed at Pete's palm.

Pete inhaled sharply as he grimaced in pain. He held his palm up, gripping his wrist tightly, and stared at Mikey with a mixture of confusion, pain, and accusation.

Mikey uncorked the vial and reached for Pete's hand. Pete recoiled, his eyes filled with apprehension. He had already been stung once; he didn't want a repetition of it.

"Easy," Mikey growled as he glared daggers at the man. He grabbed his hand and poured a few drops from the vial onto the wound on his palm.

The muscles of Pete's arms locked as he bellowed in pain. Naturally, his arm retracted from Mikey, but he stopped, almost abruptly. A quizzical look appeared on his face as he brought his palm up to inspect it. He whipped his face back to Gareth. This time around, he wore a surprised expression. Gareth saw his hand and experienced the same surprise.

A small, sinister smile crept onto Mikey's face as he corked the vial and slipped it into his pocket.

In a flash, he whipped out the gun from his holster, put a bullet into Pete's head, and sent another straight into Gareth's heart. His expression remained cold and unflinching as he shot both men.

Mikey left the hidden chamber and pushed the altar back in its place, leaving the two bodies behind and forgotten. He pulled out his phone and made a call.

"Hello," he said when the call went through, a hint of satisfaction in his voice. "I found it. You were right."

"Good," the voice on the other end said. "We've got work to do."

CHAPTER 1

CAMBRIDGE

AS NIGHT FELL, TRAFFIC snarled its way toward the local school, tension filling the air. Sandwiched between sedans and SUVs was a petite Volkswagen. Annabelle lounged in the passenger seat while her sister, Sarah, clenched the steering wheel, her knuckles white with stress.

"We're going to miss Charlie's recital, for heaven's sake!" Sarah exclaimed. "He's been rehearsing all summer, and I won't let us miss his shining moment. Had we left when I wanted to, we'd be in the front row by now. But no, I had to detour to the airport for you."

A smirk crossed Annabelle's face. "Relax, Sarah. You're morphing into Mom. Remember, Charlie's as much family to me as he is to you. Flying across Europe to be here wasn't just a whim, you know."

Nearly a decade had elapsed since their mother's passing, but Sarah was a living echo of her. Annabelle looked at her sister's dark chestnut hair and grey eyes and felt an odd sense of comfort.

Flipping down the sun visor, Annabelle met her own reflection—ebony locks, deep brown eyes, and plump cheeks. She couldn't help but smile. *I guess I drew the short straw in the gene pool, huh?*

"If I can't find parking, you're staying in the car," Sarah snapped, drumming her fingers on the steering wheel in rhythm with her rising impatience.

"Take it easy, Sarah. That scowl is adding years to your face," Annabelle chided.

Letting out a resigned sigh, Sarah's shoulders slumped. "You know, I don't think you'll ever grow up, no matter how old you get."

With a playful grin, Annabelle shook her head. "Ah, so this is what poor Charlie has to deal with every day, is it?"

Upon arrival to the school grounds, they found the car park nearly full. Annabelle's eyes widened in surprise.

"I didn't realise this was such a big event. Charlie would have been furious if we'd missed it."

"*You*, Annabelle, he'd be mad at you. It's your fault we're late."

"Fine, whatever." Annabelle shook her head, a smug grin playing on her lips.

Sarah strained to see through the darkness as she searched for an open parking space. The dashboard clock read 7:57 pm.

"There!" Annabelle exclaimed, pointing out the window. "I see a spot."

After neatly parking the car, the sisters exited and regrouped.

"Now, where to?" Annabelle asked, shaking her head and ruffling her hair before pulling the loose locks over her left shoulder.

"The hall," Sarah said, pointing in the direction they needed to go.

The hall was in one corner of the school grounds, a few metres away from the main building. It was cordoned off by a low hedge which left enough space in front for the entrance. The sound of music grew louder as they neared the hall.

Annabelle leaned close to her sister. "See, we aren't the only ones getting here now." She nodded towards the trickle of people meandering into the hall.

Sarah clicked her tongue and shook her head. "Don't make me say what I'm thinking."

Annabelle laughed and nudged her sister in the ribs, eliciting a chuckle from Sarah.

Upon entering the bustling hall, Annabelle and Sarah scanned the crowd for empty seats. Luckily, they spotted two available spots next to each other in the second-to-last row. They exchanged a series of "excuse me's" and smiles as they navigated through the seated audience.

"Finally," Annabelle sighed with relief as they settled into their seats.

"So much for the best seats in the house," Sarah muttered.

"Shush, Sarah. You're still going to be able to see your boy from here."

Annabelle looked out onto the stage just as a hushed silence fell over the hall. A child with a flute in hand emerged from behind the curtains.

Annabelle leaned towards Sarah and whispered.

"When's Charlie going to come out?"

"Soon. Now, be quiet and listen."

With a groan, Annabelle straightened up and focused her attention on the stage. The stage lights dimmed, plunging the room into darkness. Excited chatter filled the air until the lights returned, revealing a piano in the corner of the stage and a boy seated at its keys.

"Yes," Annabelle whispered excitedly. "That's our boy, Sarah. That's Charlie."

Sarah smiled and squeezed Annabelle's arm affectionately. Charlie bore a clear resemblance to his family, with his mother's brunette hair and his aunt's full cheeks.

"Hello," Charlie said into the microphone, his voice carrying throughout the hall. Annabelle nearly squealed with delight.

"Good evening to you all," he continued. "I'll be playing an elaborate triadic piece by Frederic Chopin called '*Nocturne in E Flat Major Opus 9 Number 2*'."

"I'm telling you that boy's smarter than both of us were when we were his age," Annabelle said. "Did he just say triadic? Where did he learn words like that?"

"School, Annabelle. Now, shush. Charlie's starting to play."

The audience understood their role, knowing when to speak and when to hold their words. As everyone leaned back in their seats, they listened to Charlie's performance with rapt attention.

Charlie's right hand struck the first notes, seamlessly accompanied by his left. He maintained the E flat chord and guided the tempo with the precision that came from hours of practice. His fingers danced across the keys as tenderly as his mother's kisses brushed his cheeks each night before bed. He closed his eyes and allowed the melody to envelop him.

Although only ten years old, Charlie was already establishing himself as a prodigy. His mother had enrolled him in private piano lessons, carving out a special time in his study schedule for practice.

For some, playing the piano was a gift, a talent, or a skill. For Charlie, it was much more than that. It was the only aspect of his life where he felt truly in control. When he played, he didn't merely command the melody; he became one with it, expressing his love through each note and key. Even at such a young age, it was mesmerizing to watch him perform.

As the notes unfolded in his mind, the muscles in his fingers recalled every movement from his practice sessions. This was the moment—the moment to release it all.

His left hand delighted in the freedom of movement, leaping from key to key, crafting exquisite combinations. What his right hand lacked in range, it compensated for in subtle, intricate finger movements. His fingers nimbly danced across the keys, weaving the notes together into a melodious tapestry. They sped up or slowed as the music demanded, each hand moving independently, every finger striking a different note as though his hands possessed minds of their own. It was simply breath-taking.

Charlie's music filled the silence maintained by the rapt audience, seeping into them like morning dew. Once again, when the final note resounded, there was no immediate response. The audience was so deeply immersed in the music that they didn't realize he had finished.

A surge of pride swelled within Annabelle. Grinning from ear to ear, she broke the ensuing silence with enthusiastic applause. As if on cue, the rest of the audience followed. Charlie beamed as he stood.

"He's marvellous, Sarah," Annabelle gushed. "He's truly special, that boy."

Charlie bowed repeatedly before retreating behind the curtain.

"Oh my God!" Annabelle exclaimed. "I knew he had a passion for the piano, but I had no idea he was this talented."

Sarah shrugged. "You've been away. I've been following his progress, watching him grow into the musician you saw tonight."

"Oh, please, don't be such a show-off."

"I'm not! It's just that I'm the proudest mother on Earth right now!"

As soon as the concert came to an end, Annabelle and Sarah jumped to their feet, joining the swarm of eager parents rushing to see their children.

Annabelle scoured the surrounding area from the moment they got out of the hall. Her face was static, buried in intent. She couldn't think of anything other than finding Charlie.

"There he is!" she exclaimed. "There's our little maestro!" She scurried towards him as she smiled in sweet delight.

Charlie spoke to one of his friends as he waited and was taken aback by the woman that approached him with outstretched arms. His expression transformed the instant he recognised her.

"Auntie Anna!" he cried, rushing into her embrace. "You really came!" He then burst into laughter.

"Of course, I came!" Annabelle looked dreamy as she hugged Charlie. She couldn't get enough of her little nephew.

"Mom!" Charlie squealed when he wriggled out of Annabelle's embrace. He ran into his mother's open arms.

"How did I do, Mom?" Charlie asked as he looked at his mother with glee.

"You were splendid," Sarah replied as she ruffled his hair. "Your aunt and I are so proud of you."

"You know who else would be proud of you," Annabelle chipped in.

Charlie turned to her, his eyes sparkling with anticipation.

"Your grandfather," Annabelle said. "He'd be *very* proud of you."

"Yeah, he would…" Charlie's face lit up. "Mom," he turned to his mother, "can we go see Grandpa?"

"Of course, we can," Annabelle replied, looking at her sister.

The two locked eyes, their silent disagreement playing out in their gazes.

"Your grandfather is busy, Charlie," Sarah said reluctantly.

"Dad wouldn't be so busy that he wouldn't want to see us, Sarah. I just flew in, Charlie just showed us that he's the Chopin of his generation, and you…well, I don't know about you."

"Please, Mom." Charlie tugged Sarah's hand.

Sarah exhaled deeply. She wore her reluctance like a mask. "Alright," she said. "We'll see him tomorrow morning."

Charlie smiled. "Thanks, Mom."

Cambridge University, the pride and joy of Cambridgeshire, stood as a colossal stone giant, a testament to its enduring legacy. Its essence was captured in the robustness of its walls, the magnificence of its medieval architecture, and the intricacy of its ornate spires. The university rested on a vast lawn, encircled primarily by trees and shrubs that swayed gently in the early morning breeze. Nevertheless, all the surrounding flora couldn't rival the age-restrained brilliance of the university, which exhaled silently, attracting people with awe, prestige, and the promise of immersion in academia.

Professor Young strolled down the hallway as he spoke to the small group following behind him. He was a man of medium build and average height with grey hair. A small face lined with wrinkles was at the pinnacle.

At sixty-nine, Professor Young had arguably gathered all the renown he would ever need for this life and the next if he had believed in such a thing. Not one soul shared his expertise on Charles Darwin's work and voyages – aside from the late Darwin himself.

He looked frail and whilst in good health, his body was telling of the years and his devotion to the academia. Nevertheless, his dark brown eyes, which sat behind his round glasses, sparkled with intensity. His speech was steady and measured, so that he could divulge enough without losing his audience. Regardless, those who listened in regarded him with awe. They comprised of the university's board and a few other non-members, but interested parties, nonetheless.

He had been discussing Darwin, as usual, guiding them through the department for the past forty-five minutes. He guided his captive audience toward the auditorium, where they shuffled in to claim their seats.

Unbeknownst to him, Annabelle spotted the procession from a distance. She seized the opportunity to slip in, planning to delight her father with her presence later. Sarah was occupied with Charlie and had declined to join what she deemed a 'childish escapade'.

Nimbly weaving around the back of the crowd, Annabelle chose a seat next to a captivating young man. His buzz cut, trimmed beard, and notably curious eyes made him stand out. She saw him glance at her as she manoeuvred into her seat.

Feeling her cheeks warm, Annabelle murmured, "Don't mind me; I'm not really here."

He chuckled, playing along. "Who said that?"

She giggled in reply and settled comfortably into her seat.

"If anyone has questions, I'm more than happy to address them," the Professor announced.

A woman in the front row piped up, "How did Darwin die?"

Professor Young perked up, "Ah, this is an intriguing subject. The exact cause of Darwin's death remains a matter of speculation."

Seated at the back, Annabelle couldn't help but beam with pride. She relished watching her father in his scholarly element, all while managing to remain out of his direct line of sight. She glanced sideways and noticed her seatmate appeared still amused by her covert antics.

"I'm Annabelle, by the way."

He whispered back, a teasing wink in his eye, "I thought you're not really here?" Then he broke into a warm smile. "I'm Hendrik."

The Professor continued.

"Darwin died due to heart failure and sadly had a deteriorating memory in his last few years. However, for decades he had issues with his stomach. Many believe he may have contracted a parasitic infection from his travels. Others think he may have consumed something that caused chronic stomach issues, leading to heart failure in the end. Whatever it was, the real answer died with him."

Professor Young paused as he waited for more questions. Silence remained. Something had just popped into his mind: one last bit of knowledge for his audience.

"Speaking of Darwin's writings," he said, "Darwin's first edition of *On the Origin of Species* was bought by a secret bidder at an auction, recently."

"What does that mean?" one of them asked.

"Ladies and gentlemen, it means that the location of the first—" he held a finger up "—original edition of Charles Darwin's *On the Origin of Species* is unknown."

He didn't expect them to register any emotion. Not many people were interested in his field or shared the same enthusiasm. However, he loved the feeling it gave him, and there were only few things in this world that could rival that feeling. As he surveyed the room, his eyes landed on a familiar face doing a poor job of staying incognito. A knowing smile spread across his lips; it was time to wrap up.

"So," he declared, clapping his hands together, "I believe that concludes our discussion for today. Wishing you all a splendid day ahead."

The crowd began to stir, rising to leave the auditorium. Hendrik stood, catching Annabelle's eye as he waved goodbye. Just then, Sarah and Charlie stepped into the room.

Professor Young approached the auditorium steps, meeting his daughters and grandson as they descended towards him. Their faces were a welcome sight, signalling the end of his professional duties and the beginning of cherished family time.

"Grandpa!" Charlie yelled in delight. He got up and ran towards the Professor.

"Easy, Charlie," Sarah called after him. "You're going to snap Grandpa in half if you keep up with that momentum."

Her words did nothing to faze the boy. Professor Young laughed as his grandchild ran into his arms.

"Oh, Charlie, it's so nice to see you," he said in between laughter.

He hugged the boy fiercely, and then he looked at his daughters.

"Hello, Dad," Sarah said as she hugged him.

Annabelle walked into the hug and put her arms around them.

"I couldn't wait," she said, sending them all into fits of laughter.

"I heard you flew in yesterday evening?" Professor Young asked Annabelle.

"Yes. Sarah wouldn't let me breathe before she whisked me off to go see Charlie's concert." She gazed at the boy with light in her eyes. "And boy was it worth it."

Professor Young ruffled Charlie's hair affectionately.

"You did well, eh?" he asked.

Charlie nodded.

"Oh, he played wonderfully," Sarah said.

"I'm sorry I wasn't there to see it," Professor Young said. "I had a few things to do here, and I couldn't avoid them. I didn't even have enough time to go to the toilet!"

Charlie laughed.

"I understand," he said.

"There's my boy," Professor Young patted him on the shoulder.

As the foursome chatted, a familiar face returned to the auditorium. It was the tall, attractive young man that sat next to Annabelle, Hendrik. He paused at the doorway and observed the group. He shrugged and walked down the aisle.

"Charlie and I should be going," Sarah said. "I'm going to be getting him a treat after his wonderful performance last night."

"Come on now, you lot just arrived," Professor Young said.

"Don't worry, Dad. We'll come visit you when Charlie's schedule isn't as busy."

"Don't worry, Dad," Annabelle tapped her father on the shoulder. "You and me," she pointed between both of them, "lunch this afternoon. We have plenty of catching up to do!"

Professor Young laughed. "Alright, then. Goodbye, young maestro."

Charlie smiled as he waved at him.

Sarah and Charlie walked past Hendrik with a nod and a smile, before exiting through the hall door.

"Good morning, Professor Young," Hendrik said. His eyes met Annabelle's. They may have lingered a little too long for comfort before he said with a smile, "Good morning."

Annabelle felt her cheeks flush with warmth. She restrained a sheepish smile before she replied. "Nice to meet you for the *first* time."

Professor Young squinted at Hendrik. "Ah Mr. Miller, you were with the group just moments ago."

"Yes," he smiled. "I'd be on my merry way, but there's something I couldn't quite forget. Something you said during the tour."

"Uhm," Professor Young glanced at Annabelle. "It may be best to come back later as I'm catching up with my daughter right now."

"No, no, Dad," Annabelle shook her head. "Speak with him. I can wait."

Hendrik looked at her. A small smile appeared on his face as he mouthed a little "thank you".

Leaning against the wall, Annabelle tuned out the ensuing academic discussion. Having grown up as the daughter of a history aficionado, she'd heard more than her fair share to sustain interest for one day. As Hendrik talked with her father, she couldn't help but notice how striking his features were. From time to time, he would steal glances at Annabelle. She noticed, but she dismissed them as a figment of her imagination, cursing her inner romantic.

"Professor," Hendrik ventured, "what exactly did you mean when you mentioned a hidden location that Darwin never documented?"

Ah, that delicate topic, Professor Young thought before responding with a calculated chuckle. "Well, rumours are just that—rumours. However, there are some enigmatic correspondences and notes Darwin penned during the later years of his life that could potentially validate such claims."

Hendrik's eyebrows knitted together in intrigue. "Enigmatic correspondences? What sort?"

The Professor hesitated, taking a beat to assess Hendrik's genuine curiosity. This was a subject he held close to his vest, something he only discussed when he felt the listener was worthy. A subtle glint appeared in his eyes as if guarding a secret only he was privy to.

"Hold on just a moment," Professor Young finally said, his voice tinged with excitement. "Let me show you."

He left the auditorium through the door on the left side.

Hendrik turned and smiled at Annabelle. He started towards her.

"I owe you a huge debt, for giving up your time with your father," he said.

"Oh, it's nothing," Annabelle chuckled.

"Professor Young is lucky to have such a beautiful daughter," Hendrik smiled.

Annabelle stared at him, shocked at his boldness. He maintained eye contact, holding her gaze as though he were holding her hand. Annabelle laughed quietly before looking away.

Just then, Professor Young's voice wafted in from the other side of the auditorium.

"Ah, I hope you weren't waiting too long."

"No, not at all," Hendrik turned to face Professor Young.

He walked up to them, holding a dossier filled with papers and notebooks. "I hope you can make sense of these."

"I'm probably the saviour that you need in finding out the truth."

Professor Young laughed good-naturedly and opened the dossier. "You're certainly an interesting man, Mr. Miller."

Hendrik stole a quick glance at Annabelle and raised his eyebrows. She rolled her eyes.

Show off, she thought.

Hendrik flipped open the dossier, and a unique light crept into his eyes. Annabelle moved closer, eager to see why both men were so captivated by a pile of papers and old books.

CHAPTER 2

THE HUT

"UM, EXCUSE ME, GENTLEMEN," Annabelle chimed in, nodding toward the folder Hendrik was holding. "Am I the only one who thinks it would be easier to discuss this if we were all sitting down?"

"Sorry, what?" her father looked puzzled.

"I'm just saying, we all seem pretty invested in whatever's in that folder. Maybe we'd be more comfortable hashing it out over a table?"

Hendrik grinned. "You know, she's right, Professor."

"Yes," Professor Young conceded, his smile warm. "It's not often that someone inquires about this aspect of Darwin's journey. I suppose I got carried away."

"I, too, was captivated," Hendrik admitted.

"Please, follow me," Professor Young beckoned as he began to walk. "We should continue this discussion in my office."

Hendrik and Annabelle trailed behind him. Hendrik deliberately slowed his pace, allowing Annabelle to catch up.

"Party pooper," he whispered teasingly.

"What?" Annabelle feigned surprise. "I simply wasn't prepared to stand around all day, exchanging papers and old notebooks."

"Have you seen these before?"

"No, growing up my sister and I never really got into our father's work."

"So, why the interest now?"

"Well, if you bring up secret locations and mysteries, of course I'm going to be intrigued! My dad never mentioned this stuff before..." Annabelle trailed off.

"Isn't it a good thing I showed up then? Maybe you'd never have known." Hendrik grinned.

Annabelle chuckled. "My father relishes any opportunity to share his knowledge of Darwin. He's practically helpless when it comes to his passion."

Hendrik chuckled. "You mean, in the same way a child can't resist chocolate?"

"Exactly."

Professor Young's office was rather spacious. Annabelle glanced around.

"Yep," she said under her breath. "It's still the same place." The brown rug was still there, right at the centre of the room; though the last time she saw it, there was nothing on it. Now, her father's work desk sat upon it. The walls were brown, but most of it was covered by shelves half the height of the room.

Annabelle's eyes moved around the office as awe crept in. She found herself in the midst of an academic haven that needed no further testament. No matter how many times she has been in this office, it never bored her.

"More shelves than any other piece of furniture," Hendrik observed, awestruck. "I'm beyond impressed, Professor. My own modest collection at home pales in comparison. Gazing upon this—" he gestured toward the shelves and their abundance of volumes "—makes me feel as if I've squandered my time."

"If you'd lived as long as I have, you might have amassed a similar collection."

Hendrik chuckled. "I sincerely doubt it."

Professor Young cleared his desk and set the dossier aside. He retrieved several old notes and spread them across the surface.

Annabelle playfully nudged Hendrik in the ribs. "Story time," she whispered, raising her eyebrows conspiratorially.

Hendrik laughed. "I do love stories. Don't you?"

"Well," Annabelle winced as she tossed her head from side to side. "I do, but I prefer tales that diverge from history."

"You might actually enjoy this one."

"Most of what you see here," Professor Young indicated the notes sprawled across the desk, "are original writings by Darwin." Hendrik and Annabelle leaned in for a closer look. "You see, Darwin and some of the *HMS Beagle* crew chronicled their daily activities in logbooks or diaries."

Hendrik whispered to Annabelle, "The *HMS Beagle* is the ship Darwin—"

"She knows what the *HMS Beagle* is," Professor Young interjected, glancing up from the notebooks. "She told you my stories were boring. She never said she didn't listen."

Annabelle restrained a smile and tucked in a lock of her hair behind her ear. She pretended to be too engrossed in the faint writings in the old notebook to care.

Hendrik chuckled and shook his head. "I'm sorry for the interruption, Professor. Go on."

"Darwin was meticulous in his notetaking," Professor Young resumed. "Take this, for example." He slid one of the notes closer to the pair and pointed at a page. "This entry documents his departure from the Galápagos Islands on October 20th, 1835. He recorded every detail: the ship's approach to land, his disembarkation, and the

26

fossils and animals he encountered on the island."

"Darwin certainly had an eye for detail," Annabelle remarked.

"Indeed," Professor Young agreed. He leafed through another notebook and placed it atop the previous one. "This entry, from November 1st of the same year, was written while the ship was still at sea. Darwin mentions that the crew had sighted land in the distance and anticipated reaching it by day's end."

Hendrik frowned. "But that seems to be where this particular entry concludes."

"Why?" Annabelle asked.

"You've got a good eye, Mr. Miller," Professor Young noted.

"Hendrik is fine, Professor."

"Hendrik it is then." Professor Young waved. "But if you look closely..." He traced a finger along the middle of the notebook, "you'll see—"

Annabelle gasped and her eyes flew wide open. "I see it now. Torn pages."

"Precisely," Professor Young confirmed. "And it's not just one section. Several are missing. The subsequent entry is dated November 17th, and there's still mention of a landmass in sight."

"That's two weeks of silence between the first entry and this one," Hendrik noted. "Two weeks of information, gone."

"That's not the only one." Professor Young straightened up. "There are other log entries that have been torn off in similar fashion-- right at the beginning, excluding whole pages of experience. It's not just Darwin's notes. It's that of the *HMS Beagle* as well. The crew were keeping something quiet."

Puzzlement clouded Hendrik's features, mirrored to a lesser extent by Annabelle. Hendrik scratched his forehead with a finger.

"What were they hiding?" he asked. "They documented every other aspect of their voyage; why not this?"

"Actually," Annabelle picked the note up. "They did record it. Someone just tore it all out."

"All the same," Professor Young said. "I've been asking myself the same question for years. The closest I've ever come to an answer is that there's a secret island the crew never wanted anyone to know about. It was as though they encountered something sacred."

"By the look on your face, something says you don't believe that," Annabelle said. "Do you?"

"I don't know," Professor Young shrugged. "Personally, I think something happened. Something that shouldn't have happened. And they decided to keep it quiet either for their own safety or so that others wouldn't find out"

"Hm." Annabelle pursed her lips. She looked through the notes again, and then she frowned. "Dad?"

"Yes."

"There's an odd piece of paper attached to the note here," she pointed at it. "What is it?"

"Oh, that? There are pieces of paper like that attached to several other notes. I haven't been able to make any sense out of them."

"Meaning they don't have any context?" Hendrik asked.

"I'm sure they do have meaning behind them. Someone wrote it down. I just can't seem to place that context."

Annabelle read out the words on the piece of paper:

CHARLES & ANNA, TRUTH KEPT BEHIND MOON ART

Hendrik narrowed his eyes and tucked in his lower lip. He reached out for the note. "Mind if I take a look at this?"

"No problem." Annabelle let him have it.

The trio sat around the table, attempting to decipher the paper's contents.

"Who's Anna?" Annabelle asked as she noted the shared name.

"Well, Darwin had a daughter called Annie, so it may be

addressing her as well," Professor Young suggested. He frowned and softly spoke to himself, "but that doesn't make sense. She was only ever called Annie or Anne."

"It's possible," Hendrik said, "that this line is a riddle."

"It's possible that it isn't too," Professor Young said.

"Yes."

Annabelle mulled over the words "Moon Art". *Sounds like the name of a painting,* she thought.

"Uhm," she ran her tongue over her lips. "Was Darwin close to any artists in his lifetime?"

Professor Young frowned in thought. "I'm not sure if I'd say they were close, but Darwin did share something of a friendship with the artist on board the *HMS Beagle*. I mean, they were on the same ship for some time after all. Conrad Martens was his name. He left the ship halfway through their voyage in South America in 1834. The two saw each other again when Darwin arrived at Sydney around the 12th of January in 1836, just over a year after his departure from the voyage."

"That's curious," Annabelle said. "The two of them met each other shortly after the two weeks missing from the diary. Could Darwin have told him about their mysterious experience?"

"I don't know. But it's a possibility. It all depends on how close Darwin was to Conrad.

"Well," Hendrik said, "if Moon Art is a reference to an artist's work, then Conrad Martens is a lead."

"You know," Professor Young said as he remembered an old thought. "I think I thought that too when I first came across this note. I did my research. Conrad Martens never created something involving the Moon specifically, or any other artwork that was related to the Moon. So, it seems unlikely he's the artist. Then again, I could be mistaken."

Annabelle took the paper from Hendrik and pored over it. On the back of the note was a small sketch:

"A hut?" Hendrik noted.

There's something here, Annabelle thought. *But whatever it is keeps eluding me.* She felt like she was supposed to pick out something from the note –- something that she had seen before.

Then it hit her. *Conrad Martens.*

She picked up a pen from her father's desk and took out her notebook from her leather bag. She rewrote the note and crossed out some words from the line.

"What are you doing?" Professor Young asked, now even more curious.

Annabelle handed her notebook to him, and he stared at it.

CHARLES & ANNA, TRUTH KEPT BEHIND MOON ART
~~CHARLES~~ & ~~ANNA~~, ~~TRUTH~~ KEPT ~~BEHIND~~ ~~MOON~~ ART
CONRAD MARTENS

Hendrik peered at the page and chuckled. "You're a genius, Annabelle. Anybody ever tell you that?"

"Yes," Annabelle beamed. "My father."

Professor Young gave her a smile.

"So, it's an anagram," Hendrik said. "Let's see what letters are left."

HLE NA UTH KEPT BHIN O ART

The trio segued into a variation of scrabble. They spent time rearranging and reordering the remaining letters in an attempt to arrive at something legible.

- *UNPAINTABLE? LANTERN?*
- *THE, ON, TO, AN, BUT, IN, AT BARK?*
- *BOAT? HUT?*

Just when they were about to give up, Hendrik smiled. "I think I've figured it out. The drawing of the hut is a clue. It's one of the words."

He took the pen and wrote the answer.

THE BARK HUT ON THE PLAIN - CONRAD MARTENS

"What does that mean?" Professor Young asked.

Hendrik was all smiles now. He wrested the award of most intuitive person in the room from Annabelle. "It's a painting, Professor. One of Conrad's paintings. I believe I've seen it at an exhibition."

Annabelle perked up. "And the truth, whatever it is, must be behind that particular painting!" Her heart began to race. She felt like she was back at school; back on the tracks where she prepped up for a race, feeling the pulse of her heartbeat in her ears, willing the race to be over, and sailing the wind when the gunshot went off. It was years since she last felt that thrill. Just like back then, she was eager to get off the blocks.

Professor Young narrowed his eyes as he stared into nothing. He was neck deep in a mire of thought. The recent revelation opened up a series of implications, a system of paths. It created a way where there was once a solid brick wall.

"If truly a secret island does exist," he said. Then he broke off and tittered. "The possibilities are endless. Can you imagine what that means? What it entails? Charles, the explorer, the discoverer, saw an island that he chose to keep off the books. An island probably teeming with organic life. An island untouched by external human influence."

"External?" Hendrik cocked an eyebrow. "Are you suggesting that there may be an indigent human population in this theoretical secret island?"

"It's a possibility. Not all islands Darwin discovered were uninhabited. If this secret island was large enough to support plant and animal life, it's also worth factoring in the possibility of human existence. Oh!" he gasped. He felt rejuvenated. Like fresh blood that coursed through his veins, filling him with vigour and sharpening blunt edges.

He sighed as he felt his spirits drop. It was as though his temperament had been on a wild run and was now petered out. Even as he sat, he felt his bones ache, and his body asking for rest.

"This painting," Annabelle said, "where can we find it?"

"Sydney," Hendrik said.

Annabelle was confused. "How do you know that?"

Hendrik smiled, "I paid for that exhibition I saw it in last year. It was part of a conference tour."

"Forgive me, Hendrik. I should have introduced you properly earlier, but I got carried away as usual," Professor Young apologised. "Annabelle, this is Hendrik Miller, he runs *Apate's Pharmaceuticals*."

"Oh," Annabelle replied with a hint of surprise, "you don't strike me as a businessman."

Hendrik laughed. "Anyway, let's not steer off topic. Sydney is where the painting is."

"Well, I've got to be there. I've got to be part of this."

Hendrik chuckled. "Why don't we all go together? You cracked the first code. I cracked the second, but that's because you paved the way. Who knows, your insight may prove useful going forward."

"Exactly!" Annabelle's eyes blazed with joy.

"Well," Professor Young got to his feet. "For a moment there,

I almost felt like I was a youngling again. But I'm old, you see." He smiled. "There's not a thing in the world I can do about that. This sort of crumbs-along-the-trail-travelling is over for me. The only journey I should be thinking of is the--"

"Don't you dare say those words," Annabelle blurted. Her expression was stern.

"Alright, alright!" Professor Young chuckled, raising his arms as if to surrender. "What I'm getting at is, my adventuring days are behind me. These days, I'm more at home behind a desk, in the study, or at social functions. Mr. Miller, I entrust you to venture forth and keep us informed of any discoveries."

Annabelle sprang up. "I'm going too, Dad. I want to know what's being hidden."

A look of hesitancy crossed the Professor's face. "Would you like to take Sarah with you? Or what about that friend of yours in Sydney? Nick, was it? Neville?"

"It's Nigel," Annabelle corrected, "and I'm perfectly capable of traveling solo, thank you."

Hendrik interjected, "Rest assured, Professor, your daughter will be in good hands."

Professor Young chuckled again. "Knowing Annabelle, it's you who should be at ease, Mr. Miller."

Annabelle grinned. "You heard him, Hendrik. You're safe with me."

Hendrik laughed. "I have no doubt. Let's plan for the end of the week. Contact me when you're ready, and I'll sort out the flights." He handed her a business card inscribed with his contact details.

As Hendrik exited, Annabelle lingered. She sensed her father had something more to say.

"Annabelle," he began, "if this clue leads you somewhere, exercise caution. I don't want another *Loch Arkaig* incident."

"Seriously, Dad?" Annabelle exclaimed. "I can't believe you're still holding onto that. I was only sixteen!"

"You were arrested," he pointed out.

"And released when they realised I'd done nothing wrong!"

"Fair enough," the Professor conceded. "Just be careful. Darwin encountered the awe-inspiring and the unimaginable on his journeys. If he kept something under wraps, there's likely a good reason. Keep that in mind while you're out exploring. Don't let me down."

"Don't worry, I won't. Love you." Annabelle planted a kiss on her father's cheek. "I'll swing by later and we can grab lunch."

"Love you too, Annabelle," he replied as she left the office.

Watching her go, Professor Young had one lingering thought: *Do the right thing.*

CHAPTER 3

EXHIBITION

Sydney, Australia.

THE FLIGHT FROM LONDON to Sydney unfolded uneventfully, as Hendrik and Annabelle passed the time sharing stories about themselves. Upon disembarking, Hendrik promptly called a hotel to book two rooms. Throughout the call, Annabelle stole furtive glances at him, captivated by his commanding presence. He exuded an air of authority, as though he expected the hotel to cater to his precise demands. She had encountered such individuals before—people unaccustomed to having their requests denied. However, Hendrik seemed to differ slightly from the rest; he wasn't condescending, or at least she hadn't witnessed that side of him yet. Though he initially struck her as a reserved man, he had continually demonstrated his conversational prowess.

Sighing, she gazed out the taxi window. The streets bustled with activity, as daylight illuminated the vibrant city. Sydney remained unchanged since her last visit, brimming with life, vehicles, and buildings. Such cities always shared the same characteristics—dynamic and teeming with energy.

"Thank you very much," Hendrik said, ending the call. "You'll be seeing us shortly."

He slipped the phone into the pocket at the front of his jacket. Annabelle gazed out the window. The breeze from the half open window combed through her hair, pulling it backwards. Hendrik broke the silence.

"Have you been here before?" he asked.

Annabelle turned away from the window and smiled.

"What?"

"I was asking if you've been to Sydney before."

"Yeah." A few strands of her hair flickered in the wind. She put them back in place. "I've been here several times for research. I work in environmental sciences."

"Ah. You didn't look like it some seconds ago."

Annabelle narrowed her eyes a little. There was a small smile on her face. "Did I do something that contravened the code of conduct for Sydney regulars?"

Hendrik laughed. "Code of conduct for Sydney regulars," he repeated. "You're funny, Annabelle." He smiled and shook his head.

"Really?" The small smile became a proper smile. *"Funny how? Like a clown funny? I amuse you?"*

Hendrik laughed again. "I love that line. *Goodfellas* is one of my favourite movies."

Annabelle felt as though she floated on the acoustics of his laughter. It was nothing musical. There was a genuineness in it, and that was the hook that reeled her in.

"To answer your question," he said, "it was the way you looked out the window. It was like you couldn't get enough of every single thing you saw."

"Oh, that." She stole another glance outside, where she could see the red and white trams running smoothly along the adjacent

36

streets. "Sydney's one of my favourite places. Each time I'm here, I want to soak everything up."

"Really? I feel it's too overcrowded. Most times, I'm here, it's for a pharmaceutical assignment."

"Hm." Annabelle raised her brows. "I don't think Sydney's overcrowded. Don't get me wrong. Its population is larger than others in Australia. But it's just like New York. It teems with people, and that generally means more fun, more social experiences."

"I don't like New York either."

Annabelle playfully tilted her head as she assessed him. "You don't mean that."

"I do," he said. "I prefer places that are relatively quiet. Too quiet is not good. It makes me feel like I'm a retiree just waiting out my time on earth."

Annabelle placed a hand over her mouth as she guffawed. "You're the worst, Hendrik."

He smiled. "I've been told worse."

Annabelle paused. "Do you mind if I ask you something personal?"

Hendrik's face became serious. "Sure, but I may not answer it."

"I was reading up on your company, *Apate's Pharmaceuticals*, while we were travelling here. Forgive me for asking, but didn't your company collapse after one of the failed drug trials a few years ago?"

There was a slight sting on Hendrik's face. Annabelle noticed his attempt to conceal his emotions. The topic at hand was evidently something he held close to his heart, and it was rare to see him so visibly uncomfortable.

"Well, it didn't *collapse* but it did take a significant hit. I learned from it. You see, there are protocols in place for any new drug that's going to enter the market. It must go through a series of trials before it can be safe for use. I knew our drug was safe-- and it's still safe-- but we got caught trying to hurry the process and skipped a few protocols to put it out on the market. The fine we received hurt our business. So, in turn, we've been slowly recovering from it. That's all there is to say."

Hendrik looked away from her and began to swipe through his phone. Sensing that he didn't want to discuss the matter further, Annabelle respected his privacy and returned her attention to the window.

"I'd really love to take a little tour of the city."

"I'd love that too, but there's nothing we can do until we find what we're looking for."

Annabelle faced him. "Is it always business with you?"

"No." He shook his head. "I know how to have fun too. I just think this is too important to relegate to the background."

Annabelle shrugged. "If you say so. I flew all the way to England to watch my nephew play, had lunch with my father, and now I'm sharing a trip with a total stranger after taking a twenty-hour flight to get here. So much is going on in one week that I don't know what's going to happen next."

"I'm not going to kidnap you. So, you've got no need to worry about that."

"You couldn't even if you tried to."

They both laughed.

"Why are you here though?" Annabelle asked, her eyes studying Hendrik as if he was a curious relic on one of her father's shelves.

"Isn't it obvious? I'm here because you're here." He winked. "I could ask you the same question as well."

Annabelle gave a look that wasn't satisfied with his response. Hendrik stared at her and sighed.

"It's not more than mere curiosity, if you look at it. I've always been a staunch admirer of Charles Darwin, ever since I first heard of him in school. The idea that someone could leave the comfort of his home and venture into uncharted territory was just so fascinating to me. And upon all that, he found something useful. He introduced the world to the concept of evolution. If there really is a place, he didn't let the world in on, I'd like to follow in his footsteps and discover such a place."

"You don't strike me as someone who's interested in that sort of thing."

Hendrik chuckled. "I don't strike people as being interested in a number of things."

"You can't blame them. You're practically golden boy material. Not the one that's frivolous and likes to boss over everyone in parties. The other kind, the reserved kind, the kind that's used to having everything his way, and grows into ruling an empire that's been waiting eagerly for his reign."

Hendrik laughed. "You really put a lot of thought into this."

"Nope." Annabelle shook her head. "I've just seen enough of you people to spot one when I see one."

"So... is that a bad thing?"

"That remains to be seen. But seriously. I thought you'd be focused on running your pharmaceutical company or something."

"Well, I'm here. With you." Hendrik smiled.

"Ha ha ha," Annabelle replied wryly.

They dropped by the hotel, checked in and dropped their luggage off. After lunch, they headed straight for the Art Gallery of New South Wales.

"I've never been here," Annabelle said as they stepped out of the taxi. She gazed at the imposing edifice. "Does it always have this many people?"

Hendrik surveyed the crowd gathered around the entrance. "The Art Gallery has its days."

"Let me guess. Today's just one of those days."

The Art Gallery looked like a relic straight out of ancient Greece times. Its stone façade was reminiscent of the old temples the Greeks built in honour of the Olympians – complete with an entrance with crepidoma, entablature, and pediment. The only difference was that it wasn't crumbling. Its form boasted strength.

Right on its frieze were the words "Art Gallery of New South Wales". To the left stood a black sculpture of a man on a horse. With his left arm up, he looked like he was frozen right in the middle of making a declaration.

Hendrik and Annabelle sifted themselves through the crowd gathered on the stairs, passing between the colossal columns towards the entrance.

"So, what are we looking for?" Annabelle asked as they walked in.

"The bark hut on the plain."

"I know that much. What does the painting look like?"

"Oh. It's, uhm, it's a painting of a plain. The colours are dull, mostly brown from what I remember. There aren't very many details aside from a hut and little shrubbery."

"Great."

"I spotted it back when I used to run exhibitions here for a friend."

"So, you lived here?"

"Sort of." Hendrik looked away like he had just given out an embarrassing bit of information.

"That's probably why you hate it here."

"Perhaps."

"You know where this painting is then?"

"I think so. With any luck it should still be at the same place."

They passed by clusters of people that were admiring or taking photographs of sculptures and paintings. The artwork displayed, were the most bizarre pieces of art Annabelle had ever come across. There were so many of them and all in one place. She felt as though she just walked into a shrine where each section, glass case, pedestal or corner of the wall that held an artist's work was a centre of worship.

"This place is a treasure trove," she said to no one in particular.

"It's funny how you're just noticing that. A lot of artists have their original works here. I'm talking about rare stuff that would go for millions in the market."

"You don't say."

They walked through an arched doorway into a smaller room as their footsteps echoed off the brown wooden floors. Inside, the paintings hung on the white walls.

"You see those black frames by the pillar over there?" Hendrik pointed toward three small frames hanging vertically.

Annabelle nodded and stared at the frames in question. "They're Martens' works. But none of them are what we're looking for."

They moved on and took another doorway.

"My God, this place is huge," Annabelle gasped as she admired her surroundings.

There was a sense of awe in her voice.

"They're so many rooms in here, it's so easy to get lost," she continued.

"That's why most people go with a guide. It's a good thing I've been here before. Having a guide take us to the painting would have been the worst of ideas, considering the nature of our visit."

Soon, the ambient aesthetics which surrounded them changed. It was as if they had walked into a different world. These rooms were different. As if being painted red where others were white wasn't enough, the painting on the walls didn't enjoy as much attention as others. They walked into a more secluded section of the gallery. The room was empty.

"We're here," Hendrik announced as he walked into a room with a low dark brown table in the middle. Annabelle turned and followed every painting on the red wall with her eyes until she turned full circle. She was in love with the arrangement. The frames had been kept equidistant from each other, so that viewers could focus on a particular painting long enough without getting distracted by the next. Anyone who wished to see another would simply move along.

"It's here somewhere," Hendrik said. "I can't remember its exact spot. So, start looking."

Hendrik took the left while Annabelle took the right, and they worked their way forward.

"A plain background," she muttered as she scanned the paintings. "Drab colours, a lonely hut, few shrubberies."

Suddenly, she gasped, and her eyes widened.

"I've found it," she called out to Hendrik.

"Shh," Hendrik said as he bounded across the room with quick strides. "You don't want to be calling other people in."

"I'm sorry," Annabelle whispered.

One look at the picture and Hendrik smiled.

"The bark hut on the plain."

Annabelle stared at the picture. There was a lone man on a horse looking back at a woman in front of the hut. She couldn't see their facial expressions, but she thought they were just as sad as the lonely hut and the vast plains in the backdrop. She loved the way the artist had used watercolours.

This Conrad Martens was no amateur painter, she thought.

"Now, we need to remove the painting without being caught." Hendrik ran his eyes over the entire frame. "According to the letter, the truth is hidden at the back."

Annabelle looked behind her. The room was just as it was when they walked in: empty and quiet. To her surprise, there were no cameras in this room either, only one outside, monitoring the doorway to the room. She looked at Hendrik. He could see it too. There would never be a better time.

Hendrik pulled the bottom of the frame gently from the wall. He lifted it off the hangar and whistled.

"What's the problem?" Annabelle asked as she moved her eyes from painting to the man who now turned red.

"It's heavy, too heavy considering its size."

"It's the gold framing, probably."

"Yeah. It won't be easy to walk out of here with this thing."

Annabelle stared on with burning interest as Hendrik turned the painting over. It occurred to her that she hadn't thought twice when Hendrik talked about taking the painting out of the room. *Since when did we become art thieves?* It was not possible to leave here with it. They had to do whatever they needed to do here, instead.

However, as interesting as their current task was, Annabelle couldn't stop the feeling of dread that crawled over her skin. She stole frequent glances at the door and hoped that no one would walk in. They were walking on very thin ice.

"Um, Hendrik?" Annabelle asked nervously.

"What is it?"

"You mentioned that you paid for an exhibition here before. Wouldn't this be easier if you got in touch with the owner or someone you know? I feel like that would be safer than risking being arrested."

"Let's just say I didn't end on good terms with the manager. Besides, we're going to be fine."

Hendrik turned the picture in different angles and held it against the light.

"There's nothing at the back," Hendrik said after a while. "We need to open it."

Annabelle felt her heartbeat spike. She checked the door, then bit on her lower lip. *Why does stuff like this always have to be difficult? Why can't the answer just present itself happily on the back of the frame.*

Yet, she knew she would leave unsatisfied if the clue had presented itself as easily as she wanted. The chase, the intense brainstorming, was all part of the adventure.

Annabelle sighed and tried to still her nerves. She signed up for this, and she will see it through.

Hendrik reached under his coat and pulled out a screwdriver.

Annabelle's jaw dropped.

"What the hell is that?" she asked.

Hendrik glanced at her and smiled. He began to unwind the screws holding the canvas to the frame. "It's always good to come prepared."

"You had this planned all along, didn't you?"

"No. I just like to prepare for eventualities. I had a feeling I would need this."

Annabelle looked towards the door. "I hope you have preparations for the eventuality that we're caught.'

"Of course. Why would I be here if I didn't prepare for that?"

"Alright, then what's your plan?"

Annabelle knew she should keep shut so Hendrik could work faster but talking helped take her mind off things.

"Simple. The hope that we won't get caught."

"What?" Annabelle held herself from shouting.

"See," Hendrik held an open palm in front of her. "Done." She stared at the cluster of screws that nested in the middle of his palm.

"This wouldn't have been possible if this were the Mona Lisa."

Hendrik chuckled lightly. "Tell me about it."

Hendrik removed the protective casing from the back of the canvas. He ran a finger across the back until he felt a lump. "I feel something.'

"Yeah?" Annabelle perked up.

Hendrik pulled out a jack-knife from his coat. The colour drained from Annabelle's face.

"Come on, Hendrik. We've done enough already. You could damage the painting."

"I've got this." Hendrik licked his lips and tucked the lower lip in. A small cut was made across the edge of the slight lump on the canvas. He used the tip of the blade to bring out the object underneath and looked at Annabelle. "It's paper."

"Probably, a note," she replied.

Hendrik opened it. "It's a letter. And it's dated 1867 from London."

They looked at the words scrawled across the piece of paper.

THE SECRET REMAINS WITH THE FOUR KINGS AT THE END OF THE UNARMED VISCOUNT'S SWORD.

E.L. (LONDON, 1867)

Annabelle frowned. "What does this mean?"

"I haven't the faintest idea. We need to put this back." Hendrik put the paper in his pocket, then proceeded to screw the painting and the frame together.

Suddenly, Hendrik and Annabelle looked up at the same time. They stared at each other; their eyes carried the same look – fear. They heard it at the same time, and it got louder by the second. Footsteps.

Hendrik looked at his palm. There was only one screw left. Annabelle's heartbeat surged. She felt a violent current of water beat against her chest that aimed to break free.

"Crap," Hendrik said. Immediately, he got to his feet. He grabbed Annabelle's hand and put the screw in her palm. "I'll distract whoever's coming. Put in the last screw and hang the painting back up."

"But it's heavy," Annabelle protested, but Hendrik was already off.

"Just do it," he said and disappeared out through the doorway.

"Crap crappity crap," Annabelle said, trying to compose herself.

She was aware of how hard her hands trembled. *Okay, you got this. Deep breaths. Take deep breaths.* She briefly shut her eyes and breathed through her mouth. Her hands still trembled, but not as much as before. She put in the last screw and tried to place the painting back on the wall.

"This is really heavy," she complained under her breath as her muscles ached from the effort.

The painting was just placed on the wall when someone yelled behind her.

"Oi!"

Annabelle spun around, almost carrying her heart in her hands. The doorway was filled with security guards, and Hendrik was among them.

Annabelle breathed a sigh of relief. *This will be over very soon.*

"Look guys," she raised her hands, "it's not—"

"That's her," Hendrik pointed at her. "That's the woman I was telling you about. I tried to stop her from stealing the painting, but she wouldn't listen."

Annabelle stood rooted to the spot like a statue. She stared with wide-eyed shock at Hendrik. It was as if her ability to speak had been stolen.

"I'm very good friends with the owner here," Hendrik continued. "And I won't stand for aberrant acts like this."

The security men strode into the room, put Annabelle in cuffs and whisked her away. As they dragged her out of the room, she stared at Hendrik. She couldn't get her tongue to move yet, but the look in her eyes was as clear as day. There was shock. Surprise. Sour disappointment. But above all else, disbelief.

It was a good while before Annabelle's tongue came back to life, and she tried to use it on the security guards who apprehended her.

"Look, guys. Things aren't as bad as you're making it out to be. I don't know who that guy was that brought you in, but I wasn't trying to steal anything."

Annabelle was banking on the absence of CCTV camera footage to get herself out of the mess. However, the security guards were as stoic as the Stoics themselves. Annabelle's shoulders slouched as she sighed.

"Okay, look. I'm going to lay it out plain for you. I'm going to give you the truth, okay? This is how it all happened: I'm an ardent fan of Conrad Martens," she placed a hand on her chest in self-justification. "All my friends know that. I came in here just to see his work. Then I saw that particular one, 'the bark hut on the plain', hanging at an odd angle. You simply—" she shrugged "—caught me trying to right it."

The security guard, a barrel of a man with a mean face laughed.

"You think I'll believe that?"

Annabelle stared at him. The hope already crawled out of her eyes.

"I'm not an idiot. I know what you were trying to do," the security guard said.

Annabelle sighed and let her head loll. *How did I get in this mess?* She thought of Hendrik and felt a twinge of disappointment. She had allowed someone to get close to her again, only to feel let down. *You're an idiot for being too trusting Annabelle! When will you learn.*

"Please," she lifted her head and looked at the security guard. "Help me out here, okay? I'm innocent. Just give me a phone so I can call a friend."

Reluctantly, the security guard passed her own phone back to her.

"You've got thirty seconds," he said.

"Come on," Annabelle protested, but the man shoved the words down her throat with a hostile stare. "Alright."

Annabelle tapped the digits on the touchscreen, heard the dial tone begin and waited.

"Hello, Nigel," she blurted as soon as the call went through. She was relieved. "Please, I'm in a bit of a mess, and I need your help getting out."

An hour later, Nigel showed up. He had a strong presence, with an upright posture. His dark skin showed off his muscular build. He was much taller than Annabelle.

"What is she being detained for?" he asked the security guard.

"Stealing," the guard spat.

Annabelle tried to speak, but Nigel held a hand up. She swallowed her words and reclined on her seat.

"Stealing?" Nigel chuckled. "Stealing what?"

"One of the paintings by Conrad Martens in the display room. Just to the left as you walk in." The guard stared at Nigel, unsure of where he was going with his questions.

Nigel laughed. "Come on, man. Have you ever tried lifting any of the paintings in this Gallery?"

"Erm..." The guard frowned.

"Then you'll probably start seeing how ridiculous your claim is. Look at the size of this woman—" he pointed at Annabelle "—and consider the weight of that painting. Does it look like it's something she can lift? Let alone cart off?"

The man didn't say anything. But the frown on his face had just deepened. He shifted uneasily on his chair.

"Do you have any evidence?" Nigel asked.

"I saw her."

"Saw her? Was she escaping with it or trying to put it back on the wall?

The operative remained silent.

"How then, I might ask, did you arrest her?"

"There was a witness. A man."

"Where's this witness now?" Nigel looked around the room.

"Why isn't he here?"

Silence.

"This isn't right. There's been a misunderstanding. Just like you, the witness apparently stumbled upon her trying to right the angle of the painting. If you choose to run off with the claim that she was trying to steal the painting, then you'd be acknowledging that the Art Gallery has a security problem. People can now waltz in and slink away with the world's most prestigious paintings." Nigel's eyes narrowed, and his low voice was filled with purpose.

"How do you want to explain this to your superior? How do you want to tell him that a woman held an original artwork in her hand for what? Fifteen minutes? Before you even became aware of it. Don't you think that if she wanted to steal the painting that you wouldn't have found her at all. Between your incompetence and the time a witness came to call your attention to a misunderstanding, she would've vanished into thin air."

Annabelle felt helpless, like her fate had just been wrenched from her hands. She listened as Nigel talked the security guard out of remanding her. She couldn't believe how quickly things had deteriorated.

After a while, the security guard caved in. The boring expression on his face said that he was more tired of Nigel's presence than he was convinced of his words. The painting still hung safely in its place on the walls, so he could afford to do away with both the woman and the man.

"Get her out of here," he told Nigel. "But I never want to see her face again."

Outside felt so different. The break of the sunrays on Annabelle's skin, and the brush of the air, rejuvenated her a little. She hugged Nigel tightly.

"You're okay," Nigel said as rubbed his hand over her back.

"Thank you," she said.

"Do you want to sit?" Nigel asked as soon as they broke out of the hug.

"Yes, please."

CHAPTER 4

REUNION

ANNABELLE SAT HUNCHED OVER, elbows digging into her lap, using her arms as a prop for her chin. Her eyes darted nervously, unfocused. She was usually cheerful and witty, an unstoppable force, but right now she felt more like a wilted flower.

She was aware of the Art Gallery still within reach, its silent bustle still palpable. The unsettling events from earlier replayed in her mind. Nigel was there, drumming his fingers on his knee and inhaling deeply. She could sense his concern, even his curiosity, about what had happened, but she knew he wouldn't press her for answers here and now.

Annabelle felt Nigel's gaze on her, and then he reached out with a hand and tapped her gently.

"Hey," he said.

She turned slowly, offering a weak smile.

"Come on, you don't need to put that up for me," he said. "I know when your smiles are real, and when they're not."

A small peal of laughter escaped through her lips.

"Yeah," he smiled. "Now, that one was real."

Annabelle turned away, shaking her head gently. Nigel always had a knack for breaking through her defences. Regardless of how angry or sad she was, he would find a way to reach her. It wasn't his persistence; it was about the air of calm and gentility about him. It was like the happy ocean on the kind of sunny day that recommended a sunbathe – quiet and subtle, but still eating into the sand at the edge of the shore.

"How're you doing?" he asked.

Annabelle sighed. "I don't know what to say. I still can't believe Hendrik did that to me."

"Who's this Hendrik guy anyway? I don't recall you mentioning him in any of our recent conversations."

"Well, that's because, he only came into my life after our last chat."

Suddenly, there was a loud cheer from the direction of the Art Gallery. Annabelle turned, and the light that started to creep into her face, bled away.

"Belle," he called. She flicked her eyes towards him. "Why don't we step away from here."

"Yeah," she said. "A change of scenery sounds nice, right?"

"Yeah. I think it'll do you some good."

"I hope you've got ideas that don't involve walking through the city. I doubt if I have the strength for that now."

"Come on, are you kidding me? You've been here countless times. There are lots of places we can go that are outside of the city."

Nigel got to his feet and stretched his hand towards her.

"Come on," he beckoned. "I know just the getaway."

Annabelle, still stooped, turned her face until she could see Nigel's face. He towered over her like a skyscraper, but not in the looming, imposing, Goliath-over-David kind of way. Quite the opposite. She lowered her eyes to his offered hand and placed hers in it.

Annabelle felt a tinge of relief as she took Nigel's offered hand. For a moment, she had considered staying back, burdening herself further with guilt. She could sense that Nigel didn't know the full extent of what had happened, but she felt his understanding all the same. His gaze met hers, and she knew he could see the lingering pain deep within her eyes.

He lifted her up, bringing her full height up to his shoulders. Annabelle looked at him and smiled.

"So, where to?" she asked.

"Let's have that be your little surprise."

Annabelle shook her head, and they walked away. Away from the Art Gallery. Away from the agonising reminder of Hendrik's full-faced betrayal. It would take some time before she would ever see the grand building the same way again.

Royal Botanic Garden, Sydney.

The sun at that time of the day was soft and warm. At 4pm, its light danced daintily along with the breeze, creating shades out of the colony of trees on the expanse of the manicured lawns. Nigel and Annabelle strolled next to each other. Nigel had both hands in his pocket while Annabelle leaned against his shoulder and looped an arm through the crook of his elbow. In her other hand, she was holding a hot drink that Nigel had bought her along the way. She was pleased that he still remembered her favourite – dark hot chocolate with marshmallows and no cream.

Their shadow cast a soft but bizarre impression on the tarred road that abutted a stone wall at the right, and the rest of the garden by the left. The stone wall held its testament of age in the countless chips that adorned its surface. But its greatest significance lay in the lake that it cordoned off. Under the sunlight, its surface shimmered, like an endless ocean of sapphire. The lake ran on, greeting the curve of the Royal Botanic Garden's landmass and a conglomeration of buildings at the other side of town.

By the left, the Garden spoke of itself in the verdure of its different shades of green. The lawn was a sprawling canvas lighter than the darker coiffure of the trees. It wasn't just the flora. There was an embodiment of harmless quiet floating in the air, permeating every pore, crack, and crevice like the light of the sun. In the distance, a man lay on the lawn with a book in his hand. A couple, a few meters away from the man, sat against the trunk of a tree as they swapped stories and enjoyed the tree's shade. The calming scenery was the reason why the dark cloud that hung over Annabelle's head dissipated. Ahead of them, the path panned out into a backdrop of skyscrapers, part of which was the Sydney Opera House.

"Hey," Annabelle nudged Nigel. She had a soft smile on.

Nigel tilted his head down a little and stared at her.

"Thank you," she said. "The walk's doing me a lot of good."

Nigel smiled. "I'm glad it worked. You don't know how much of an uninteresting person you are when you're glum."

Annabelle chuckled.

"So, are you ready to tell me what all this is about now?"

"Do you want to do that sitting or standing?"

"Either one," he shrugged. "It's entirely up to you."

Annabelle tucked her bottom lip in as she contemplated over the options.

"Let's head over to that bench there," she nodded towards a free bench at the corner. "We could walk the entire park, and I'd still not be done with the story."

Nigel laughed. "A story that's worth the entire width and length of this garden? That's a story worth hearing."

Annabelle unlinked her arms from Nigel's as they sat. She turned and faced him.

"You know about my dad's obsession?" she began.

"You mean with Darwin, right?"

"Exactly," she continued. "This all began with some speculation that Darwin might have been onto something big."

Nigel's brows arched. "Really?"

"Yeah. I flew back to the UK because Charlie had a piano concert in his school."

"Charlie is what? Ten by now?"

Nigel's voice had spiked momentarily with surprise.

"Yeah, he is." Annabelle nodded.

"Last time I saw him was— "

"When you came to pick me up a couple of years back, so we could go see a movie."

"Yeah..." Nigel nodded as his eyes took on a light shade of dreaminess. "Charlie was so young back then, no bigger than my little finger."

Annabelle laughed. 'Well, he sure is bigger than your little finger now. He plays the piano wonderfully."

"I'm glad."

"Anyway. When Charlie was done playing, I figured it was a great idea to go say hello to our dad at Cambridge. We walked in on him, taking a small group of people through a tour of the department. After he was done, a *striking* young man walked in, interested in his work."

Nigel couldn't help but notice Annabelle's tone at "striking young man". The sarcastic intent was unavoidable.

"As always, my father dives headfirst into impassioned conversations about Darwin with him, particularly his theory of evolution and the intricate details of his voyages. This time, they were so engrossed in their discussion that even I got captivated. What really caught my attention were these tantalising claims Darwin made about a mysterious, undocumented island."

"Claims?" Nigel's brows furrowed.

"Yeah. Something about the island being hidden, like it was sacred or something."

"That sounds antithetical coming from someone like Darwin."

"Yeah. It's also what's making our minds tick. What could be on an island that Darwin, the father of evolution, would consider mysterious and forbidden to share?"

Nigel didn't answer. He didn't think he needed to. Annabelle continued.

"This island, wherever it is and whatever it is, refused to be disclosed to anyone..."

Annabelle pulled Nigel into the depth of her experience as she recounted the events that led her to Sydney.

When she was done, Nigel gazed into the open.

"Wow," he said. "So, two grownups decided to gallop across the continent and across the ocean for the glory of a quest." He said the words like he was repeating to himself as a measure of reality, of fact.

"Are you doubting me?"

"No. I'm not. I believe you. What I can't quite wrap my head around is how you let yourself travel with a stranger. You just met the man, Belle."

"It's not my fault. We got to talking on our way here. I was thinking I knew enough of him to get by. I'm sure I've more than learned my lesson."

"I know he was a *striking* young man and all, but couldn't you have at least brought a friend or your sister with you?"

"There was simply no time."

Nigel shook his head and threw his arms mid-air in exasperation.

"It's like South Africa all over again, remember? That time I feared you were eaten or kidnapped!"

Annabelle burst into laughter. "Oh, my God. I can't believe you still remember that.

"You were missing for hours!" Nigel's eyes spread a little.

"I only went for an evening stroll.

"Yeah," Nigel nodded shrewdly. "In a place inhabited by lions."

Both of them launched into a bout of laughter.

"But it's not entirely bad," Nigel said. "You've always been wild."

Annabelle sipped her hot chocolate.

Nigel sighed. "What have you been up to, before all this?"

"Nothing much. I'm living in Copenhagen now. I've been moving from place to place, you know. I was in the Netherlands for a few months and Germany before that. Being an environmental scientist, isn't easy. But I'm grateful it's given me the opportunity to explore new things in new places. It's almost like spending a holiday abroad."

Nigel tittered and shook his head.

"What?" Annabelle asked with the shell-shocked expression of someone who had just been accused wrongly.

"Nothing." Nigel shook his head. "It's just great to see that you haven't changed."

Annabelle bobbed her head in understanding.

"What about you?" she asked. "What have you been up to? Please tell me you're not still doing the skydives on weekends."

Nigel chuckled. "I try to whenever I get the chance."

"So, you're still crazy then?"

Nigel laughed.

"I got work in a conservation park for wildlife here in Sydney for the last eight months."

"Hm." She nodded. "Away from South Africa then?"

"Yeah. My time with them came to an end. I didn't think I could do anymore."

"Yeah, I understand that. What's the name of this conservation?"

"The Sanctuary."

Annabelle whipped her face towards him. Her brows arched.

"The Sanctuary!"

Nigel chuckled and looked away.

"Come on, Nigel," she bumped him gently on the shoulder. "You're not kidding with me, are you?"

"Why would I?" He looked at her.

"Wow," she said, flustered. She reclined further onto the bench and folded her arms across her chest. "I'm jealous, Nigel." He chortled. "Do you know how long I've been trying to get in with the Sanctuary? And here you are, working there already."

"Yeah, their recruitment process was long and tedious. Too many poachers have tried to sneak in as staff in the past. They're just being extra mindful, so they don't have another case on their hands."

"Whatever," she said. "They're just rude."

He laughed, shaking his head.

"How's your brother?" Annabelle asked, trying to change the subject.

"He's doing well. I haven't seen him in a while but we're going to be catching up again in Cape Verde on my next vacation." Nigel let out a short sigh. "Hey. I feel like we've sat for too long. Want to stretch your legs?"

"Sure, why not?"

They got to their feet and continued down the path.

"See that tree over there?" Annabelle pointed.

Nigel looked in the direction of her finger. "What tree, Belle? This is a garden, there are about a million trees here."

"I said that tree, didn't I, silly? Look." She was more insistent this time. "The tree with the pink flowers."

"Ah. I see it now. It was wedged between trees then."

As they walked, the tree emerged from the rest.

"It's beautiful," Nigel said. "As full of pink as the other trees are of green."

"It dared to be different."

"And it's getting the attention it deserves. Just like you."

Annabelle kept her eyes stuck on her converses as she beamed.

Damn this guy, she thought.

It had been close to three years since they decided to end their relationship -- not on any particularly bad note, but on the difference of location and occupation. Their jobs required them to live across different time zones. While they considered the distance a new test to their relationship, Annabelle found it strenuous to keep, so she ended it.

Even though so much time had passed since they split, she still felt like no one understood her better than Nigel.

"So, is there any lucky gentleman in your life at the moment? Outside the *striking* one that just ditched you."

Annabelle punched Nigel playfully. He recoiled as laughter rolled out of his mouth. Annabelle, on the other hand, tried to restrain her smile so she could maintain a scowl.

"So, my question...?" Nigel said as soon as he was done laughing.

"Nope," Annabelle shook her head. "I've been on a few dates, but none of them ever stretched beyond the date. I've been moving around too much, I guess. What about you?"

"Yeah. I was seeing someone for just a few months, but then it didn't fly."

"Was she nice?"

Nigel flashed his eyes on Annabelle. "She was lovely, but there was no connection in the end, so we both decided to end it."

Annabelle nodded.

"Remember how much we used to love it here?" she asked. "How we'd stop by the wall and look across the lake." Nigel smiled. "You said something that was beyond cheesy. I think you said something like, 'if truly anything was possible within the limits of love, then our love would allow us to walk across the lake one day.' I thought it was hilarious."

Nigel chuckled and blushed. "Yeah. I remember all of it. I was young and tried to be romantic." He placed his palm over his face. "I've never forgotten a single moment." Nigel sighed. "The truth is I never get the chance to visit here in the city since we were over. I always thought that if I was coming back here, it would be for... well something different. Something other than breaking someone out of jail."

Annabelle frowned in jest.

"First of all, Nigel, it wasn't a jail. It was a stupid holding room!" He chuckled. "And I'm sure I'd have got myself out in the end."

"Yeah. Keep telling yourself that. Why did you phone me then? Why did you ask me to come break you out, Miss I-Had-Everything-Under-Control?"

Annabelle grimaced. "Oh, shut up."

Both of them laughed until they had to bend over to cushion their aching sides.

"Oh, God," Annabelle said. "If I have to laugh some more, Nigel, I swear I'm going to burst. My tummy is sore."

Nigel chuckled.

Annabelle sucked in air through her lips and exhaled deeply.

"I should go, Nigel. Thank you for everything, it was really good to see you."

"Are you not going to stay a few days?" He looked a little affected by her news.

"I wish I could, but I can't. I need to get back to the UK. My father would be worried sick. He'd want to know what we've done with the information he furnished us with. And he, no doubt, will be furious when he hears what transpired."

Nigel looked disappointed. Annabelle wasn't exempt either.

"Very well then," he said. "You tell your father I said hi, okay?"

"I will."

"One more thing, Belle."

"Yeah?"

"Let's keep in touch more regularly. It's been too long, and I'd like to know how're you doing. I wouldn't want 'busting you out of jail' to be the only occasion where we can see and talk to each other."

Annabelle smiled. "Yeah, that sounds like a great idea. Who knows?" She shrugged. "I may get a turn to rescue you."

Nigel laughed. "I highly doubt that. I'm more about finesse, you know, subtle moves that no one notices. You, on the other hand, are the barge-into-the-room-and-accept-my-fate sort of girl. You'll always get caught."

Annabelle laughed. "Get out of here, Nigel."

They laughed and then they wrapped each other up in a warm hug.

As she watched Nigel leave, Annabelle couldn't deny the burn in her heart. He had wiped away the effect of Hendrik's betrayal. He left an impression in the process, and now she missed him terribly.

She checked the time on her phone.

"Shoot," she exclaimed and spun on her heels. "I need to get out of here before I miss the next flight out."

Back in the UK, Annabelle called Sarah.

"Hey," Sarah said. Her voice was hushed, almost like she was trying to keep from being heard. "What's up with this artwork hunt? Dad's livid over here."

Annabelle sighed and looked at the ceiling. "Just as I expected," she said. Her father had texted her back in Sydney when she left to pick her things from the hotel. She gave him a brief reply but apprised him of Hendrik and his betrayal.

"You can't blame the old man," Sarah said. "That's part of his life's work right there, and now he's hearing that someone he trusted has run off with some precious new details. He would be beating himself up for trusting Hendrik so quickly."

"Yeah. I understand. I was thinking I could talk to him. I could tell him more about our discovery, you know. But it's a good thing I called. I can't face him when he's all temperamental. I might just as well be speaking to a wall."

Sarah chuckled.

Annabelle remembered what it was like during their childhood. Their father was sulky and bull-headed when he was furious.

"Anyway," Sarah said. "What are you going to do now?"

"Continue with the hunt."

There was a brief pause from Sarah's end.

"I thought the guy that betrayed you and remanded you in prison ran off with the next clue?"

"It wasn't *prison*, Sarah," Annabelle rolled her eyes. "It was a holding cell." *God, I'll kill myself if I have to point out the difference again.*

"It doesn't matter. You get my point."

Annabelle shook her head. "You forget that we solved the puzzle together up until the moment he decided to stick in a knife in my back. I know the next clue just as much as he does."

"Yeah?"

"Yeah."

"What is it?"

Annabelle made to speak, but she stopped herself. "I'll tell you when we meet. All I can say now, is that it's in London somewhere, and we need to start looking."

CHAPTER 5

THE FOUR KINGS

ANNABELLE EXHALED AS HER gaze fixed on her laptop screen. She scoured the internet, searching for any hint or lead on the mysterious clue. For hours, just like yesterday and the days before, she had come up empty-handed. Her passion for finding answers remained undiminished, but she couldn't help feeling weighed down by disappointment and mental fatigue. Annabelle had stayed up all night, and for what?

She sighed and began massaging her temples with her fingers, feeling a slight ache at the front of her head.

"Damned coffee is supposed to be doing its job," she murmured, "not giving me headaches."

If Sarah was with her, she would probably point out that Annabelle had been on two consecutive twenty-hour flights and that her brain was bound to protest the lack of rest. But rest was the last thing Annabelle wanted—not while Hendrik's betrayal still haunted her thoughts. She had come to terms with the pain of his actions and the foolishness of her own misplaced trust. Now, her curiosity about Darwin's enigmatic island and the litany of clues he left behind had turned into an intense eagerness to find it and stay one step ahead. Each tick of the clock seemed to remind her that Hendrik had taken the lead while she languished in the security hold, waiting for some miraculous intervention. She wished she could take back those moments, but all she could do now was strive to beat him at his own game.

The cryptic clue replayed in her mind like a neon sign on the side of the road: *"The secret remains with the four kings at the end of the unarmed Viscount's sword"* – *signed E.L.* The message, penned in 1867 London, hailed from a time when people would have dismissed concepts like the internet or online archives as the work of the devil.

Annabelle groaned in exasperation and slammed the laptop's lid shut.

"I give up." She flung her arms up. "I'm stumped. There. You happy now?"

It was a good thing she was the only one in her apartment, otherwise, she might have been considered mad.

"So much for getting the drop on him," she murmured, shaking her head. Pushing herself away from the table on her swivelling chair, she eyed the bed across the room, which seemed to beckon her to lie down and rest. It was tempting.

"No..." She ignored her much needed sleep. "I need a drink."

She walked over to the fridge in the kitchen.

Just last week, she and her father had visited St. George's Cathedral, Windsor, the burial site of former British monarchs. Despite examining every inch of the cathedral, short of vandalising the tombs, they had come up empty-handed. The exhaustive search had taken a visible toll on their minds and bodies. As they left the cathedral, they seemed only a few breaths away from joining the dead entombed within its walls.

The disappointment had only mounted since then. She

considered calling Nigel but didn't want to disturb him unless absolutely necessary. She had already bothered him once and didn't want to make a habit of it.

Annabelle poured herself a glass of orange juice, and after finishing it, finally decided to listen to her body and take a nap. As she crawled into bed, she made a mental note to visit Sarah later in the day. She hadn't seen her sister since they had gone to watch Charlie's school concert.

No sooner had her eyelids touched themselves than she was carried hastily in sleep's arms.

Annabelle hit the doorbell three times in quick succession and stepped back. She looked around at the quiet, conservative neighbourhood. It still looked the same way as it had all those years ago when Sarah first moved in. The estate was abutted, for as long as it ran and intersected, with low-rise buildings and bungalows which sat prettily within picket fencings or hedges. The estate had the kind of dead-quietness obtainable in a cemetery. Annabelle couldn't help but detect the mindful silence that hung in the air. It was like a statement, a decree to keep one's nose into their business and never into another's.

"Charlie," she heard her sister call out, "please, get the door, will you?"

"Yes, Mum," Charlie replied in a singsong voice.

Annabelle beamed as she heard the patter of approaching footsteps behind the wooden door. The lock clicked, and the door swung open.

"Auntie Anna!" Charlie enthused. He rushed in and wrapped his little arms around Annabelle's waist.

Annabelle chuckled as she ran her fingers affectionately through Charlie's hair. Sometimes, especially at this time in her life, she forgot she was even his aunt. There were just too many things having a go at her, and recently, it felt like they were finally beginning to get her under, just right where they wanted her. She was a fighter, or at least she liked to tell herself she was. She wasn't going to give up just yet. The ice sheet under her was gradually thinning. Annabelle could feel it. Unless she stumbled across a fresh lead before the week ran out, she was scared the ice might cave in.

"Hello, Charlie," she said. "How're you doing?"

Charlie smiled and looked up at her. "I'm doing good. I'm glad you're back."

"Were you just practicing piano or playing videogames?"

"Can't I do both?"

Annabelle laughed. "Oh, wait till your mother gets you."

Entering the room, Annabelle sniffed and hummed with pleasure. A delicious aroma filled the air.

"Is your mum in the kitchen?" she asked.

"Yeah." Charlie nodded. "We're having roast chicken for lunch."

"Wow," Annabelle rubbed her stomach, feeling a slight rumble. "I could do with some of that. I'm really hungry."

"So, you're going to be with us for a while?" Charlie asked, his eyes gleaming with excitement.

"Yeah, something like that. Until your mother decides I've overstayed my welcome and need to get going."

"I was just about to call you," Sarah said, entering the living room. She wiped her hands on a small towel and stuffed it back into one of the large pockets on her apron.

"Hi, Sarah," Annabelle greeted.

"Welcome back," Sarah replied. "I'm preparing lunch. Care to join us?"

"Of course," Annabelle smiled. "I could eat up this entire house right now."

Charlie grinned. "I would suggest seasoning it first. It'll taste disgusting otherwise."

Annabelle laughed. "You're hilarious, Charlie."

Giggling, Charlie headed towards the dining table.

Shortly after lunch, the three of them settled in the living room. Charlie lay on the floor, drawing pictures in his notepad, while Sarah and Annabelle sat next to each other on the chaise lounge.

"So..." Sarah faced Annabelle. "How's the search going?"

Annabelle exhaled and rolled her eyes. "It's been frustrating. It feels like all I've been doing since Sydney is hitting dead ends."

"What exactly are you looking for?"

"Four kings and a viscount."

"What's a viscount?" Charlie asked. He was still sketching away on the notepad.

Sarah smiled at him. "A viscount is part of a ranking system in British nobility. The system of nobility involves dukes, marquesses, earls, viscounts, and barons. All these titles are given by the British monarchy."

Charlie shrugged indifferently and continued with his drawing. Annabelle burst into laughter. She remembered how her father had bored her with similar details when she was younger.

"Do you know where it is, yet?" Sarah asked her. "The four kings and the viscount?"

"It's not as straightforward as that, Sarah. This is a riddle. It's almost like Darwin is taking us on a joyride from the depths of his grave. The four kings in question may not be actual four kings."

Annabelle thought about King's Cross. It had four points. It made her wonder if she could come across a statue or something of swords – viscounts' swords – being linked together to form a cross sign. Only a few days ago, she had combed the entirety of King's Cross station and came up with nothing.

"Hendrik must have found something," Annabelle said.

"Hendrik? Oh, you mean the tall dashing guy you fell head over heels for?"

"Sarah," Annabelle cautioned.

"Sorry," Sarah held her hands up in surrender. She stared at Annabelle and sighed. "You simply worry too much. What if he's having as much luck as you?"

"And what if he isn't?"

Sarah shook her head. "Sometimes 1 wonder why you took this quest up in the first place. If you ask me, it seemed like a bad idea, running around the world and grabbing at wisps like a child."

"Well, 1 didn't ask you, Sarah."

Sarah chuckled and shook her head. "Could you do me a favour, Annabelle? Just a tiny little favour."

"Shoot."

"1 need you to look after Charlie for me today. I've got somewhere 1 need to be."

"That's not going to be a problem. Charlie and 1 are going to have so much fun. Aren't we, Charlie?"

Her young nephew looked up at her and beamed with a smile.

"Yes, we are," he replied enthusiastically.

Annabelle patted him on the shoulder. "Maybe we'll get some sweets, hot chocolate and then go to the cinema afterwards?"

Charlie nodded his head frantically. Annabelle faced Sarah.

"You heard the young man," she said, nodding towards Charlie. "You're good to go."

Trafalgar Square.

If Annabelle's experience at the Royal Botanic Gardens in Sydney had been natural and organic, then her time at Trafalgar Square was the opposite. Though to be clear, it wasn't the opposite in the true sense of the word. Trafalgar Square was definitely a wonderful experience. In appearance, it paid attention to far more stone structures than it did to greenery. It was natural in that kind of way that pulled people in and left them in perpetual awe. Perhaps, it was the infamous four large black bronze lions, depictions so accurate they might have well been the real thing. Or Nelson's Column that stood tall in the middle of the lions as it thrusted itself from the shadow that wreathed its stockier stone base, up out into the sun's gaze. The fountains on either side of the sculptures, shone alluringly blue like portals to another world. The clean stone grounds were littered with pigeons that cooed and trotted about, expecting little treats from the tourists in the square. The tourists, on the other hand, turned the other way, leaning up against the statues to get pictures.

Annabelle sat at the stone edge of the fountain and looked over at Charlie as he played around with other children. She thought her nephew always found a way to shine wherever he was. A dreamy smile sat on her face as she watched, interested in the boy than the game he played.

Charlie squealed with delight as he raced with the other children to the statues. Annabelle chuckled, unsure if she had ever seen him this happy at home.

I can imagine Sarah's keeping him choked up with lessons all the time, she thought. *I've told her multiple times; the boy is brilliant already. Let him play and have injuries like the kids his age. But no, she wants him to be the world's greatest pianist at only ten.*

She sniggered and shook her head.

"Look, Auntie Anna," Charlie called out. Annabelle turned to see him riding one of the lions as if it were a horse. "I'm riding the king of the jungle."

Annabelle giggled.

She stopped abruptly.

All the mirth in her face vanished in a second, as her eyes misted over with realisation.

"Oh, Charlie, you're a genius," she said as she whipped her phone out of her pocket. *King of the jungle. There are four lions. Four kings!* It had never occurred to her to look in this direction. She always thought of kings in their literal sense. How could she have been that restrictive?

Always think outside of the box, Annabelle. Outside of the box.

She ran a quick search on her phone. *Who designed the Lions of Trafalgar Square?*

The results pooled in a second later. *Edwin Lanseer designed the four lions which opened to the public in 1867.*

Edwin Lanseer! Annabelle's face perked up. *The initials! The signature at the end of the clue. That's E.L! 1867 is also the date on the clue!*

Her heart kicked off a marathon sprint of its own as it nudged her more and more into the exuberance of excitement. In a flash, her eyes moved up to the top of Nelson's Column. She squinted as the sun fell into her eyes. She placed a hand horizontally just above her eyes to cut off the sun's rays.

I'd bet anything this too is a clue, she thought.

Annabelle wasn't about to wait to seal that bet. She got off the edge of the fountain and walked towards the small stand in front of the column. There was a black plaque fixed onto a small stand, placed in front of the column. However, her concerns were not with the magnificence of the structure, but with the words etched into the plaque. They briefed anyone curious enough to look about the history of the statues. Annabelle was more than curious, and she read along.

"The Column was built to commemorate Admiral Horatio Nelson, who died at the Battle of Trafalgar in 1805. Admiral Nelson was a viscount..."

Annabelle paused. Her head reeled with excitement. She dug her fingers into the heel of her palms, until her nails began to bite. It was all she could do to keep from running around like Charlie and the rest of the kids.

The answer is here, she thought. *It has to be. I need to be sure.*

Annabelle took her eyes back to the top of the column where Nelson's statue stood. She could see him, but her vantage denied her access to finer details of the statue. She took out her phone and tried to take a picture, but the quality was too poor as her camera was damaged. Annabelle had never been one for expensive phones. Mysteriously, none of her phones had ever died from staying with her too long. Most of the time, the screen would end up shattered after a few months of purchase. Going for cheap allowed her to switch phones quickly if the need arose. Now, her decisions had turned full circle to bite her in the backside.

But Charlie! Charlie has got a good phone.

She spun around as the fringes of her hair swished around the base of her neck.

"Charlie!" she called. She saw him up ahead, just near the fountain. She covered the distance between them in quick strides.

"Charlie," she called again. "Can I borrow your phone?"

She must have come on stronger than she expected because the little boy frowned. He was confused, but he still gave the phone to her.

"I don't know why a ten-year-old should have a phone, especially one this good," she commented.

"All my friends have phones," Charlie replied.

"Hmm. Still not crazy about it."

She walked back to the column and tried to retake the picture. This time around, it worked. As she zoomed in on Nelson's miniature sculpture, she felt a huge pod of happiness burst inside her. The ensuing flood was so much, she felt quite giddy. She laughed. Nelson was leaning on his sword with his left hand, but his right arm was missing. Everything pointed to him. Admiral Horatio Nelson was the unarmed viscount.

She repeated the words of the message out loud. "The secret remains with the four kings at the end of the unarmed viscount's sword."

Suddenly, an idea sparked to life.

She turned back towards the fountain. Thankfully, Charlie hadn't run off yet.

"Charlie," she called. He turned. "Do you mind helping your aunt out for a bit?"

Charlie shrugged, said a few words to his friends and trotted towards her.

"What do you need help with?" he asked.

Annabelle pointed towards one of the black lion statues. "I need you to get back up there. Tell me if you see any message or symbol on the lion. Tell me if you see anything at all."

As Charlie moved towards the statues, it occurred to Annabelle that the body of the statue would be too obvious for a hiding place.

Charlie called back after a while. "I can't see anything, Auntie Anna."

Annabelle's brows knitted together. Her mind was a hive with thoughts for bees. She ran through tons of possibilities as she tried to sift through for something tangible.

The message talked about a secret, she thought. *The only relation the four kings and the viscount have to this quest is the secret they hold.*

Out of the blue, another thought fell into the puddle. *A secret is hidden unless someone speaks it.*

"Charlie," she called, her face lighting up again. "Check its mouth. That's where you would keep a secret."

Charlie felt around its open maw, and then he froze.

"Auntie Anna," he called. Annabelle started to move close. "I feel something. Up here at the roof of the mouth, there are dents. Like a pattern of lines or something."

Annabelle dipped her hand into the small black bag she carried with her and brought out a notebook. *You never know when these things will come in handy,* she thought. Thankfully, she was about to be rewarded for her decision. She tore a clean sheet from the notebook and handed it over to her nephew along with a pencil.

"Place the paper against the roof of the mouth, Charlie, and scratch. Just like you would when you scratch a paper over a coin to get its picture."

"Alright," Charlie bobbed his head, and obliged his aunt. He stuck his tongue out the side of his mouth, as he worked, completely engrossed in the process. He pulled out the paper. It was done.

The moment he looked at it, he flashed eyes, filled with amazement, at Annabelle. Annabelle rushed and stooped over him.

"Let me see," she said.

"I got something," Charlie said. "It's a word." The excitement in his voice rushed like a brook.

On the piece of paper, there was an image of the word 'Sea' covered in the dark shade of a pencil.

"Let's do the same to the other lions," Annabelle said.

She followed her nephew from lion to lion, and at each one, they got a word from the roof of its mouth.

"This one says 'Sun'."

"A longer word, 'Moon'."

"Last one. This says 'Stars'."

When they were done with the last one, they stopped to look at what they had on paper. The image of four huge words stared back at them. SEA, SUN, MOON, STARS.

"Let's go show this to Grandad," Charlie suggested.

Annabelle pulled him in for a short embrace.

"Yes, darling. Thank you very much. Let's go meet Grandpa." If there was anybody who knew the meaning of the words they just got from the lions, it was going to be Professor Young.

Annabelle and Charlie took the Tube straight to Professor Young's home.

Professor Young had just finished staging a lecture online at an annual conglomeration of historians from different universities in the UK.

"What can I do for you two?" he asked, peering at them curiously through the rim of his glasses. Anyone would share the Professor's curiosity if his visitors wore the kind of unabashed grins that Annabelle and Charlie wore.

"This," Annabelle said as she thrust the pieces of papers towards him.

The Professor received it and peered at the paper. He looked up. "Where did you get this?"

"At Trafalgar Square," Charlie replied, unable to maintain a tight rein over his excitement. "Auntie Anna and I uncovered a very hard puzzle today."

"Ah." Professor Young smiled. "Is that so?"

"Yes, Grandpa," Charlie said.

"I'm proud of you. I always knew you had the knack for being a great adventurer."

Charlie's grinned so hard, he could feel the side of his lips stretching.

Professor Young returned to the words on the paper. He squeezed his face a bit, as he rummaged through his mind. After a seemingly endless stretch, he spoke.

"It looks like this is hinting towards a particular apparatus. An apparatus a sailor might use for guidance."

Annabelle stepped forward a little.

"How so?" she asked.

"At sea, the sun, stars and moon are used for navigation. So, perhaps an apparatus such as a sextant is what we're looking for.

Now, if I remember correctly, Darwin had a pocket sextant that he used for his voyage. Smaller than an actual sextant but still applies the same function."

Charlie donned a quizzical look. He was a smart kid - there was no doubt about that - but he still struggled to keep up with the adults.

"What does a sextant look like, Grandpa?" he asked.

"Good question," Professor Young replied emphatically. "I have an example of one that's been used by previous navigators. Come, I can show it you."

Daughter and grandson followed Professor Young as he led them to his home office. Inside, he headed over to a locked cabinet, unlocked it, and brought out a cylindrical object with a dull gold shine.

"This is what a sextant looks like. It's not exactly a perfect duplicate of Darwin's. Still, it's hard for a lay person to spot the difference."

Annabelle was fascinated with this new device. She took out her notebook and drew a sketch for reference later. Her camera and phone were too unreliable to get a good quality image.

"So, we need to find Darwin's sextant then," Annabelle said. "How are we going to do that?"

"I don't think finding it would be an issue," Professor Young said. "Getting hold of it will be."

Annabelle was confused.

"Where is it then?" she asked.

The Professor held her gaze, and then he smiled.

Later that day, Sarah dropped by her father's, to pick up Charlie. The boy ran over to her, giddy with excitement.

"Guess what, Mum!" he said. "Guess!"

"What?" Sarah asked him. "You know I'm not good at making guesses."

"Auntie Anna is going to break into the Natural History Museum to steal something," Charlie blurted.

Sarah's face became a mix of horror and confusion.

"What!"

CHAPTER 6

NATURAL HISTORY MUSEUM

Natural History Museum, London.

THE NATURAL HISTORY MUSEUM, an imposing Baroque masterpiece nestled in South Kensington, set itself apart as a world of its own. Its ornate stone architecture and low white picket fencing that encircled its perimeter created an atmosphere of grandeur. Professor Young, as always, marvelled at its breath-taking aesthetics and sheer size. Standing at the base of the steps leading to the arched entrance, he gazed up at the magnificent façade, admiring it like a priceless gem in a treasure chest. The building bore no signs of its 140-year history. Instead, it exuded a quiet assurance, an unspoken determination to endure for centuries to come. Often, he would joke with his colleagues by saying,

"If there's anything I'm certain will see the end of days, it's the Natural History Museum. That thing is a well-kept beast."

Today, he was not entirely in awe of its structure. He walked in through the entrance with a twinkle in his eye. Deep in his mind, the Professor housed a keen awareness of his surroundings. He couldn't afford to mess the plan up. The blowback would be just too hot to handle.

The entrance opened into a huge inner courtyard with glossy brown embellished floors. The vault was comprised of a unique blend of wooden panes through the middle and a series of glass screens by each side, offering a clean view of the sky above. Regardless, none of that was as grandiloquent as the huge skeletal frame of a whale tethered to the vault's beams by cords. The skeleton was a welcome statement, a pointer to the museum's heritage, and the things that could be expected of it.

Ascending the main stairs, Professor Young confronted the white marble statue of Charles Darwin. He scrutinized the figure as if appraising an adversary, his curiosity palpable. From the moment he delved into the realms of academia and the enigmatic history of Darwin, countless questions had remained unanswered. The mystery of the hidden island stood out among them all. For years, he grappled with why Darwin had singled out this island from the numerous others he had discovered, why he had chosen to shield it from the public eye and gone to great lengths to ensure its secrecy.

"Is what you're protecting really true, I wonder?" the Professor mused quietly to himself as he stroked his chin. "Or am I the only one that may believe your mad discovery?"

"Ah, Anthony," a voice chimed in beside him. "Always the ardent Darwin scholar. I see you've wasted no time reacquainting yourself with the museum's rendition of the man himself."

Professor Young chuckled as he turned to face his colleague.

"James," he greeted as he shook his hand.

James was an inch shorter than the Professor and spotted a bald patch at the middle of his head proudly. His lips were a bit lopsided, creating the impression that he had a mouth at the corner of his face, rather than at the middle. He had been appointed as curator to run the Darwin exhibition for a couple of months, though typically he was a colleague of his at the university. Professor Young had reached out to him a couple of hours back, and James was swift to respond.

"Thank you for accommodating my request, James, especially on such short notice. I genuinely enjoy teaching children about our history from time to time. They're like endless wells of curiosity; you can keep pouring knowledge into them, and they never tire. Always so inquisitive, so eager. Sadly, university students often lack that same zeal. It's a pity, really."

"Don't mention it, Anthony," James responded, waving dismissively. His voice carried a slight rasp, as if his vocal cords grated against each other intermittently during speech. "It's no trouble at all. Besides, you're more knowledgeable about Darwin than anyone here." He placed his right hand on his chest. "We're fortunate to have you."

The Professor nodded at his appreciation.

"Very well then," James said. "Let's get on with it."

As if on cue, a group of school children entered, chattering excitedly. Professor Young smiled, sensing their enthusiasm radiating like beams of sunlight. The sight of these young, eager minds invigorated him.

Think of the seeds I could sow in these young minds, he thought. *You can think about it all you want, but don't forget why you're here,* he chided himself.

"Well, there is your flock, Anthony," James gestured towards the group. "Have fun."

Professor Young nodded and walked towards the group.

"Hello, children."

They stopped and stared fixatedly.

"Welcome," Professor Young said as he glanced from face to face. "I understand that you all came here to participate in the ultimate experience. I won't disappoint you. This way," he started to walk, and they followed, "is the Darwin section. Charles Darwin, the father of evolution, is one of the greatest discoverers that ever lived."

He spoke slowly, taking extra care to enunciate and elaborate on some terms. This tour was a meal, one that he wanted to think he prepared well for, and he wanted them to swallow every bite of it.

He took the group towards a group of fossils held in by crystal-clear glass panes.

"This, here," he pointed at what looked like a huge mass of brown rock, "is one of the mammal fossils Darwin collected while he was at the South American coast." The group huddled together in front of the glass, peered at the fossil, and chatted excitedly among themselves.

"Over here," the Professor continued, "is an armadillo that Darwin and his crew collected from Bahia Blanca during the first year of their voyage."

He guided them onward when he felt they had absorbed enough. Stopping by a sculpture of a stuffed pigeon, he said, "Did you know that Charles Darwin also raised and cared for pigeons?" He feigned a look of surprise before nodding. "I bet none of you were aware of that. Darwin bred pigeons for experiments, crossbreeding them to better comprehend the mechanisms of evolution. Charles was an incredibly diligent worker. Do you want to be diligent workers too?"

The children responded in unison.

"Good. Then you need to pay extra attention to what I'm saying and study your books hard afterwards."

Professor Young forayed into the navigation section, where several navigation tools from the *HMS Beagle* rested untouched behind the glass panes. The museum supervisor hung around like a shadow as he watched the tour. The Professor noticed the gloves on the supervisor's hands and pulled out his own. He put them on and turned to discuss the display of the next tool when he came face-to-face with the sextant. He froze, but only for a few moments.

As I live and breathe, he thought. *Darwin's pocket sextant. I'm so close to it. So close to putting an end to this charade.*

He stole a glance at the museum supervisor. He was engaged in a light conversation with another group. Professor Young prepped himself, the opportunity had come.

Gently, he slid the pane that protected the sextant and pulled it out gingerly. He launched into a small lecture on how the sextant worked. He got to one knee as he held the sextant by the bottom and gestured with his free hand.

"The sextant is primarily used at sea to determine directions. It relies on the sun, moon, and stars..."

Professor Young spoke convincingly, yet a persistent thought nagged at him. He couldn't believe how effortless it had been. He had anticipated more of a challenge, especially considering the difficulties his daughter had faced in her own endeavours. Silently, he counted his blessings. Now, all he needed was a plan to exit the museum with the sextant in hand.

"Excuse me, sir," a young boy in a blue cap raised his hand.

"Yes," Professor Young smiled at him.

"Can I get a closer look?"

"Of course. Why not? Come closer, please."

The boy began to wade through the group to make it to the front.

"Make way for him, please," Professor Young pleaded.

"Here," he said, when the boy came up to him. "I'll even let you hold it." He gave the boy the sextant. "See how light it is?"

The boy grinned and exposed his grown big teeth.

"Oh no, sir, you can't do that," the museum supervisor called out.

Professor Young looked up as the supervisor quickly approached him.

"That can't be handled like a toy," the supervisor said. "Please, put it back."

The Professor got to his feet.

"I apologise, I was merely showing them how light it is."

"You can't!" the supervisor shot back. He walked past the Professor and snatched the sextant from the boy.

The boy's expression dissolved into disappointment.

"I'm sorry, sir," he said. "I didn't mean to hold it."

"No, no," the supervisor replied. "That's okay. Some adults just choose to turn deaf ears to protocols." He glared at the Professor.

"Forgive me," Professor Young said. "I think I got a bit too enthusiastic."

The supervisor shook his head. "You know what? I think it's best we let everything stay behind the glass for the rest of the tour. We can't risk having any damage done to these artifacts."

"I understand," Professor Young nodded. "I don't want to cause any trouble." He turned to the children who still remained gathered around. "Children, shall we?"

The Professor led the group away from the navigation section. He appeared disappointed, but inside, he bubbled with delight. Darwin's sextant was still very much within reach. He had harboured a little fear that it may not be in the museum's possession. For once in his life, he was glad to be wrong.

During lunch time, the children sat in groups at the round white tables in the museum's restaurant. The teacher, leading the group, sat at one of the tables and kept a watchful eye over her students. The last thing she wanted was one of them acting out of line while in public. The atmosphere in the restaurant was cool and calm, almost like the place commanded its own respect.

As the pupils pulled their lunch boxes out of their bags, Sarah walked into the restaurant with a tense expression, combing through the place with her eyes. Suddenly, she saw the teacher, and her face lost some of its tautness. She walked towards her.

"I apologise," she said. "I forgot to pack his lunch for today. The morning was a bit hectic."

"It's nothing," the teacher chuckled. "Some days are like that. You didn't even need to come all this way. I'd have got him something myself."

"Thank you." Sarah patted her affectionately on the shoulder. "You're too kind. But I've already gone through all the trouble. I'll just say a quick hello and give him his lunch box."

"Alright. He's over there," the teacher pointed at a boy with a blue cap sitting three tables away. "Hey, Charlie, come greet your mother."

Charlie looked up and smiled when he saw Sarah.

Sarah got on one knee as he approached.

"Hi, Mum," he said and hugged her.

Sarah cradled his head in between her hands and looked him over, as if she was searching for something inconspicuous on his person.

"I have your lunch," she said. Sarah flashed a look at the teacher, who returned to her table, and leaned in close to Charlie.

"Did you do it?" she whispered.

A wide grin grew on his face as he nodded. He handed his bag over.

"Good boy," she said as she received the bag. She patted him on the cheek. "As promised, you can get any treat you'd like later. Go and eat now."

Sarah watched Charlie until he returned to his table. As soon as he settled into his seat, she turned and made a beeline for the bathroom. She walked into the closest cubicle, put the lid down, and sat down. A few moments later, she rapped her knuckles twice against the cubicle to her left. The hollow sound rang, and then it was followed by silence. Two heartbeats later, there was a response. An equally loud rap in three quick successions. Sarah stooped and slid Charlie's bag under, and through to the next cubicle.

Annabelle received the bag from the next cubicle. She unzipped it quickly and peered inside.

"Yes," she whispered as she pumped a fist in the air. The sextant was inside. She pulled it out and fit it into her own bag. Carefully, she slid Charlie's bag back to Sarah.

Without a word, Annabelle got up, walked out of the bathroom, out of the museum and into the fresh air of freedom. Outside, she turned and headed towards South Kensington's Underground Station.

She was chuffed. They stuck with the old switcheroo trick. She didn't expect the plan to go so well. She had doubts of her own as the plan was constructed. Given her experience in the past, the incident with Hendrik being the most painful reminder, she half-expected something to go wrong. Everyone had played their part like properly oiled components of a machine, and the outcome was simply magic.

Take that Hendrik, Annabelle thought. *I hope you rot in hell.*

As Annabelle descended the stairs into the station, she felt an enormous amount of pride swirling in her chest. All she could think about was how impressive Charlie had been through everything. She had a hard time getting Sarah on board, especially as their plan hinged on Charlie doing the switch. Her boy was ten, and she feared that he was too young to pull off something of that nature.

"He's just a child, Annabelle," Sarah had screamed. "Can you hear yourself?"

"I know, Sarah. I know," Annabelle moved forward. Her voice was calm. Placating. "I wouldn't be doing this if it wasn't absolutely necessary."

"Absolutely necessary?" Sarah scoffed and shook her head. "You're asking a ten-year-old child to steal an artifact from the Natural History Museum." Volumes of incredulity bled from Sarah's voice. She couldn't understand how Annabelle didn't understand the gravity of what she was asking.

"Not steal. Just switching two items, that's all. Charlie's smart, Sarah."

"You think I don't know that. I'm his mother."

"That's not what I was trying to say. He's smart enough to not do anything that'll get him caught. He only has to play a very little role. We'll be doing the heavy lifting."

Sarah gasped and kept her hands akimbo.

"Sarah," Annabelle stood right in front of her as she gazed into her eyes. "Please. I know this is a very big thing to ask."

"Big is an understatement," Sarah scoffed.

"I know. But I wouldn't be asking this if it weren't necessary. This thing isn't just important for me. It's important for Dad, and for the whole world. We don't know what it is, but you're familiar with Darwin's work enough to know that his discoveries changed the world. I believe, Dad believes, that this hidden island will change the world more than we know it. You saw what happened the last time I was stupid enough to trust a stranger. He betrayed me and would have preferred I rot in that holding cell. I can't take the same risk again. The only people I can trust are family. You, Dad, and Charlie; you guys are the only family I've got left. Hendrik already has the head start. We're lucky he didn't find out about the sextant before we did, but that's no guarantee that he isn't on to the lead this very instant. If we want to act, we need to act now, and that entails making do with what we have. I promise you; Charlie will come to no harm. We'll deflect attention away from him so he can do what he needs to do. Please, Sarah, I'm begging you."

Annabelle looked at her sister, her eyes filled with a desperate sincerity that she hoped Sarah couldn't ignore. She could sense Sarah's resistance waning as she pleaded with her. When Sarah shook her head, Annabelle wondered if she'd finally broken through.

"Alright," she said.

Annabelle squealed with delight.

"But," Sarah held a finger up, cutting Annabelle's squeal abruptly. "We're going to do this on one condition."

"Anything you want."

"I'm going to be a part of this plan."

"Oh, consider it done. You were already a part of it."

As Annabelle walked along the platform, she was thankful that she hadn't been wrong.

She stood close to the rail with a growing mass of other people waiting for the Tube. It would be months before the museum realised that the sextant in the glass case was a duplicate. The chances that they would discover it were very slim. Annabelle sighed and breathed in the underground air. A fresh draft blew in from the entrance, constantly dispersing the cloy of heat and body odour in the air.

Suddenly, Annabelle heard a commotion to her left. She turned, along with a few more heads towards the source of the row. She saw a skinny man running down the platform with everything he had. A couple of security men ran after him, yelling and threatening him. The skinny man had a half-wobble to his gait. It seemed as though he would break on the slightest contact with anything.

Annabelle tried to get out of the way, but the mass of bodies around her made that near impossible. The fleeing man crashed into her and knocked her straight to the ground. He stumbled to the ground and flailed around desperately as he tried to get himself up. The crowd around made it difficult for the security men to catch up, and just before they got to him, the skinny man got to his feet, and continued down the platform.

Annabelle sighed and shook her head. She started to pull herself up when she caught movement above her. She looked up and saw a tall man holding his hand out to her. She put her hand in his, and he pulled her up. He handed her bag over.

"Thank you very much," she said and held the bag close to her chest.

"No problem. It's rush hour. These things happen all the time. Are you hurt?"

"No," Annabelle smiled. "I'm fine. Thank you."

The man nodded and looked ahead. Annabelle couldn't help but notice his Australian accent. It stood out like grass in the snow.

The Tube arrived just then. Annabelle walked in as soon as the doors slid open. She took a seat, leaned back, shut her eyes, and heaved a sigh. She wasn't aware of how hard her heart was beating until then.

Damn him, she cussed as she thought about the lanky man who crashed into her. *Of all the people to run into, you chose me.*

She opened her eyes and got accustomed to the environment within the Tube. It was already full of passengers. Some, especially ones among the younger demographic, sat with earphones plugged into their ears. Others buried their eyes in a book or a magazine. Many more sat, more interested in minding their own business than doing anything else.

The doors bleeped and then they slid closed.

On impulse, Annabelle opened the bag, and peered inside. Immediately, her heart thumped. She looked out of the bag, a shocked expression in her face, and stared back in. Her eyes weren't lying the first time. The sextant was gone.

No, no, no, no, no, no.

She got up and headed for the doors, but they were closed.

"Crap crappity crap."

She placed both hands on the door and looked out through the glass panes. A few feet in front of her, a tall man stood looking in her direction. Annabelle stepped back from the door by a few paces and squinted.

Isn't that—

She was right. That was the Australian man who helped her up from the ground. He had a nasty scar running down the right side of his face, and the top part of his ear was chopped off. Annabelle wondered why she hadn't seen these the first time.

Why's he smiling at me? she asked herself.

And then she saw it.

It was right there in his palm, open for her to see.

Annabelle leaned against the door and seethed with anger. She wished the doors would just open. The Australian man held the sextant.

Annabelle felt a wave of helplessness wash over her, replacing the pain and desperation she'd been harbouring.

The man smiled and waved as the Tube began to move.

CHAPTER 7

DOWNE AND OUT

IT HAD BEEN OVER a month since the Tube incident. Yet, the memory of it still stung fresh in Annabelle's mind. There was a perpetual cloud of guilt that hovered over her. It was as if there were memorabilia everywhere she turned, like the incident was hell-bent on her never forgetting; on always feeling the pain of her care-lessness to details. Many times, she asked herself how she had let that happen? How did she let herself be swindled in that manner? Her father, for the very first time since they started to chase the prospect of Darwin's mystery island, decided to get actively involved in the mix. He orchestrated the heist, saw his own part through, only for her to go and mess it up. She trusted a stranger again.

"There's no way you could've known that it was going to happen," Sarah reassured her. "You were knocked to the ground, and you were offered a helping hand. It's not wrong to accept it."

"Neither is it wrong to reject it."

"Oh, please. Like that's something people do normally."

"That's the point, Sarah! Stealing a priceless artifact from the Natural History Museum isn't normal. I should've been on high alert. If I hadn't let my guard down, this wouldn't have happened."

"You'd already made it to the Tube with the sextant," Sarah argued. "I'd have relaxed too, thinking I was nearly home."

"But I wasn't, was I?"

"Annabelle, you keep finding ways to blame yourself, but it's not your fault."

"Does Dad feel the same way?"

"I know he wouldn't blame you, and so do you."

"Has he said that?"

Sarah hesitated.

"Has he said that to your face?" Annabelle pressed.

"Dad understands."

Annabelle sighed. "You're not answering the question, Sarah."

Sarah didn't say anything else.

Their father probably would not say anything to her face, but she felt she had let him down. Her task was simple. She didn't get her hands dirty like others did. All she had to do was just bring the sextant home, and she messed it up.

Sarah and Annabelle reclined on chaise lounges on the patio. Sarah held a book over her face, absorbed in Darwin's autobiography, while Annabelle considered taking a cold shower, craving the refreshing sensation of cool water on her skin.

"You know," Sarah said, lowering the book from her face, "I think I finally understand why you and Dad are so fascinated by this Charles Darwin guy."

Oh, sure, Annabelle rolled her eyes. *The last thing I need right now is talk about Darwin and Dad. Rub it in.*

She understood that Sarah's intent wasn't to make fun of her. However, the hurt that spurted within her at the mention of Darwin obliterated every iota of reason.

Following the theft incident, Sarah had grown increasingly

intrigued by Darwin, immersing herself in books about him. She'd been at it for a month now.

"Listen to this, Annabelle," Sarah said, sitting up and flipping through the pages of her book until she found the passage she sought. "I found this part where Darwin addressed his children, talking about the later stages of his life. I'll read it for you:

IF I HAD TO LIVE MY LIFE AGAIN, I WOULD HAVE MADE A RULE TO LISTEN TO POETRY AND LISTEN TO SOME MUSIC AT LEAST ONCE EVERY WEEK. THE LOSS OF THESE TASTES IS A LOSS OF HAPPINESS, AND MAY POSSIBLY BE INJURIOUS TO THE INTELLECT, AND MORE PROBABLY TO THE MORAL CHARACTER, BY ENFEEBLING THE EMOTIONAL PART OF OUR LITERATURE. MY CHILDREN, DO NOT ABANDON THESE VALUES. IF YOU WISH TO EMBRACE ENDLESS TREASURES AND HEALTH, FIND THE RIGHT COMBINATION OF KEYS TO UNLOCK THEM."

Sarah cleared her throat and stared at Annabelle.

"Do you think there's something hidden behind that message?" she asked. "A clue perhaps."

Annabelle wanted to tell her that just because Sarah had recently taken an interest in Darwin didn't mean every word he wrote concealed a clue to a new lead. Sometimes, words were simply words.

"I don't know," Annabelle replied after some time.

"I'm just thinking that Darwin's home might be an ideal place to get answers. A safe or a locked chest, perhaps. He mentions a combination of keys. If we find what needs to be unlocked, we might find what we're searching for."

Annabelle stared at her. "Are you serious?" Since losing the sextant, Annabelle had adopted a defeatist attitude, which had impacted her efforts more than she realised.

"Of course. Does it look like I'm joking? Darwin clearly spent some part of his life in Downe. I know we're desperately clutching at thin air now, but desperate times call for desperate measures. Short of miraculously stumbling across the sextant again, and going back on the old lead, the only way we can get back in the race is by grabbing blindly in the dark."

Annabelle hated grabbing blindly. It didn't speak of control, neither did it speak of expertise or knowledge. She wanted to have as much of her fate in her hands as she could. When she breathed, she wanted to be certain that there would be a next one, and she wanted it playing just to her tunes. What they were about to do was not the ploy of someone who was in control.

But I relinquished control that day at South Kensington's underground station, she thought.

Annabelle sighed. She knew she would do it. What other option was left?

"It's worth taking a look," she conceded. "After all, we don't have anything else to go on. However, I doubt we'll find anything. If there were a safe or chest, it would've been discovered by now."

Sarah's brows knitted as she kept her eyes fixed on the book's pages. "Oh look! It says here that Darwin's wife, Emma, was taught by Chopin himself." Her face sparkled with interest and curiosity. "Charlie would love to hear this," she said to herself more than to her sister. Annabelle shrugged. The last time she roped Charlie into the mission, Sarah had protested vehemently against it. Now, she was the one pulling Charlie along.

"How times have changed," Annabelle remarked, her words laced with bitterness.

"Oh, come on, Annabelle!" Sarah retorted, picking up on the sarcasm. "Don't be childish. This is an incredible opportunity for Charlie. Chopin's one of his favourite composers, and he personally taught Emma. Isn't that a place he'd want to visit?"

"Who am I to say anything?" Annabelle shrugged.

Sarah sighed in exasperation. "Sometimes, I forget how much of a pain you are."

The trio arrived at a small village in Downe, just outside central London. An aura of serenity hung thickly in its air, almost like the village tried to define itself by separate standards. It was beautiful, like a surreal scene from right out of a painting. It commanded attention with its cosy country roads as it spliced through the lawns and arrays of trees, growing without apparent tutelage. Horses and their riders trotted along the roads, creating a tinge of pastoral nostalgia that pulled everyone back in time.

Sarah, Charlie, and Annabelle hopped off a bus by a small roundabout in the centre of the village. They made their way up the road to Darwin's house. They passed by some locals who walked with neighbours or their dogs, exchanged nods in greeting or an amicable how-do-you-do? It didn't take much to feel the underlying sense of connection that ran through the entire village. It was like walking among members of an extended family.

Down House was a beautiful piece of a statement. It was an enormous white house with vibrant tufts of plant life around its windows. The gardens, a scenic spread of varying shades of green, surrounded the house that exuded deliberate care and love, like the gardener was especially attentive to pouring a part of his love into his work.

At the door, the trio were met by a friendly lady and an older gentleman.

"Hello, gentleman," she nodded curtly at Charlie, "and ladies," she looked at Sarah and Annabelle. "Welcome to the Down House. I expect you want to have a tour of this place," she gestured towards the house. "It's not every day we get to tread the same paths that the father of evolution once walked."

"Of course," Sarah replied.

"Alright," she said and produced a small notepad. "Just sign in here, and then Albert here," she gestured towards the older man, "will take you on a tour of the house."

The trio complied, and soon they stepped through the doors into the living space of Charles Darwin, one of history's greatest explorers, the father of modern biology, and a figure who had both captivated and vexed them for months.

Albert led them into the main hallway downstairs.

"I apologise, but you folks won't be able to take pictures in here."

Charlie's face lost some of its colour.

"Why?" he asked.

"I'm sorry," Albert smiled politely. "It's just the policy here. The house is open for tours, but some of the items in here are original, and we want to protect them as much as we can."

"That's understandable," Annabelle said.

"Thank you for understanding."

Sarah leaned in close to Annabelle and whispered,

"Like we have any choice."

Annabelle smiled. It was the first time she had smiled in a month. It was a little one, a shadow, but it was something. Much of the room downstairs had been cordoned off with red ropes so they could only stand at strategic positions to listen and watch as Albert spoke. He took them into the drawing room where Emma, Darwin's wife would play the piano and knit. The room was relatively smaller than the other rooms they had been in, but it had an exquisite touch to it. The floor was a mosaic of pink, red, and white designs, thrown against the grey and floral patterns of the wallpapers. The furniture around was sparse, but enough for a personal retreat.

"I don't know who Darwin's wife was," Annabelle said. "But she sure had an eye for good things."

"Yeah," Sarah agreed, nodding. "The decor here is charming."

"And what a cool piano she had..." Charlie pointed at the brown piano at the far end of the room.

"Yeah," Sarah ruffled his hair. She turned to Albert. "This one is a piano prodigy."

Albert smiled. "Is that so? Emma would have definitely been happy to have you. She loved people who could play the piano."

Charlie beamed.

Next, Albert led them to Darwin's study room. The walls here were made of burnished glossy brown wood.

"Here," he said, "you can see and understand why this house is important. This," he spread his arms and gestured at the entire room, "is where the great Darwin wrote the *On the Origin of Species*."

"Grandpa would be stoked to be here," Charlie said.

"With a place like this," Annabelle said as she scoured the room, "who's to say he hasn't been here already? He's had much more time to study about Darwin than any of us put together."

"True," Sarah nodded.

Out of the corner of her eye, Annabelle noticed a painting on the wall just by the door. She turned away from Albert and squinted at the paining. She could swear that the artistic style was familiar.

"Excuse me, Albert," she cut him off. "Sorry. But who's painting is that?" she pointed at the frame.

"Oh, that." Albert's face lit up. He walked towards the frame, and the trio followed. "This is a painting of the *HMS Beagle*. It was given to Darwin as a gift. It's a painting by Conrad Martens."

Annabelle's eyes flew wider. They began to fill with sparks of hope. She and Sarah exchanged a glance, and then she focused on the painting. It was a scenic depiction of the sea cutting through a league of mountains, moving towards a white snow-capped mountain range at the backdrop. There was a ship with full white sails at the foot of one of the mountains, and a canoe a few miles in front of it.

Charlie had left the group a while back, intent on finding something else in the room that held more interest.

"I believe on good authority," Albert continued, "that this is the only painting of his here in the UK. The rest are in Australia."

"Besides paintings," Annabelle said, "is there anything from Martens here? Anything at all?" She hoped she didn't come off as too desperate.

"Well, not here exactly. I do know that they wrote each other on multiple occasions. They were good friends. Sadly, we don't have those letters with us at the moment. This painting is all we have of Conrad Martens."

The light in Annabelle's eyes dwindled. Sarah noticed and gave her a gentle squeeze on the shoulder. Annabelle thought that she was beginning to have her first headway in a month. She couldn't have been more wrong.

"What about a safe or a compartment with multiple locks?"

"I beg your pardon?" Albert asked, confused by the question that was asked.

"Never mind," Annabelle said and realised shortly after that it was not a normal question to ask.

They continued upstairs, unintentionally leaving Charlie behind. Alone, he decided to exercise his newfound freedom. He walked over to other rooms, peeping and trying to ascertain if they held anything of interest to him. He peeped into what he guessed was a dining room. It held a large dark brown table in the centre with multiple chairs around it. Charlie carried on.

He made his way back to the drawing room and looked straight at the piano at the far corner. He took a quick glance at the corridor to ensure he was alone. Carefully, he walked into the drawing room and stepped gingerly over the roped fence. Soon, he stood in front of the piano and admired the artifact. It wasn't any different from what he had at home; it was just older. It must have been undergoing regular maintenance because there was not a drop of dust on its surface, and it still looked workable. He raised the piano lid and exposed the array of yellowed and black keys. The piano stool was already adjusted to the right height, and he sat down on it.

His mother had seemed excited with the idea that Darwin's wife had been taught by Chopin. She made the mistake of thinking this fact excited her son just as much. Chopin didn't enjoy the celebrity status in Charlie's eyes. He was a great composer, no doubt, but Charlie couldn't just bring himself to fawn over him. Perhaps, it was because he spent seemingly endless stretches of time, practicing Chopin's compositions for his concert at school, and finally nailing it.

Charlie felt his fingers tingle. They wanted to play. It had been several months since he last played an elaborate piece of musical composition on the piano. He wanted to see just how much he remembered.

He hit the C note gently, and he cringed. The sound was off.

There's no way in the world that's a C, he thought. He reappraised the instrument. *This piano probably hasn't been tuned since Darwin lived here.*

Regardless, he had to feed the tingling in his fingers otherwise, he would have no rest. So, he continued as he keyed in the rest of the notes, just as he remembered them. Just as he practised. His muscle memory kicked in, and his finger movements became fluid, every note they created, melded with enviable silkiness into the other. It was an exquisite symphony. He segued into the fast, rippling section of the composition, and he let himself be carried by the thrill of it. Then, something really unusual happened.

The piano gave off a loud click and caused Charlie to pause mid-movement. His eyes bulged like balls.

What was that! he thought as he feared he damaged something.

He looked around the piano and ran his hands around the surface until he felt something underneath. He paused. He got on his knees and looked under. There was a small open compartment, the size of a book just under the piano. Inside, there was a piece of paper neatly rolled up and tied with a string. Charlie ran his tongue over his lips, reached into the compartment and pulled out the roll of paper. Then he closed it.

He just got to his feet when Albert ran in through the door, livid with rage.

"What do you think you're doing, young man! Get out from there! Now!"

Startled, Charlie quickly slipped the roll of paper into his pocket. He turned and gently lowered the piano's lid.

"You don't touch things in places like this!" Albert continued. His face glowered so much he might have been a steam engine.

"I'm so sorry," Sarah apologised to the tour guide as she ran into the room. She faced Charlie. "You heard the man, Charlie. Get out of there. Oh, God, what were you thinking? This is why I can't bring you to places like this."

Annabelle stood back, more mentally than physically, and observed the situation like a third wheel. She knew something was up. She had seen Charlie at the very last moment slip something inside his pocket. The boy was shaken. It was as clear as day.

"I'm sorry," he said. "I didn't break anything."

"You better not have," Albert spat. Annabelle stared at him. She wanted to tell him to keep his mouth shut; that he didn't have to yell at Charlie in that manner. For some reason, her lips didn't work.

"I'm afraid you all have overstayed your welcome," Albert said with a tone of finality. "I must ask you to leave."

"Please, sir, it hasn't come to that," Sarah said. "It was just a little curiosity on the boy's part. Please, let's continue with the tour, I'll make sure it doesn't happen again."

Annabelle saw the flint hardness in the man's eyes, and knew Sarah was wasting her time. She could plead with him from now till the end of time, and he wouldn't budge.

"Hey," Annabelle touched Sarah on the shoulder. "I think we should leave."

Sarah tried to say something, but Annabelle gave her a quizzical look. She shut her lips and swallowed her words.

"Thanks," Annabelle muttered, leaving the room without waiting for Albert's response.

They walked back to the village in silence.

"I found something," Charlie worked up the courage to say after some time.

"It can wait," Annabelle replied. "Not here."

They made their way to a small restaurant in the eye of the village. Its architecture was modest; it's seating arrangement, a little congested, but they couldn't exactly hold the management to blame. The restaurant was only small enough to fit about twenty people. They settled into one of the tables and ordered tea and coffee.

"Well, Charlie..." Annabelle said as she faced her nephew. "Do you mind getting your Mum and I up to speed? What happened in there?"

"I didn't mean to cause any trouble. I'm sorry."

"It's okay," Sarah said. "That man was just mean. I did tell him that you were a piano prodigy after all. What did he expect?" She scoffed and shook her head.

"Charlie," Annabelle cocked a brow.

"Oh, alright." Charlie leaned forward and let the entire story fly. He spared no details, intimating them of the off key as well as the hidden compartment at the piano's underside.

Annabelle smiled and was impressed. "So that's what Darwin meant by the '*right combination of keys*'. He was talking about piano keys."

Sarah looked mortified. She sighed and pinched her forehead. "I knew it," she said. "I've turned my son into a thief. I knew that encouraging him to swap that sextant was a bad idea, and now I've created a domino effect." She looked at the ceiling and threw her arms up in frustration. "My son is going to grow into a criminal and I'm responsible for it."

"Shut up, Sarah, and stop quibbling," Annabelle said.

"See? Even his aunt supports him."

Annabelle shook her head, and looked at Charlie, who was already near tears.

"Can I have it?" she asked as she stretched her palm forward.

Charlie nodded and gave her the roll of paper.

Annabelle proceeded to untie the string gently. Then she unravelled the paper. There was a smaller piece inside, torn, but neatly folded.

Charlie picked up the paper and unfolded it. Suddenly, he pulled his head back in surprise.

"Woah," he exclaimed.

"What is it?" Annabelle asked. Unable to contain her curiosity, she took the paper from him. It was a map, but an incomplete one. The other half, wherever it was, had been torn off. Her eyes rekindled with hope.

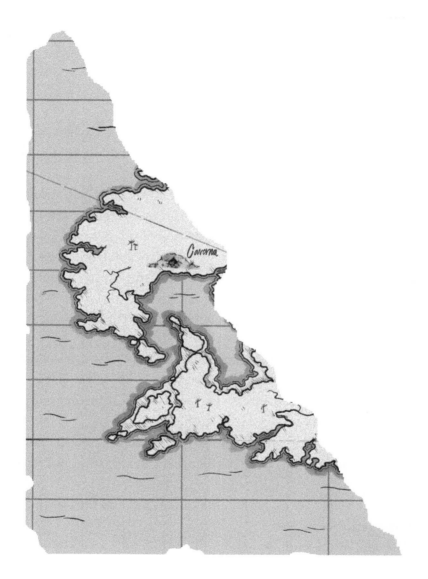

"Well, what does it say?" Sarah asked.

"I thought you weren't interested, seeing as you were turning your son into a hardened criminal."

Sarah sniggered and made a face, throwing Charlie into laughter.

Annabelle handed the torn map to her, then she focused on the bigger piece of paper. It was a letter. A letter from Darwin himself. Annabelle looked around the restaurant. Thankfully, it was still largely empty. She drew her chair closer to the table and read the contents of the letter in a low voice.

MY DEAR CHILDREN,

I AM PROUD THAT YOU HAVE USED THE BEAUTY OF CHOPIN TO OPEN THE PIANO. AS PROMISED, I HAVE PROVIDED YOU WITH PART OF THE MAP. UNFORTUNATELY, ONE THIRD OF THE MAP IS ALL THAT I CAN PROVIDE FOR YOUR QUEST.

WHEREVER THE EUROPEAN HAD TROD, DEATH SEEMED TO PURSUE THE ABORIGINAL. TO PROTECT THIS PLACE, I CANNOT RISK THE MAP BEING WHOLE AND IN ONE PLACE.

MY DEAR FRIEND, MR. MARTENS HAS USED ONE OF MY DEVICES FROM THE VOYAGE TO HIDE THE OTHER PIECE. HOWEVER, I AM NOT SURE OF THE WHEREABOUTS OF THE THIRD PIECE. HOT COFFEE HAS REFUSED TO STAY IN TOUCH. REMEMBER, IF YOU SUCCEED IN OBTAINING ALL THREE, THE PURPOSE OF HAVING THEM SHOULD BE FOR GOOD INTEN-TIONS ONLY. SINCE THE PASSING OF OUR DEAREST ANNIE, WE HAVE LOST THE JOY OF THE HOUSEHOLD, AND THE SOLACE OF OUR OLD AGE. OH, THAT SHE COULD KNOW HOW DEEPLY, HOW TENDERLY, WE DO STILL AND SHALL EVER LOVE HER DEAR JOYOUS FACE. I DO NOT WISH THE SAME FATE FOR YOU, MY CHILDREN. FIND THIS PLACE IF YOU EVER GET STRUCK WITH ILL HEALTH.

CHARLES

Annabelle was stoked. Her face shone like a candlelight in swathes of darkness.

"I can't believe it," she said. "Oh my God. There really is a place."

"I'm confused." Sarah blinked. "Why would Darwin want to send someone who's sick to an unknown place?"

"I don't know," Annabelle shrugged. "But that's something we're going to find out."

"I think we both know what Darwin may be referring to when he said Martens used his device to hide the second location of the map."

"Yeah." Annabelle's shoulder slouched. "The sextant. I wonder if the guy who stole it has already found the second piece."

Sarah turned the map over and inspected it, like she sensed something odd with its pale appearance. Suddenly, her face perked up.

"Look," she said, pointing at the back of the map. "There are numbers here. *12036'3...*" She trailed off. "That's where it ends. The rest have been torn off."

Annabelle stared deeply into the air. "They must be co-ordinates. We need to get the other pieces in order to find this place."

"Who's *Hot Coffee*?" Charlie cut in. "It's such a weird name."

Annabelle and Sarah nodded in agreement. It was quite a name, but whoever they were, they had the third piece. It was a requisite if they were going to find Darwin's mysterious island.

CHAPTER 8

THE HUNTER AND THE HUNTED

Santiago, Cape Verde

NIGEL SQUINTED AS HE stepped out of the taxi, shielding his eyes from the relentless sun. Its fiery heat seemed to thicken the air, transforming the entire town into a sweltering oven. He placed a hand over his eyes as he inspected the noisy street. The zinc roofs atop the pallid low-rise buildings didn't help to alleviate the sun's glare. Little tufts of light bounced off them, jumping into his eyes.

Why didn't I bring my damn sunglasses? he thought.

He walked to the driver's seat and leaned in to address the man inside: a stout, middle-aged fellow with weathered cocoa skin and tobacco-stained teeth.

"Are you certain this is the place?" Nigel asked.

"I'm sure," the driver nodded. "This is just inside town. Visitors find very good accommodation here."

Nigel surveyed the bustling street. At the far corner, a cluster of stalls accounted for most of the activity. Vendors stood behind vibrant displays of vegetables, shouting and haggling with customers. A group of boys sprinted past the taxi, giggling and shouting in Portuguese. Nigel marvelled at how effortlessly they ran under the sun, their bare upper bodies glistening with sweat. Despite wearing thin clothes, he felt stifled by the oppressive heat, his sweat-soaked garments clinging to his skin like a second layer.

"Hey!" the driver called. "You going to pay me or what?"

Nigel looked at the driver and hesitated a bit. Then he dug into his back pocket and brought out his wallet.

"You'd better not be playing with me, my friend."

The driver smiled as he revealed an entire row of crooked yellowed teeth.

"Me? I don't play with visitors," he said. "Visitors give good money. I take them wherever they want to go."

As Nigel counted out a stack of Cape Verdean escudo, the driver's cracked lips parted in anticipation.

"Here," Nigel handed his payment over to the driver.

The driver smiled. "That's my man." He started the engine. "I'm always around for some business, eh? You know where to find me if you want to go to the beach, or the trees and mountain range, all of the places where you visitors like to visit."

Nigel smiled and nodded, watching the taxi disappear down the narrow street. As he strolled along, he observed that most of the houses were made of stone, many adorned with a smattering of handwritten names—some familiar, others not.

Up ahead, a rusty sign caught his attention. As he drew nearer, his eyes lit up with recognition. Though Nigel's Portuguese was far from fluent despite his multiple visits to the island, he easily identified the words for hotel.

The hotel stood slightly taller than the surrounding buildings, its exterior predominantly white, save for patches where the paint had weathered away to reveal the grey stone beneath. The edges around some of the windows were chipped, but only slightly. The windows themselves appeared newer, suggesting recent renovations.

Having spent so long under the sun, Nigel had almost forgotten what it felt like to be without its scorching presence. As soon as he stepped onto the hotel's clean floorboards, a wave of cool, refreshing air washed over him. It ate through him like a canker, almost weakening his legs. Nigel closed his eyes and sighed.

"The sun is hot, right?" the hotel receptionist asked. A native of the island, she had smooth, almost luminous skin and a stunning set of pearly white teeth. Her hair was neatly tied in a bun, and her brown khaki uniform fit her impeccably.

Nigel smiled in return.

"Yes," he agreed.

"Don't worry. You'll get used to it. All tourists do after a day or two. What brings you here, sir?"

"I'm looking to get a room for a few days."

"You could have checked downtown for some accommodation. They've got accommodation that is better suited for tourists."

Nigel looked around. "Are you saying this isn't up to par?"

"No. That's not what I'm saying. But you know tourists and their thing for aesthetics."

Nigel chuckled. "My brother and I have been here several times in the past. I thought I'd try out another part of town this time around, you know, for a more immersive experience. He's arriving tomorrow, so I might get him to check this place out too."

The receptionist smiled warmly. "Well, welcome."

After processing a full payment for his room, Nigel was assisted upstairs by a bellboy—a young, wiry teenager with a spark in his eyes and an eager smile. Grateful for the help, Nigel handed him a few escudos. The boy's eyes widened in appreciation, and he stared at Nigel as though he'd just performed a miracle.

"Thank you, sir," the boy said.

Nigel smiled as he nodded.

He closed the door behind him the moment the boy ran down the stairs. Nigel turned on his heels and inspected the room. Though slightly smaller than the rooms he'd stayed in before, it had a certain charm. The minimalist decor featured neatly painted walls—three sides a warm shade between yellow and brown—while the fourth wall, opposite the bed and bearing the television, showcased a leopard skin-patterned wallpaper. A small shelf beneath the television, a table and chair near the bed, and a coffee table on the other side of the bed completed the furnishings. Nigel nodded approvingly.

"Not bad," he said. "Not bad at all."

If one was tired of staying inside, the balcony through the light caramel curtains would offer some reprieve. They wouldn't need to step outside unless the need was dire.

Nigel walked through the billowing curtains out to the balcony. The effect of the sun was milder here, as it hung at the other side of the building. The ravishing flora of the island sprawled out before him, with a few more buildings getting caught in the mix. He saw a few hills in the distance. Later in the day, Nigel made a mental note to go sightseeing. He needed to touch down by the beach and explore the rest of the island. First, he needed something to eat. One of the island's local delicacies came to mind. Rather than order them from the hotel's restaurant, he would get them from the street vendors. Food gotten from off the streets were usually the sweetest and gave the most authentic local experience.

Returning to his room, Nigel quickly ducked into the bathroom to wash away the day's sweat, grime, and heat. As he stepped out, he felt revitalized, as if he had just donned a fresh new layer of skin.

The street hadn't changed since Nigel had got into the hotel. Vehicles crawled across as they tooted endlessly. People milled about as their voices created an endless buzz that hung in the air. A woman by one of the street corners hawked some pieces of cloth to another, another carried a smaller basket of colourful chickens, while a man to his left displayed an array of fresh vegetables to a customer. Nigel walked over to him and bought one huge apple. He paid in local currency and bit into the apple as he walked away. He almost moaned from the juice that filled his mouth. Santiago might be quieter than Sydney, but it had just as much life and activity buzzing through its veins.

Suddenly, Nigel's heart lurched. A man in a polo shirt and shorts had emerged from a building a few meters away. He wasn't a local; his white skin marked him as a tourist or visitor to most. But those who knew him would recognize the sinister scar on the right side of his face. The man stood in front of the building, hands in his pockets, surveying the streets with a menacing smirk.

Nigel hastily pressed himself against the nearest wall, praying he hadn't been spotted. He cautiously peeked out at the street again— the man was still there. Nigel didn't need further confirmation. He knew that even without seeing it, the upper section of the man's right ear was missing, completely severed.

What could be of interest to Mikey in Santiago? Nigel wondered.

There could be only one thing. Poaching.

In his career dedicated to protecting animals from the malevolence of poachers, Nigel had encountered Mikey's name more often than any other. Mikey was the Don Corleone of poaching; no one else came close to his level of skill. Elusive, he had managed to keep a low profile, evading arrest despite his audaciousness. Mikey was a brash, arrogant man, openly boasting about his trade while somehow managing to stay one step ahead of the law. Nigel had figured it out a couple of years back, but it still hadn't brought him any closer to thwarting Mikey.

Mikey catered to an elite clientele—people with money to burn. When a wealthy individual desired a rare, exotic animal as part of their collection, part of the money Mikey earned ensured his own security. He infiltrated and escaped from locations with the stealth of a stalking cat and the silence of a graveyard.

Mikey posed a significant threat, and Nigel couldn't believe that fate had just delivered him right into his hands. He kept his eyes on Mikey as he followed a safe distance behind, making sure he didn't attract any unwanted attention.

Well, he thought, *there goes my vacation. It's a good thing my brother isn't arriving today.*

He didn't know where Mikey was going, but the island boasted a bank of exotic animals. It was clear that Mikey was up to no good, and Nigel was determined not to let him succeed.

Mikey continued walking as the buildings around them grew sparse. Nigel had purchased a sunhat and sunglasses from a roadside store a few minutes earlier, providing the perfect disguise. He checked his wristwatch and wondered if Mikey had become aware of his presence.

They walked now for close to thirty minutes. *Where exactly is he going?* The road up ahead led to a cluster of larger trees at the base of a hill, surrounded mostly by shrubbery. The ground appeared dry, stony, and dark brown.

Suddenly, Nigel caught Mikey looking behind him. Quickly, he whipped out his phone and pretended to be taking pictures of the surroundings. The road wasn't exactly a deserted one. People moved around in trickles, and it helped him blend in. All the while, Nigel kept Mikey within the sights of his peripheral vision. The man looked around some more. Nigel thought he detected some purpose to the man's inspection. Mikey didn't stay long for Nigel to make sure. He turned and took a winding bend away from the road.

Nigel counted fifteen heartbeats before he followed him down the bend.

Mikey had disappeared by the time Nigel got on the road.

Oh, come on, don't tell me I've lost him, Nigel thought in dismay. Fortunately, he didn't have to search long before spotting Mikey entering a small local church on the hillside. The church was a modest rectangular structure with a triangular roof, topped by a blue cross. The windows and door were smaller than any he had seen on a church before. A similar building without a cross stood a short distance away.

Three dirt bikes were parked next to the house. Nigel glanced at them briefly. He made a mental note to go for a ride on these bikes during his time here later. It had been years since he last rode a bike, but the thrill of the ride never got old whenever he mounted one. He took his eyes back to the church.

The white and blue painting of the façade made the church stand in hard contrast against the surrounding brown sun-baked earth. Nigel crept closer to the building, careful not to make his presence known just yet. Suddenly, he heard collective but disjointed cries of horror. He felt icy pin pricks run all over his skin.

Mikey's voice was loud and clear.

"Where is it?" the man shouted. "Where's the damn thing!"

Nigel moved closer to the church doors.

"I know you have it," Mikey continued. "Where is it! If you don't give it to me, I'm going to blow your brains out. Don't try me. I'll scatter your brains out on the floor and walls, right here."

Another wave of disconcerted cries floated out of the church towards Nigel.

Nigel glared at the church while he gritted his teeth. He couldn't stay put any longer. He needed to see what Mikey was up to. Besides, the people in there were in trouble.

Nigel bent down and approached the church from the side. He climbed its blue stairs and peered through the door. The entrance opened into an aisle that scythed through two rows of chairs and stopped only at the altar at the opposite end. It was right at the feet of the altar that Nigel saw the cause of the commotion. A group of about four of five nuns, dressed in black and white, were on their knees, huddled up close to a priest, a middle-aged native with full black curly hair. Mikey towered over them as he pointed something at them.

"I'm warning you for the last time," Mikey yelled as he thrusted the object in his hand forward. The nuns whimpered and startled with fear.

It's a gun, Nigel realised. *The bastard is holding them at gunpoint.*

He looked at how helpless the group on the ground looked. They were just quiet natives, content with doing their work in their church until Mikey came running, asking for something that they obviously didn't have. Nigel could see the terror in their eyes; it was nearly palpable.

Nigel's jaw tensed and moved as he ground his teeth together. His eyes grew steely as he stared into the church. He knew what he had to do.

He climbed the stairs and walked through the doors.

For a few seconds, Mikey was entirely oblivious to Nigel's presence. He contemplated creeping up to Mikey and snatching the weapon from his hands. On second thought, he decided to try another approach. He didn't put it past Mikey to freak out and do something nasty to his victims.

As Nigel walked, he looked around the church and searched for something – anything – he could use as a weapon. Like outside, the

114

walls continued the white colouration. Rather than transition into blue painting, the walls had a wallpaper with floral patterns at its bottom. There was a door just in front of the right pew, but it looked shut. The ceiling was naked and bared its burnished wooden beams.

Nigel's search was futile in the end. He couldn't find a thing. It was as though the church itself tried to steer clear of any iota of violence. Barring the cross that hung on the wall at the centre of the altar, there was nothing else.

Nigel stopped at the centre of the aisle and stared at Mikey. Some of the nuns had already spotted him at that point.

Nigel cleared his throat.

Quickly, Mikey spun the gun around and faced him.

"Woah," Nigel raised his hands, "take it easy, man."

His speech, his movements, were gentle, not too hastened, not too slow either. His demeanour was calm, unperturbed. Almost like he already knew how things would pan out.

"Look man," Nigel continued, "let these people go. Whatever you think they have, they don't have it."

"And who do you think you are?" Mikey asked as he put his finger closer to the trigger. He had an astonished look on his face. One of the nuns broke into a sob.

"Shut your mouth," Mikey barked, stifling the woman's distraught sound almost immediately.

Nigel carefully removed his sunglasses and hat. Mikey drew his head slightly backwards as his face brightened with recognition.

"You," he said, with a hint of annoyance in his voice. "You're that bloody thorn in my side that sabotaged me in Kenya."

"That's right, me." Nigel nodded. "What's the problem? Why are you bothering these good folks?"

"If you know what's good for you, you'll walk right out of here and mind your own damn business. There are no rhinos for you to save this time."

Nigel didn't respond. He remained still and kept his eyes fixed on the gun that was aimed in his direction.

Mikey faced the priest.

"You'll tell me where it is right this instant," he growled.

"Or what?" Nigel asked.

Mikey grimaced and inhaled through his teeth. He faced Nigel.

"Do you know how many people want you locked up?" Nigel continued. "Maybe I can fix that."

Mikey stifled a laugh. He trained the gun on Nigel. "Yeah, good luck with that."

He glared at Nigel and dared him with the flame in his eyes to make just one heroic move.

Nigel tittered. "You know, I've faced people like you countless times in the past."

"People like me?"

"Yeah. Pricks. They always have something going for them. You know, something other than real strength. You," he stabbed a finger in Mikey's direction, "have a reputation that precedes you, Mikey. Look at you, powerless without your gun."

He chuckled. "Is that what you think?"

"You're a hunter, aren't you?"

"The best in the world."

"Then prove it. Stop cowering behind a gun. It's a very quick way to dispatch your prey. Surely, there's no honour in that. Come, fight me without the gun. A true hunter should be able to dispatch an ordinary man in no time."

A menacing grin snaked onto Mikey's face. It crumpled up, squeezing the scar and made him look like a one-eyed street cat.

He combed his fingers through his blonde hair and smacked his lips.

"Alright," he said as he dropped his gun. "You've chosen death.

You're going to get it exactly how you want it."

Mikey stooped and drew out a dagger from a small bag next to him.

"Alright," he played with the dagger between his fingers. He turned to the priest. "Say a prayer for my friend here, will you? He's done so many good deeds in his miserable life, he may need to go to heaven after here."

"Put your mouth where your hands are, brother," Nigel said, as he cracked his neck. "That's all I want to see."

Mikey spread his legs apart and lowered into a crouch. He held his dagger poised and smiled menacingly at Nigel. Nigel drew closer, holding out bowled fists. The nuns and the priest at the ground didn't know whether to intervene on the impending bloodshed or stay back and watch as spectators. The fear, despite the ambivalence in their minds, helped them decide. It rooted them to the spot.

Mikey slashed the dagger countlessly through the air, hoping to see fear steal into his opponent's eyes. But he got the opposite reaction. Nigel's eyes were as hard as flint.

"Come on," Mikey egged him on. They circled each other. "Stop acting like a child and come forward."

Nigel stared at the dagger in Mikey's grip with no emotion. He would have taken the fight to Mikey if he didn't have the dagger on him. The dagger gave him the advantage of offense. Nigel, on the other hand, would have to go on the defensive and hope for offensive openings during the brawl.

Nigel stepped to the side as he tried to circle Mikey – though he was no fool. Mikey moved along. Accidently, he kicked his small bag.

The sound of metal clattered against the church's concrete floor as it splintered the tension in the air. Nigel followed the metal object as it bounced across the ground, rolled and stopped at his feet. He squinted.

This looks familiar, he thought.

The object was a dull golden colour, and it was structured like a compass. Except it was bigger, didn't have a glass screen. Although, it did have external dials. Nigel tilted his head slightly to the left. He knew he was staring at a sextant. It was unusual as much as it was familiar. It had delicate, calligraphic writings on its body. All of a sudden, it hit him.

This was the same sextant Annabelle had described to him when she told him about the heist at the Natural History Museum.

"Hey," Nigel stared at Mikey. "This isn't yours."

Mikey stared back, frightened by a fraction.

"It's not yours either. So, don't do anything stupid."

At that moment, Mikey wished he still had his gun with him.

"Yeah?" Nigel dared him with his eyes. "Try to stop me."

As he stooped to pick up the sextant, Mikey made a mad dash forward. He collided into Nigel and threw him backwards. Nigel grunted as his shoulder hit one of the pews. He pulled himself up and heard the sound of footsteps run past him. He whipped his head around in time to see Mikey jump out of the doors. The spot where he last saw the sextant, was empty. It was gone.

Nigel jumped to his feet and dashed out the doors. An engine roared to his left. He spun around and saw Mikey speeding away on a dirt bike as it left behind a trail of dust. The dirt bike made little jerky movements as he tried to maintain his speed on the rough terrain. Quickly, but calmly, Nigel bounded towards the remaining dirt bikes he had seen earlier. He mounted one of them. Thankfully, the keys were still on the ignition. He kicked the bike on and took off after Mikey.

Their bikes gave off a constricted roar that cleaved through the air like an assault. One pushed his bike to get away from the other, while the other throttled to cover up the distance between him and the escapee.

Nigel squinted to keep the dust from his eyes. He throttled the bike, feeding it with more juice, but enough to keep it from going past its limits.

Given that he had a few seconds' head start, Mikey was still a good bit beyond Nigel's reach. Nigel didn't give up. He knew how these things worked. One mistake from Mikey was all he needed to cover the distance.

Soon, they made their way into a little wooded area. Mikey swerved sharply to the left and avoided a rut in the middle of the road. Nigel missed it until the very last moment. Upon impact, the bike lost its stance. It pitched forward on its front wheel.

Nigel moved backwards a bit, adjusted his balance on the bike, and landed on one wheel. He gunned the bike's engine, riding on the front wheel for a few seconds longer. The back wheel bounced back to the ground and Nigel increased the bike's acceleration.

Mikey had gained more distance in the time it took him to right himself.

"Damn it!" Nigel cussed.

He gunned the engine some more.

Nigel spotted a right bend on the dirt track up ahead. An idea dropped in from the blue. He swerved off the road and into the trees. He kicked the bike into another gear and pushed the throttle as far as it could go. The bike weaved through the trees elegantly, with Nigel occasionally putting his foot on the ground to gain a smooth turn. He kept a strong grip on the bike as it rolled across stones, roots, and twigs. As he looked up ahead, he saw that the bike was heading back towards the dirt track again.

Suddenly, his eyes fell on a berm right where the edge of the woods met the dirt track. He couldn't afford to slow down, so he pushed the throttle to its limits.

The engine gave a whiny roar as it sped forward, desperate to not get caught. Nigel kept his hands firmly on the bike's handles as he prepped himself for a move. Just as the bike climbed the berm, he pushed himself downwards and gave the bike an extra bounce. The bike rose clean off the ground.

At that same moment, Mikey drove by. His eyes met Nigel's as he and his bike vaulted over him. Mikey sped past. Nigel turned the bike's head a little so he could right himself as soon as he landed. The tires hit the ground with no more than a little bounce. Nigel pushed the throttle and continued to give chase.

Now, he covered much of the distance that existed between him and Mikey. This time around, he kept a watchful eye on the track, to keep from making mistakes like the one he made a few minutes ago.

The dirt track eased into a tarred road. They got into the populated areas of the town now. Nigel was much closer than before and got closer with every second. Mikey began to tire.

Suddenly, Mikey twisted backwards. Nigel had just enough time to see the gun aimed in his direction and veered off course. A gunshot rang out. The natives around screamed and scrambled for safety.

"Move!" Nigel yelled as he sped forwards. He couldn't afford to slow down for anything. "Move, move, move!"

His warning dawned on some of them too late, and they had to dive out of the way. Nigel moved through a few stalls and then got back on the road. Mikey found it difficult to move through the streets - there were just too many people and vehicles to avoid. Regardless, the chase went on. It couldn't stop.

Mikey turned and fired more shots behind him. Nigel would veer of the road each time, avoiding pedestrians and skirting around stalls that held fruits, vegetables, and other groceries. Some of the natives, profoundly shaken by the jarring experience, would scream curses after them.

He got back to the road and saw that Mikey had a close call with a taxi. The driver had just pushed the door open into Mikey's path and Mikey skidded to a stop. To Nigel's surprise, it was the driver who dropped him off earlier.

Perfect timing, Nigel thought. He felt a spurt of excitement, he was so close to Mikey now. *You'll get a bigger tip from me once I catch him.*

The driver started to pelt Mikey with heated words and other forms of curses in imperfect English and fluent, perfectly accented Portuguese. Mikey, panicky, and aware of Nigel's engine growing louder, whipped the muzzle of his gun across the driver's face and sent him to the ground in a heap.

He pushed the taxi door closed and started to move away. Nigel stretched his arm and intended to pull Mikey off his bike. He was so close now.

With the speed of light, Mikey turned and fired a shot at Nigel. Nigel's mind froze at that moment. Mikey had shot so unexpectedly that he didn't have the luxury of evasion. He saw his headlights spark and exploded different shards of glass.

Phew. He just missed death by a hair's breadth.

Mikey tried to shoot again, but the gun clicked. The chamber was empty.

"Damn it!" he cussed and flung the gun at Nigel's head. Nigel bowed quickly and evaded the projectile.

The two bikes continued to speed through the streets, creating chaos and instability. They left the town again, going uphill into the mountains. The terrain here was stony and full of hardened ruts. The bikes shook and bounced as it moved upwards. Mikey almost fell, but he placed a foot on the ground almost immediately and throttled the bike. The back tire spun with the speed of lightning and kicked up a cloud of dust in Nigel's face.

Nigel squinted as he burst through the cloud. He stretched his arm out, trying to see if he could get a hold of Mikey's bike. He was only a few inches away. He tried again, but the effort seemed to be giving Mikey more distance. So, he stopped, and deferred to trying to catch up with him.

They climbed the mountain until they got to the peak.

Mikey saw the edge of the platform coming up ahead at the very last minute and jumped off the bike. The bike hit the ground, skidded across the surface and then went over the edge of the mountain as it plummeted to the bottom.

The engine of Nigel's bike purring behind Mikey. He shut his eyes tight and sighed in disappointment. He turned and faced Nigel.

"Finally," Nigel said. Both men were covered in sheets of dust. Their eyes shone with the truth of finality. Nigel wasn't going to let Mikey leave the island with that sextant. Mikey wasn't eager to let Nigel have it either. There was only one way this could end.

Nigel killed the engine and stepped off the back. Both men had their eyes trained on each other the entire time.

"You know," Nigel said. "You can still walk out now before it's too late. Just hand over the sextant."

Mikey chuckled and drew out his dagger. "What do you take me for, huh? A coward? I've slit more throats than you can count. Yours is just going to be the latest that kisses my blade."

If Nigel was put off by the threat of imminent death, he didn't show it. He just watched Mikey with icy clarity.

Without warning, Mikey dashed forward and took a swipe at Nigel with the dagger.

Nigel bent backwards like a stalk of maize in the wind. He side-stepped Mikey's assault and pushed him on the back.

Mikey stumbled forwards, nearly falling. He turned and ran at Nigel like a mad man. Nigel took a few hurried steps backwards as Mikey lunged at him with the dagger. He waited patiently, like a lioness in ambush. He evaded Mikey's thrusts and swipes, keeping his eyes on his dagger arm, and waited for the opportune moment. It came.

Mikey lashed out with his hand, and Nigel brought a bowled fist down on his arm. Stung by the blow, Mikey hesitated a moment too long, and gave his foe the chance to land a blow across his face.

Mikey grunted in pain and staggered backwards. Nigel came for him.

That was his mistake.

Mikey had got away with poaching for far too long not just because of his clientele, but because he was a sly fox. He pretended to be in far more pain than Nigel had inflicted, hoping to draw Nigel in. The moment he saw Nigel bound towards him; his lips spread into a small smile.

"Gotcha," he said.

With a quick thrust, his dagger found Nigel's lap and buried itself in, almost to the hilt. Nigel screamed in pain but reacted quickly. He whipped up his knee and smashed it into Mikey's jaw. Mikey's sight went out of focus. He staggered backwards, dizzy, and completely disoriented. Blood dribbled from the sides of his mouth onto his clothes.

With a start, Nigel realised the man was heading towards the edge of the mountain. He quickly moved forward and stretched his arm to grab for Mikey. It was too late.

Mikey's foot left solid ground, and he pitched backwards, falling off the edge of the platform.

Nigel hissed and shut his eyes. After reopening them, he realised that Mikey had really fallen off. There was no way anyone could survive a fall from such a height. Nigel peered over the edge and saw Mikey's lifeless body lying across the rocks next to his damaged bike. *Damn it!*

Nigel stepped back and sucked in air through his teeth from the pain. The dagger was still sticking out of his thigh. He wrapped his fingers around its hilt. Took one sharp breath and yanked it out. He grimaced as he gave a sharp cry. He let the dagger clatter on the ground. The blade gleamed red with his blood. He looked at his lap. Blood spread rapidly as it seeped into his clothes. He tore off a portion of his shirt and tied it around the wound, stemming the blood flow. He turned and cast his eyes about.

"Where is it?" he wondered out loud.

Out of the corner of his eye, the little bag sat close to the edge. He limped towards it, wincing slightly as he moved. In one swoop, he picked the bag up. The sextant was right inside it.

Just then, a phone rang. It came from inside the bag. The late Mikey had left his phone behind. Nigel rummaged through the bag for a few seconds before he found the phone. He pulled it out and gazed at the screen. The call was from an unknown ID. He picked it up and put it to his ear.

"Did you get it?" the voice at the other end asked.

"Who's this?"

The caller hung up immediately.

Nigel stared at the phone and shook his head. He threw it back into the bag, slung it over his shoulder and walked towards the dirt bike.

CHAPTER 9

ON THE ORIGIN OF SPECIES

THE PRIEST STOOD AT the entrance of the church and watched as Nigel brought the gurgling bike to a stop. Nigel grimaced as he swung his leg over the bike.

"Holy Mary, Mother of God!" the priest exclaimed as he saw the blood on Nigel. One half of his denim pants was tinged red with blood.

Nigel smiled through his grimace of pain as he limped towards the priest.

"You'll say the foreigners have brought trouble to the house of God," he quipped.

With a compassionate expression, the priest stepped forward, draping Nigel's arm over his shoulder to support him. Together, they ascended the church steps.

"The house of God is a sanctuary for the troubled, my son," the priest replied.

"Ah, yes," Nigel chuckled, the sound strangled by his pain.

The priest helped him onto one of the pews.

"You stay put," the priest said. "I will only be a minute."

Nigel dropped the bag beside him and watched the priest disappear through the door to the vestry. Exhaling, Nigel leaned back, adrenaline still coursing through his veins from the exhilarating chase. He hadn't expected to ride a motorcycle again, but today's events had shattered that notion. It had been years since he last straddled one.

"I hope you didn't have to wait long," the priest, reappearing to kneel beside Nigel.

"No, you were only gone for a minute, just like you said."

The priest's lips curved into a gentle smile. In one hand, he held a small bowl of water, while the other grasped a first aid box. A towel draped over his shoulder completed the ensemble.

"Do people get injured around here often?" Nigel inquired.

The priest chuckled. "Why do you ask?"

Nigel gestured at the first aid box. "You seem well-prepared, as if you're running a clinic or something."

"You think because this is the house of God, we shouldn't be prepared for injuries?"

Nigel smirked, "Well, isn't there a verse about angels holding you up lest you strike your foot against a stone?"

"Hm." The priest smiled. "You know your Bible, it seems."

Nigel looked away as the priest cut through his pants with some scissors. "I used to read the Bible."

"What happened?"

A cloud settled over Nigel's face. "I don't want to talk about it. Religion isn't really my thing anymore."

"Very well," the priest replied, taking no offense. "Just know, whenever you decide to return, that God is always there."

Nigel didn't say a word.

The priest cut the area around the wound and dropped the blood-soaked piece of cloth into a plastic bag. He then used the water to clean the wound.

Nigel hissed as he did so.

"Please forgive me," the priest said. "I've been very rude. I'm Father Fernandes, and my nuns and I thank you for saving our lives."

Nigel looked towards the altar. "Where are they? The nuns."

"I sent them back home as soon as you ran after that man."

Nigel nodded.

"This is going to hurt," the priest said as he placed a tuft of cotton wool into a bottle of spirit. He daubed it on Nigel's wound.

Nigel recoiled sharply and grunted in pain.

"I'm sorry," Father Fernandes apologised. "I just need to disinfect the wound. Then I'll stitch it up and we'll be done."

"You seem to have a lot of experience doing this," Nigel said.

The priest smiled. "Before I came here, I had a very different life. I treated injuries like this quite often." He paused, looking thoughtful, "I chose to serve God, and it seems my past skills have proven useful in this new life. Especially since the church decided to start hiring out dirt bikes to tourists and locals who wanted to explore the mountains. It brings in income that takes care of some of the church's basic needs. You know, I couldn't believe my luck when I was assigned here. I knew it had to be nothing but the hand of God."

Nigel was curious. "What did you do before this?"

Father Fernandes ignored the question. He just continued treating the wound.

Nigel raised an eyebrow. *I guess you wish to remain mysterious then.*

He looked around and inspected the interior of the building. Father Fernandes spoke again.

"The church doesn't look like much, I know. But it's not the church's looks that is its value. It's the centuries' worth of memory that it holds." The priest looked around at the church. "This place owes its existence to Darwin."

Nigel's eyes widened. "Darwin? Like Charles Darwin?"

"Exactly the one. Santiago, Cape Verde was the first place the *HMS Beagle* stopped at during its journey. The church remembers Darwin's charitable work. He did what other members of his crew would not. He helped nurse the sick natives back to health during his brief stay on the island. You see, a single act of kindness can go a very long way."

Nigel winced and sucked through his teeth as Father Fernandes commenced the stitching process.

"What did Mikey want from you?" he asked.

"Mikey?"

"The guy who held you all on gunpoint."

"Oh. He didn't even introduce himself before he pulled his gun on us..." Father Fernandes gave Nigel a cursory glance. He had never met the man before now and didn't know whether to trust him. However, after his display today, he decided to go out on a limb.

"He was after the original copy of *On the Origin of Species*," he replied.

"That's Darwin's book!" Nigel replied. "I didn't know it was for sale. It's here?"

"Yes."

Nigel sat up abruptly.

"Easy now," Father Fernandes said, "you don't want to spoil your stitches."

"Sorry," Nigel said. "It's just hard to believe that this church has the original copy of one of the books that revolutionised science and the world."

"Not the church," the priest said as he placed a gauze on Nigel's wound and wrapped it around his lap. "Me."

Nigel's brows rose in surprise. "You bought the original copy of *On the Origin of Species?*"

"Yes."

"My God, that must have cost—"

"A fortune, I know."

Nigel frowned. He was still unable to wrap his head around it. "How could you have possibly afforded such a purchase?"

"In the same way you judged the church in error by looks alone, you'd be making the same mistake if you do same with me. I try to live humbly now and spend money where I can. There was an auction not so long ago. I bought it anonymously and have kept it ever since."

"Why buy it?" Nigel asked.

"I bought the book as a reminder of Darwin's help. It will give the church a greater cause – the charge to protect the book and keep it away from those who decide to abuse it."

"I'm a little confused. Why would you protect a book like that when the theory of evolution contradicts the church's teachings? Seems a bit ironic for a priest to have that in his possession."

"A valid point. However, just because you don't agree with someone, doesn't mean you can't help and protect them. You said that you were not religious anymore. Yet, you protected the nuns and me from danger today, inside the house of God. Wouldn't you find that ironic?"

Nigel chuckled. "Touché."

Father Fernandes finished wrapping the final bandage around Nigel's thigh. The pain in his leg was still present but much improved than before.

"May I have a glimpse of the book?"

"Of course." Father Fernandes got to his feet. "Let me get you some crutches and you can follow me then."

He scooped up the first aid box and the bucket of water. The water in it had been tinged red with Nigel's blood.

Nigel looked at his lap and sighed. "I just bought these pants. Now, look how ruined they are." He would have to ask the priest for a change of clothes before he left.

The priest returned holding a pair of wooden crutches. "Take these and follow me."

Nigel tucked the crutches under his armpits as he stood up. The pain in his thigh was sharp and it throbbed. Father Fernandes waited patiently for Nigel to follow. The moment Nigel moved and swung his body forward, the priest led him through the doorway and down a stairway. They descended further down until it looked like they reached a dead end. Father Fernandes placed his hands on the sone wall and gave a slight push. To Nigel's surprise, the wall retreated and moved slowly to the side, creating an opening.

"As I said, there's a lot more to this church than meets the eye. Come." The priest gestured.

Secret doorways. Rare historic objects concealed. Honestly, it wouldn't surprise me if a large boulder came rolling down on us. All I'm missing is a whip! Nigel chuckled to himself.

They entered a lowly dimmed room. The room was cool with curtains of cobwebs hanging on its walls. Father Fernandes walked to the centre of the room where there was a chest situated. He bent down and unlocked it.

Inside, he took out a large green book and held it in his palms. The delicacy with which he carried it informed Nigel of how much importance he attached to it.

Nigel received the book with the same delicate treatment the priest had shown. His eyes were full of wonder. He held one of the most significant books in history. The only one of its kind that still existed. He could feel the fragility of age on the book. Its cover was already beginning to flake, and the pages of the book were a dirty brown. Besides these, he could say without doubt that the book was in perfect condition.

He flipped the front cover over, revealing a carefully written scribble on the very first page. It was a note, written by Darwin himself.

> MY DEAREST ANNIE,
> YOUR FIRST DAY GUIDES THE GOLDEN WAY TO THE TRUTH.
> IT TAKES A SCIENTIST, AN ARTIST, AND A CAPTAIN TO PROTECT
> THE TRUTH.
> CHARLES

The words in the last sentence flung Nigel back to last week. He was on the phone to Annabelle when she intimated him on the details of their trip to Darwin's home. She had said something about a mysterious third person who was involved in the codification of the truth that Darwin had chosen to exclude from his journal. In a flash, it dawned on Nigel just who the third person was. The first person was Darwin, the Scientist. The second was Conrad Martens, the Artist. The third person was the Captain.

"I'm sorry, would it be possible for me to take a picture of this note on the first page?"

"Sure. Knock yourself out."

"Thank you." Nigel smiled.

Nigel took out his phone and took a picture of what was on the book. He handed the book back to the priest as soon as he was done.

"Thank you, Father Fernandes. I'm quite grateful for your help."

"You gave it first. I owe you more."

The priest took the book back to the chest and locked it. A few moments later, they returned to the pews. Nigel sighed and leaned back into the seat. His wound still ached, but not as sharply as before. He pulled out his phone again and placed a call to Annabelle.

"Hello, Belle," he said when she picked up.

"Nigel?"

"Yeah. I think I have something for you." Nigel thought about the picture of the note he took on his phone. He glanced at the sextant in the bag. He smiled. "In fact, it's actually two things. Let's meet."

CHAPTER 10

THE CAPTAIN

ANNABELLE GLANCED AT HER slender silver chain watch for what felt like the millionth time that afternoon. She sighed, wiping a bead of sweat from her brow. Up until now, the day had been a dreary affair with the sky keeping the sun firmly hidden behind a veil of clouds. At last, the clouds had loosened their grip, allowing the sun to make its presence known with a dazzling display.

Annabelle watched a classic black British taxi depart from the airport, colourful balloons spilling from the passenger window. She couldn't help but stifle a laugh, wondering if she should have done something similar for Nigel.

Why don't you carry a placard while you're at it? She teased herself.

Her shoulders relaxed as she released a deep breath, her fingers drumming lightly on the steering wheel.

Maybe I should have gone inside to welcome him, Annabelle pondered. *No.* She shook her head. *It would've looked desperate, like I can't wait to see him or something. Or maybe it would have warmed his heart instead. Come on. You two are still friends regardless of your history.*

Annabelle spotted Nigel limping out of the airport, a brown

backpack slung over one shoulder. She was concerned; Nigel wasn't one to get injured easily.

Stepping out of the car, Annabelle greeted him with a sympathetic smile. "What did you do to yourself?" she asked as he approached.

"Well, let's just say I won't be riding a dirt bike again for a while. I don't want to give you the pleasure of saying 'I told you so,' especially since you warned me against riding them."

Laughter bubbled up from Annabelle as she playfully smacked his shoulder. "I told you they were dangerous!"

"It's nice to see you too, Belle," Nigel said. The two embraced.

"You don't look too bad for someone who's had a rough go of it lately."

"Oh, please," Annabelle rolled her eyes. "Don't get me started on that. You don't know how hard it is to be haunted by two failures at quick succession."

"Well, go on, say it. What would I do without you, Nigel?"

"If you're here to gloat, go ahead. I give up."

Nigel followed Annabelle into the car. "I'm starving."

"You're in luck. Sarah had just started prepping something when I drove out to get you. She should be almost done by the time we get back."

"Good. I need a cup of coffee so bad. I have a feeling I'm about to step into a whirlwind of activity, and I need to be prepared."

"Don't worry. I've got you covered. I'll throw the kettle on as soon as we arrive."

Annabelle and Nigel spent just over an hour at Sarah's before saying their farewells and heading to Professor Young's house. They found him in his study, pouring over a stack of musty old books.

He raised his head and smiled.

"Hi, Dad."

"Annabelle," he said as he got to his feet. "It's been what?"

"Only two days, Dad," she replied shrewdly. "Stop making it look like I've been away for years."

He chuckled and turned to Nigel. "Sometimes, it's hard to accept that your children have grown up and don't need to be around the house as much anymore. Do you have children of your own, Mr..."

"That's Nigel, Dad," Annabelle interjected.

Professor Young paused for a moment. Then he lapsed into a spell of laughter.

"My, oh, my," he said. "I must really be getting old. It's all coming back to me, now, Mr. Moloi. I'm so sorry."

"It's nothing, sir," Nigel reached out to shake the Professor's hand. "You must have a lot on your plate and it's been some time since our last meeting."

"Yes, indeed. But to forget the man for whom my daughter would have once turned the world upside down, that's quite an oversight, don't you think?"

"Dad!" Annabelle protested, her eyes wide with disbelief.

"What?" Professor Young replied, giving her a knowing look. "You think I didn't notice? You're my girl, Annabelle. I'm more aware of things than you might think. I just don't always discuss them."

Annabelle opened her mouth to say something but found herself at a loss for words. Instead, she pressed her lips together and remained silent.

Professor Young and Nigel exchanged a few more pleasantries, and then the trio got down to the business of the day.

Annabelle helped her father clear the big old books from the thick dark brown mahogany table and piled them in a corner on the floor. She placed the note and the map piece she had got from her visit to Darwin's home at Downe.

"A few days ago, Sarah, Charlie, and I went over to Darwin's home in Downe."

"You actually did that?" Nigel asked, unable to keep the surprise from showing in his voice.

"Yes," Annabelle nodded curtly. "Try to keep up, please."

Nigel gave her a wry smile and then let her continue.

"His house wasn't too exciting, except for Darwin enthusiasts, I must say. But it did provide us with an unexpected discovery."

Annabelle dug into her pockets, brought out two neatly rolled up pieces of paper, and spread them out on the table. Nigel squinted as he leaned over the pieces of paper, while Professor Young adjusted his glasses before joining the examination. Annabelle stood back, observing them like a teacher who had stumbled upon a critical discovery and allowed her students to examine it.

"You found these at Darwin's house?" Professor Young asked as he looked up in wonderment. "Why didn't you tell me?"

"I wanted to wait until you were back from Scotland, Dad. It was going to be a surprise." Annabelle smiled.

"It's the last place anyone would look," Nigel said. "It's a brilliant move. Everyone would be expecting him to hide the items far away from him."

"Well, not everyone," Annabelle said.

"Yes. I'm sorry. I forgot. You're one in a million."

Annabelle suppressed a blush.

"Well, you've seen the note and the map," she said. 'What do you think?"

"Well, what else is there to point out?" Nigel said. "Darwin loved to create elaborate schemes just to impose Chopin on his household."

Professor Young chuckled and Annabelle gave Nigel a pointed look.

"We have to find the remaining two-thirds of the map. By the way—" Nigel frowned, "—who the hell is *Hot Coffee*?"

"Charlie asked the same question," Annabelle said. "Got nothing."

Professor Young sighed and pinched his forehead. "I think I might know who it could be. But if you had asked me a year ago, after all my studies on Darwin, I would have told you that, aside from his strange reluctance to reveal details about this mysterious island, the man was quite straightforward. Now, look at how he keeps revealing puzzles."

"Wow." Nigel raised his eyebrows. "Who knew Darwin was a fan of pirates and treasure hunts."

The trio shared a laugh.

"You know," Nigel began, "I came across the original copy of *On the Origin of Species* a couple of days ago."

Professor Young's mouth fell open in astonishment. He blinked, then quickly recovered and approached Nigel, as his eyes gleamed with excitement like a child who had just discovered a hidden stash of sweets.

"Come on, son," he said. "Tell me, what does it look like? Is it old? Musty? Is it still in good condition? What does it smell like? Was it the one bought from the auction? Did you meet the secret buyer? Who was it?"

Nigel had never seen the Professor this excited.

Wow, he thought. *His enthusiasm for Darwin has never dwindled after all these years. No wonder they're both so invested in figuring this all out.*

Annabelle caught his eye and burst into laughter, as if she had read his thoughts.

"Come on, Dad," she said. "Relax before you scare Nigel off."

"Sorry, sorry." Professor Young took a few steps back. "It's just I've been studying him for years, and I've never got the chance to look at his original piece."

"I understand. It's only by a stroke of fortune that I stumbled on it. It's too far removed for people to even waste their time going after it. They wouldn't even think to look there."

"It's a shame how some things stay out of reach until your dying breath," the Professor sighed.

Annabelle shook her head, as if breaking free from a trance. It was time to change the subject. She turned to Nigel.

"Nigel, you mentioned you had two things to show us?"

"Yeah." Nigel opened up his backpack. "I think you may have lost this." He produced a small golden cylindrical object from the bag.

Annabelle gasped and took an involuntary step towards him. Her eyes roved between him and the object in his hands for seconds before she mustered the words to convey her shock.

"It's the sextant," she said. "H-how did you get this?"

"Right from the guy who stole it from you. I stumbled upon him while I was in Cape Verde. His name was Michael White, but he went by Mikey. He was a ruthless poacher with secret benefactors who kept him in their service to procure exotic animals, many of which are on the brink of extinction. I've encountered him several times throughout my career, but he always managed to escape. This was the first time I actually engaged him."

"What did this Mikey want with the sextant?" Professor Young asked.

"I think he was working for someone," Nigel said. "I got access to his phone, and luckily, someone called asking if he had procured the object. I bet the mystery caller was a benefactor, intent on finding this mysterious island to exploit its rare animal life. If this place has never been discovered, as you've said, think of the undiscovered species it might harbour. It would be a goldmine for a lowlife like Mikey and the people who buy from him. Thankfully, he'll never be able to do so. He died from a fall the other day."

Nigel decided it was best to omit the details of his pursuit and fight with Mikey. The last thing he wanted was for them to think he had killed him.

Nigel handed the sextant over to Professor Young, who held it tenderly, as if unsure whether to touch it yet fully aware that he was handling it.

"I can't believe I'm holding it at last without a museum supervisor breathing down my neck," he said.

Annabelle placed a hand on Nigel's upper arm. She locked eyes with him and mouthed a thank you. Nigel smiled, placed his hand over hers, and gave a gentle squeeze. Annabelle felt reassured by his touch – a silent promise, a commitment of sorts. He would have her back for as long as she needed. She felt enveloped in a cocoon of comfort.

"What's the second thing?" she asked.

"This." Nigel turned his phone on and showed her the picture he'd taken of the note from On the Origin of Species.

Annabelle read it out loud. "My dearest Annie, your first day guides the golden way to the truth. It takes a Scientist, an Artist, and a Captain to protect the truth."

"What do you think it means?" Nigel asked.

"Well," Professor Young began, "Annie was Darwin's favourite daughter. Sadly, she died of tuberculosis when she was only ten. This deeply affected Darwin. I don't think he was quite the same after her death."

Annabelle's eyes took on a distant look as she contemplated. After a moment, they came right back into focus. "Her first day would be the day she was born, I presume. I wonder what he means by the golden way to the truth?"

Nigel's eyes fortuitously fell on the sextant Professor Young had gently placed on the table. His brows knitted together as he frowned lightly. He picked the sextant up and weighed it gently on his palm as he mulled over something.

"Uhm…" he said as he tilted his head a little to the side. He held the sextant up. "This is brass that's coated in gold. Is there any chance it could be related to our puzzle?"

Annabelle's expression perked up. "Yes! Nigel, you're brilliant!" Nigel beamed. "He said Conrad Martens used one of his devices to hide the other map. This must be its purpose!"

Professor Young picked up the sextant and examined it, peered at it intensely through his glasses and turned it over in his hands.

"How do we get the second piece?" he asked. "More importantly, how do we get it out of this? There seems to be no oddity here. Nothing out of the ordinary."

"Has anything been straightforward so far?" Annabelle asked.

"Yeah, you're right," he replied.

"Nigel," Annabelle called. "I've got an idea – a little thing that just came out of the blue. Can you quickly look up the date Annie Darwin was born?"

"Right on it," Nigel said as he tapped his phone's touchscreen.

Annabelle held the sextant, lavishing it with attention. It seemed like an ordinary navigation tool, but she knew by now that nothing was ever just itself.

She stared at the index arm and the scales that arced full circle around the edge of the sextant, marking the degrees of measurement. She had never used a sextant before, but she got the intuition that she could work it by moving the arm to corresponding degrees on the scale.

"I've got it," Nigel said, drawing Annabelle's gaze. "It's…" he looked at his phone as he spoke, "the 2nd of March, 1841."

"Of course, everything's going to have to be digits if they're going to work on that," Professor Young said.

"That's true," Annabelle replied. "So, that's going to be. 2-3-18-41."

Professor Young and Nigel bobbed their heads simultaneously.

"Here we go," Annabelle said, and then she moved the arm according to the digits, in the order she just called out. Professor Young and Nigel huddled around her and looked on with bated breath. Every click got a jump out of their hearts, and it teased a bifurcated prospect. It was either failure or success. They could pray for the latter, but their emotions trod on this uncertainty.

Annabelle carefully moved the arm to the last digit, 41. They paused and watched the sextant with bated breath, each heartbeat feeling like an eternity. For a moment, it seemed as though nothing would happen. Then, there was a soft click at the bottom of the sextant, followed by a faint thud on the ground. They glanced down, their eyes widening as they spotted two neatly folded pieces of paper on the floor.

"Yes!" Professor Young pumped his fists enthusiastically into the air.

Annabelle turned the sextant over. Her eyes beamed with amazement. A fairly sizeable rectangular aperture was at the bottom which revealed an even larger compartment.

Nigel shook his head as he stooped and picked up the paper. "Our man is certainly one for surprises."

"Indeed," Professor Young replied.

Nigel unfolded the paper carefully. A part of him was scared that it had grown brittle with age and could crumble with the slightest mishandling. The first paper was torn, but it was a map. The second part of the missing map had been discovered.

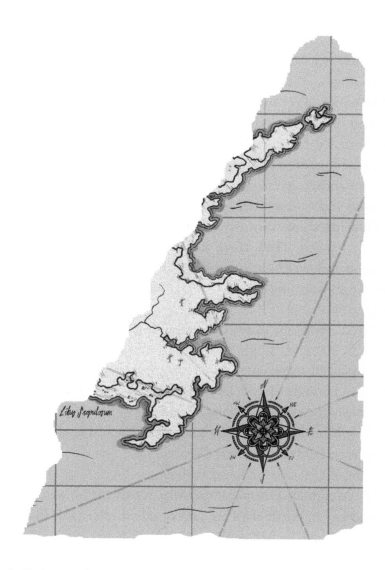

Annabelle hurriedly put the first piece side by side.

"It's a perfect fit," she said, the relief in her voice more evident than the excitement. She turned the second part of the map around, and just like the first, there were coordinates written at the back.

5'02.7"W.

Professor Young and Nigel chuckled.

"This is great," Professor Young said. "I've never felt we were closer to our goal than now. We've got two-thirds of the map."

"I reckon it's only a matter of time before we get the third," Nigel said.

"If there's someone out there after this island as much as we are, I'm pretty certain we can beat them to it."

Nigel bobbed his head.

"But let's not get ahead of ourselves now," Professor Young advised as he picked up the letter. "It looks like Conrad Martens left us something extra." He adjusted his glasses so that they could sit comfortably up his nose. He read the contents of the letter out loud.

MY DEAREST FRIEND, CHARLES,

I HOPE THIS LETTER FINDS YOU IN GOOD HEALTH. YOU WILL SEE THAT I HAVE KEPT THE SECOND PIECE HIDDEN SAFELY IN YOUR SEXTANT. I TRUST YOU HAVE HIDDEN YOUR PIECE JUST AS SECURELY.

I HAVE RECENTLY BEEN IN CONTACT WITH OUR FORMER FRIEND, HOT COFFEE. HE REFUSES TO CO-OPERATE WITH US. YOUR REMARKABLE RECENT WORK HAS INSULTED HIS RELIGIOUS BELIEFS, I'M AFRAID, AND BETRAYS THE PURPOSE OF PROTECTING THE ISLAND. HIS PIECE OF THE MAP IS NO LONGER IN HIS POSSESSION.

IN OUR LAST CONVERSATION, HE HAD GIVEN IT AWAY TO THE NATIVES OF NEW ZEALAND, THE MĀORI, IN THE NORTH ISLAND. THE REASONS FOR DOING SO, I AM NOT CERTAIN, BUT I DO BELIEVE THAT IT WAS INTENDED AS A PEACE OFFERING. PERHAPS HE FAILED THEM DURING HIS TIME AS GOVERNOR. WITH THE PIECE NOW OUT OF REACH, WE MAY NOT BE ABLE TO JOIN ALL THREE TOGETHER AGAIN. THE ISLAND WILL BE

PROTECTED FROM THE OUTSIDE WORLD FOR THE FORESEE-
ABLE FUTURE.
    TAKE CARE OLD FRIEND,
    CONRAD.

"Hot Coffee," Annabelle repeated as her eyes lost their focus to contemplation. "That's the second time I've heard that name."

"My best guess? It must be someone who's a captain. You know," Nigel began as tilted his head this way and that, "it takes a Scientist, an Artist, and a Captain to protect the truth."

"Who's the Captain?"

Professor Young laughed. He looked at them and his eyes sparkled with awe. He stumbled across something big; it was clear to see.

"They're referring to Captain Robert FitzRoy."

"I'm sorry," Nigel said. "Who?"

"Captain FitzRoy," Professor Young repeated. "He was the captain of the *HMS Beagle*. It's all just coming back to me. They call him 'Hot Coffee' because of his temper. People thought he was mad whenever he was angry.

"As Mr Martens pointed out, he was a governor in New Zealand for a few years. If I recall correctly, his performance at the time was questionable so he was sent back to Britain. FitzRoy was a deeply religious man. Naturally, like many other religious people at the time, was appalled when Darwin published *On the Origin of Species*. I believe FitzRoy felt guilty as he felt he contributed to the theory's development.

"Anyway, on top of all that, along with financial issues and depression, he died by slitting his throat with a razor. Such a tragic way to end a life."

Annabelle sighed. "There we have it. We've hit another dead end then. The third piece is gone."

"Don't give up just yet," Nigel said. "At least we know it's somewhere in the north island of New Zealand."

"Yeah. We'll just walk in there, and the third piece will present itself to us."

Nigel chuckled softly.

"But the letter mentions he gave it to the Māori people. Surely, if we locate any of the communities that existed in Robert FitzRoy's time, we'd have an idea of where to look," Nigel suggested.

"Do you know what this means?" Professor Young asked as he picked up the two map pieces. "It means the existence of the island is confirmed. It's not just myth or rumour."

"Why are they protecting this particular island, though?" Nigel asked. "What's all the fuss about? They've been to uninhabited places and still documented them."

"I've got no idea," Annabelle replied. "Although Darwin did tell his children to look for it if they should ever fall ill. It seems quite—"

"Unusual," Nigel completed.

"Yeah," she nodded.

Professor Young leaned against the table, quiet, with worry lines etched on his face. *Should I tell them?* he thought.

"What's the problem, Dad?" Annabelle asked.

Professor Young snapped out of his thought and smiled. "It's nothing, darling. Just an old man lost in the maze of his mind. Whoever hired this Mikey is looking for something, and we need to go to New Zealand before they discover the island first."

"Does anyone have any idea who this sponsor could be? I mean, outside my wild guess."

Annabelle was quiet. She had a hunch, a feeling that clawed incessantly at her heart. *Hendrik.*

CHAPTER 11

WHAKAREWAREWA VILLAGE

ANNABELLE SHIELDED HER EYES from the sun's glare, squinting out the window of the aged brown Jeep, its bodywork chipped and worn. She and Nigel had rented it from a local agency after disembarking from their flight. Despite being the priciest option among the modest collection, it didn't look much better than the others. They paid for it anyway, figuring it would be the most reliable way to travel between the Māori communities scattered across New Zealand's North Island. Their first visit had been fruitless – FitzRoy had no history with that community. Their next destination was a small village called *Whakarewarewa*.

"My God," Annabelle groaned, "I should've brought a hat. This sun's going to blind me."

Nigel chuckled. "Don't be silly. I packed a couple of baseball hats in my backpack. Here, take one."

"Thank you!" Annabelle exclaimed, delighted.

She hesitated between the black and blue hats, ultimately tossing the black one back into the bag and donning the blue one.

"I don't really know what we're going to find in this Whaka, uhm, Whake, uh... Damn, this name's impossible to pronounce."

Annabelle guffawed. "It'll just take some time that's all. It's Whaka-rewa-rewa. Easy-peasy."

"Easy for you to say," Nigel grumbled. "Why couldn't we choose another community in New Zealand with an easier name?"

"Because only a few Māori communities that existed during Robert FitzRoy's governorship are still around today. And this is one of them." Annabelle had extensively researched the various Māori communities and had become fascinated by their diverse cultures.

"Look!" Her brows arched. "I think we're here already. There's a signpost and a little monument up ahead."

The signpost stood beside the footpath, surrounded by shrubs and trees. Below the village's name, a longer name in the native language was inscribed, which Annabelle attempted to pronounce but failed. They slowed down and exited the vehicle as they approached a gleaming white arched gateway. The pillars were adorned with jet-black granite tablets bearing inscriptions in white, as well as small figurines perched atop each pillar. Bold block letters stretched across the arch, which Annabelle assumed meant *"Welcome to Whakarewarewa."*

They strolled through the gateway, entering a landscape where houses nestled amid a verdant expanse of trees and shrubbery. They crossed a bridge just past the gateway, the stream below it running serenely through the village. Despite the presence of tourists wandering the pathways and snapping photos, the village retained its tranquil ambiance. The ground was hard and rocky where plants didn't flourish. From their vantage point on the elevated bridge, the village appeared as a harmonious blend of nature and human ingenuity.

As they ventured further inland, they observed pillars of vapour rising towards the sky. Some dissipated during their ascent, transforming into misty sheets that drifted over houses and treetops like spectral apparitions. This vapor lent the village an otherworldly aura.

"Did I mention that this place is also a geothermal village?" Annabelle asked.

"Nope," Nigel replied, his attention still captivated by the mesmerizing scenery.

"There are numerous geysers and hot pools here. I mean, loads of them."

"Ah," Nigel nodded, understanding dawning. "So that's the vapour floating all around us, huh?"

"Exactly."

They exchanged knowing glances and smiled.

"This place must be heaven," Annabelle mused. "Think about it. It's got natural jacuzzies, hot baths, and so much more. Plus, the sun shines bright throughout the day. You can sunbathe whenever you want."

Nigel chuckled. "True. Just don't stand atop a geyser when it erupts. It'd scald your skin right off."

"Nope," Annabelle agreed, grimacing. "No one wants to experience that."

They strolled past several streams, their surfaces alive with dancing wisps of vapor. Some areas were cordoned off with wooden fences.

"There are so many more of these," Nigel commented, nodding towards the streams.

Annabelle agreed, her head bobbing in response. They even walked past a boiling one, the sound of the turbulent water bubbling up from the rocky ground below.

The houses they passed were modest, their simplicity exuding a unique aesthetic charm. Most were wooden bungalows adorned with tasteful paint choices. Some featured multi-coloured zinc roofs, while others were more unassuming. Enclosed by fences, the homes were surrounded by neatly trimmed lawns and stately trees. Each dwelling seemed intentionally spaced to maintain the serenity and tranquillity that permeated the air. Yet, despite their distance, the houses shared a visual connection, unifying the village. The villagers and tourists mingled seamlessly, the former distinguished by their casual familiarity with their surroundings. While the village might seem like paradise to visitors, for the natives, it was simply home.

Annabelle and Nigel strolled past a group of children, playing and laughing, filling the afternoon with the delight of their voices.

Annabelle smiled dreamily.

"What's the smile for?" Nigel asked.

"It's just that watching them play just reminds me of a time when I was this little, without anything to worry about. Well," she conceded, "I did have to worry about my father—" Nigel laughed, "—and his attempts to immerse us in Darwin's theories and adventures."

"And years later, look at you – neck deep in the same thing you were running away from."

"What can I say?" Annabelle shrugged. "Life happened."

"And a great deal of curiosity too."

"Yeah." She nodded. "That too."

Nigel looked across the lanes as if searching for something.

"You know," he suggested, "I think it's better if we ask some locals a few questions."

"Agreed," Annabelle replied, her eyes darting inquisitively between the houses. Her face brightened. "I think I've found someone we can ask."

She pointed at a young boy walking out from between two houses in the corner. He had dark skin, black hair, and what Annabelle thought were curious brown eyes. They approached closer, but not too close, to avoid scaring the boy.

Please speak English, Annabelle thought.

She bent forward a little, and put on the type of smile that said, "we're strangers, but we're also friends".

"Hi, we're tourists – visitors - and we're looking for someone to speak with. Perhaps, someone who's in charge of the village."

Nigel stood back and watched Annabelle as she spoke to the boy. His demeanour sparked with the suspicion of laughter. Inwards, he was bursting with it, but he applied some effort to keep the outside calm. She enunciated every word and gesticulated a lot, waving her arms like a flailing duck.

The boy smiled.

"That would be Tui Waerea," he said.

Annabelle withdrew her head slowly, her brows arched as she stared open-eyed at him. He had just spoken impeccable English. His mother tongue had left trails on his accent though, but they weren't thick enough to constrain his speech. Now, she felt embarrassed.

Nigel finally left the laughter out as he threw his head backward. The boy's smile increased.

I've gone and made a fool out of myself, Annabelle thought.

She turned to the boy. "I'm sorry, okay? I was just trying to get through the language barrier."

"No, no." He shrugged. "It's okay. We go through it all the time."

Wiping the remnants of laughter from his face, Nigel stepped closer to Annabelle.

"Could you direct us to this Tai...uhm...Tia-"

"Tui Waerea," the boy supplied.

"Yes—" Nigel nodded gratefully, "—Tui. Could you give us directions to where we'll find her?"

"No," the boy shook his head.

Nigel and Annabelle's spirits fell, their hope of finding assistance in the village seeming to evaporate.

The boy sighed. "I'll take you there myself."

Oh, thank God, Annabelle thought as she recovered some of the light that had been on her face.

"I'm Ari," the boy said as he led them forward.

"I'm Annabelle," she replied. "This," she tapped Nigel on the shoulder, "is my friend, Nigel."

"What do you want to meet Tui Waerea about?" he asked.

Annabelle was about to tell him, "Private matters," but Nigel said something better instead.

"We want to understand better of the village with the help of someone who's versed in the lore and history of Whakarewarewa."

Ari nodded. "You pronounce the name well. It's a good thing. Too many of your folks murder it."

Nigel chuckled. "Annabelle just taught me how to say it only moments ago."

"We'll turn left here," Ari said, and they all turned left on the pathway.

They spent several minutes, taking bends on the road on Ari's instruction. They even walked past a flock of trees. It was the most soothing moment of the journey. Not that they had had their fill of the rural and natural aesthetic of the village, but the shade and cool offered thrown off by the trees were so markedly different from what they had experienced throughout, and most welcoming.

"Here," Ari said as he pointed at a small semi-detached house sitting on a manicured lawn. "This is where Tui Waerea lives."

The bungalow's lawn blended seamlessly with the surrounding landscape, with no fence or hedge to set it apart.

"I hope this goes well," Nigel muttered under his breath.

"So, what next?" Annabelle asked.

Ari pointed at the semi-detached. "You said that you wanted to meet with Tui. She's the leader of this village. I'm going to lead you inside, and perhaps, do some introductions?"

"Sounds good to me," Nigel agreed.

All three of them approached the house.

Ari rapped his knuckles gently on the door. A few seconds later, the door swung back, and a large middle-aged woman walked out. She had light brown skin, but it was the scowl on her face, and the tattoo covering her bottom lip and spilling down her chin, that was the most prominent. The scowl on her face wasn't much of a scowl as it was an expression of distanced studiousness. She wasn't trying to scare the visitors, but she wasn't trying to welcome them either. Not until she knew their true intent, or at least, scrutinized them enough to know that they would be of no harm to the village.

She cast disinterested eyes on Nigel, and quickly moved them to Annabelle, and then finally, Ari. On Ari, she seemed to delay a little more, and the boy turned his face away. Suddenly, his shoes held more appeal for him than anything in the environment.

Annabelle and Nigel exchanged a quick glance. But it was enough for one to spot the reflection of their uncertainty in the other.

Annabelle harrumphed and stepped forward a little. Tui's eyes flicked towards her instantly. Almost like a cat pouncing on dinner. Annabelle could feel the questioning in those eyes, the judgement, the strained tolerance. Still, she got on with her business.

"Please," she said, "we're researchers, and we stumbled upon credible information that there's an item that was gifted to you and your people by Robert FitzRoy back in the late 1800s. We're looking for that very item."

Tui had looked steady since the strangers climbed on to her porch; unmovable, just like a mountain. But at the mention of

Robert FitzRoy, she seemed to have blanched temporarily. Within the next second, she righted herself. The steely expression that had been on her face from the get-go, slid back in.

"I don't know what you visitors are after," Tui said, "and I don't think I care. You'd only bring trouble here with your inquiries. I'm afraid I'd have to ask you to leave now."

"Leave?" Annabelle asked incredulously. "But we just got here. And we've done nothing wrong."

The woman squared up to Annabelle, deepening the frown on her face.

"I'm the leader of this village. If I say you leave, you leave."

"Alright," Nigel said as he raised his hands in a peaceful gesture. "We don't want trouble, Ms. Waerea. We'll just leave."

Annabelle and Nigel turned to go, but Annabelle felt conflicted. Almost like she was leaving behind a part of her on that porch. Nigel kept glancing at her on their way back to the pathway. Her unease was written plainly on her face. He heard a harsh hiss behind, and he turned to find Tui glowering at Ari.

"She must be scolding him for bringing us here," Nigel observed.

Annabelle pulled her lips backward, and then she turned and hurried back to Tui.

"Annabelle!" Nigel cautioned in a hushed whisper, but she was off already.

"You know you shouldn't be talking to him that way," Annabelle said.

Tui looked up, genuinely confused for perhaps, the first time since they walked up to her door.

"Excuse me?" she asked.

"You shouldn't blame him for bringing us here. He was simply doing what he thought was good."

Tui's nostrils flared as she stared daggers at Annabelle. She drew herself straighter and folded her arms across her chest.

"What I choose to do in my village doesn't concern you," she said.

"Of course, you've set that plainly in stone," Nigel said, rushing in with a polite smile. "I'm really sorry for my partner. We'll be heading out now."

"No," Annabelle shrugged his arm off. "I don't know what you think you're hiding from us, but I know about the island." Annabelle stabbed a finger downwards.

"What?"

"Yeah, that's right?" Annabelle said as she stood confidently. She was growing bolder. "I know about Darwin and FitzRoy's secret. And about the things they tried to hide out of the public eye."

Tui stared at her, lost at first. Then she compressed her lips and heaved a sigh.

"Come in," she said, and walked inside.

Annabelle gave Nigel a smug smile.

"Ok," he said wryly. "Just keep your I-told-you-so to yourself."

Tui's living room was small, but it was about the most exotic living space Annabelle had ever seen. A row of flowerpots stood beside the entrance, running along the wall until the end. There were four windows in the living room, and one huge flowerpot stood just below it. She saw figurines, just like the type they had seen on the arched gateway. There were lots of them here, arranged on shelves, and hung on the wall like picture frames. The sofas had been pulled to the centre of the living room to form a quadrangle, while also leaving space around. There were frames hanging on the wall, a few monochrome pictures, and paintings of native motifs and objects.

"What did you mean when you said you knew about the things Darwin and FitzRoy tried to hide from the public eye?" Tui asked as she plonked down on the nearest couch.

Annabelle and Nigel helped themselves to the long couch.

"We know about the mysterious island. I don't know what the name is because Darwin and his friends cleverly left that out, but we're trying to discover it. We've been following clues Darwin left behind. There's a map of this place that he split into three pieces. We've got two-thirds of it, and we've got reason to believe the third part's here."

"And why should I believe you're any different from regular tourists who come here masking their intent to exploit and manipulate.

Nigel leaned forward, locking eyes with Tui. "Look, I understand your scepticism. From your perspective, we might as well be invaders. But hear me out. If we wanted to exploit or manipulate, why would we come to you? We could've just continued our search covertly."

Tui remained silent, considering his words.

Nigel pressed on, "This isn't just about discovery; it's about stewardship. Whatever is on that island, if it falls into the wrong hands, we're all worse off. This isn't theoretical; there are people, organizations, with resources you wouldn't believe, who are after the same thing. They have technology, manpower, and a complete lack of moral compass. Hiding the third part of the map won't stop them; it'll just take away the one lead we have to beat them to it. And when they find the island, do you think they'll take the time to consult with the Māori or consider the ecological implications? No, they won't."

He paused, letting his words hang in the air. "Look, I get it. We're outsiders. But sometimes it takes an outsider to protect what insiders take for granted. We're asking for your trust, not forever, just long enough to prevent the worst from happening. If, after that, you want us gone, we go. No questions asked."

Tui looked at Annabelle, then back at Nigel. It was clear she was weighing their sincerity against her scepticism. "Give it a few days, if you're still unsure," Nigel added. "When these other people show up—and they will—you'll see we're the good guys."

Tui laughed. "*Good* guys," she repeated. She looked at Annabelle. "You should have destroyed both pieces of that map when you got the chance. The Māori people are protecting that island from the world, from the likes of you. I cannot trust you two."

Annabelle gasped desperately. She felt like she was clawing at thin air, but she would rather have a go at it, than do nothing.

"I promise you, Tui," she said, "we've got no ill intent. We're not intent on exploiting the animals that'll be there."

"Animals?" Tui frowned with disbelief. "The Gibbaki? Is that what you think we're protecting? They can protect themselves."

Annabelle and Nigel flashed confused glances. They came here to get answers. Yet, it felt like they were stepping into another puzzle.

Tui narrowed her eyes. "You two have got no idea what Darwin and FitzRoy were trying to protect, do you?"

Nigel blinked rapidly and shook his head, trying to get the look of puzzlement off.

"What's on the island?" he asked. "What's the Gibbaki?"

"Hmmm." Tui tutted and pulled her lips backwards. She was hesitant. "The island-"

BANG!

She was cut off immediately by a loud explosion outside. The trio turned towards the door simultaneously. Suddenly, they began to hear screaming. Lots of it.

They exchanged troubled glances. Tui couldn't think of a reason why there would be that much fuss in the village, so she immediately got to her feet and strode towards the door. Nigel and Annabelle followed behind her.

The moment they opened the door, it was as though they had walked into another world. It was utter pandemonium. Villagers were running to and fro, confused and lost. One of the houses in front was on fire. Flames flickered from the roof as smoke climbed out of the windows. A group of men were yelling at the top of their voices, threatening and flashing the muzzle of their guns on the villagers.

But none of them commanded so much attention, even in the ensuing chaos, than the young man with dark hair, a neat sky blue shirt, and pinstriped trousers, walking in their midst.

Annabelle's breath caught in her throat.

"How the hell did he find us?" she asked.

It was Hendrik.

Immediately, a disappointed and embarrassed expression stole into Nigel's face. Something had just flashed into his mind.

"Oh, come on," he groaned as his shoulders slouched. "He tracked me."

"What!" Annabelle looked at him. "How?"

Nigel dug his hand into his backpack and brought out a phone. "This was Mikey's," he held it out in front of her. "I held on to it, thinking it might help us because he was in contact with someone back in Cape Verde."

He sighed and shook his head. He felt regret cloy over his skin like a sheet of cold. Its sour sting sank in his heart. He let the phone hit the ground and crushed it with the heel of his boot.

"I'm so sorry," he said.

Another gunshot rang in the air. Annabelle and Nigel flinched and cowered.

"You need to get out of here," Tui seethed. "This is a peaceful place, and you just had to bring trouble along with you."

Annabelle's face was clouded with emotion. She was apologetic. "We didn't mean to. I'm really sorry."

"I don't care about your apologies. My village is on fire. My people are in agony. You need to leave this place and carry the trouble you've brought with you."

Tui stepped out the house shouting in her native language to the villagers running away from the commotion.

Annabelle heard a cry for help nearby. It was Ari. He was crouched down at the base of the tree, crying. Annabelle ran over to him.

"I'm here!" she shouted over the noise as she held her hand out. He grabbed her hand and she led him back to Tui's house. "Stay here and hide, you'll be ok."

The boy, who was visibly scared, nodded and went inside. Tui came rushing back. More alarmed than moments before. She approached Annabelle and grabbed her by the shoulders.

"Destroy the map. Those men—" she looked at the group as they gradually made their way through the village "—cannot find that place. If I tell you where the third piece is, will you promise me you'll destroy it altogether? As soon as you get your hands on it?"

Annabelle paused. This was a tricky decision. It was like being caught between a rock and a hard place. Her heart raced. She didn't come all this way to start destroying the very things that would lead her to the island. Still, destroying them was the only way she would be led to the destination of the third map.

Isn't that ironic, she thought.

She sucked in air through her teeth and combed her fingers through her hair.

"Easy," Nigel said, trying to placate her. He understood the kind of heat she was going through.

Someone screamed, and Annabelle looked. Hendrik and his men were drawing closer. Too close.

"You didn't destroy the map?" she blurted. "So why are you asking me to do it?"

"I swore an oath to protect the island," Tui replied. "Not destroy the map. I must go and protect my people now. If I don't survive this, the protector of the Great Cloak of Tia holds what you seek. Follow the Koru."

"What?" Nigel frowned. He tilted his head. The last thing he needed now was another puzzle.

We're in the eye of a storm for God's sake, he thought. *Couldn't things get any simpler.*

Annabelle stared at Tui. Her eyes flashed with clarity, she read enough about the Māori before coming to understand what Tui was saying. For the first time, since they arrived through the welcome sign, she had a clear cut purpose. Without taking her eyes off Tui, she said,

"Don't worry. I know what she means. Let's go."

In that stare, she seemed to communicate silently with Tui. It was the look of a person who had been pushed to the last resort.

Annabelle turned to go.

"We need to stay and help them," Nigel said. "It's the least we can do for bringing trouble to their village."

"No." Annabelle shook her head. "Tui made it clear. And she knew what she was asking when she told us to destroy the map. We need to do exactly as we're told. Hendrik's already on our tail. He's a dog. He might sniff what we're onto and leave the village alone."

"No Annabelle! We need to help them. Fight back! They're killing them!"

"Nigel, trust me. We'll be saving them if we leave. Hendrik wants us, not them!"

Nigel was reluctant, but he gave in to Annabelle's request. Some part of him would rather he stayed and fought, but another part just wanted to stick to the plan.

"What's the plan?" he asked her.

Annabelle looked at him. "We need to find a boat."

CHAPTER 12

THE THIRD PIECE

ANNABELLE AND NIGEL DUCKED their heads, sprinting towards their rented Jeep, desperate to evade any stray bullets. They took an alternative route to the entrance, determined to outsmart Hendrik's men. Upon reaching the Jeep, Annabelle leaped into the driver's seat and swung open the passenger door for Nigel.

"Get in, quick!" she urged.

Nigel hurled his bag into the back and clambered inside. Annabelle turned the key in the ignition, and the engine roared to life. She slammed the gas pedal, tires screeching and spitting gravel as they made their escape. They left the turmoil in their wake, but Nigel couldn't tear his eyes from the side-view mirror. A gnawing unease coiled in his chest, and he hoped distance would quell his guilt. But the image of the villagers—fleeing, suffering, their homes ablaze—haunted him.

They didn't ask for this, he thought. *They were just going about their simple lives and trouble came knocking. Tui was right. We're all the same. What really makes us different from the guys who're shooting up the place? We only went there because of what we needed, and we ditched them like cowards as soon as we got what we wanted.*

Annabelle cast a sidelong glance at Nigel.

I wonder what's got him all worked up, she thought.

She flashed him another look, like someone trying to gage the nature of a stranger seated next to them.

"Are you okay?" she inquired.

"Do I look okay?" Nigel snapped, his glare icy.

"Hey!" Annabelle raised her eyebrows. "Talk to me."

Nigel huffed and averted his gaze. "We should've stayed behind," he muttered.

"What?" Annabelle's brow furrowed, and she cocked her head slightly, careful not to lose focus on the road as the Jeep hurtled onward.

Nigel clenched his jaw and faced her. "I said, we should've stayed behind and helped the Māori people. Fought back against Hendrik and his men."

Annabelle sighed in exasperation. "Not this again. I thought you understood why we left."

"We abandoned innocent, defenceless people to be hurt, Annabelle. How can I move past that? We could be there now, protecting them."

"And what good would that do?"

Nigel scoffed, his voice dripping with disbelief. "Can you even hear yourself?"

Annabelle sighed, her heart pounding wildly as a twinge of guilt mingled with her rising anger. The rage began to simmer beneath her skin, threatening to boil over. She fought to contain it, unwilling to ignite an argument at this critical moment. At the same time, she couldn't bear Nigel's reproachful demeanour any longer, especially when she couldn't shake the feeling that she was partly to blame.

Top of Form

"I admire your bravery, Nigel. I understand that you wanted to help those people, but what could we have done? We didn't have the means to hold back Hendrik's men. No guns. Not a single weapon."

"The natives didn't have anything either. Tui didn't have anything. Yet, that didn't stop her from trying."

Annabelle's restraint waned as irritation swelled within her.

Why's he being so stubborn? she thought.

"Tui herself told us to leave. We need to protect that map, and you know it. If it falls into Hendrik's hands—"

"Maybe she was clouded by fear," Nigel interrupted. "Maybe she didn't know what she was saying."

"Enough, Nigel!" Annabelle's anger erupted, the flimsy barriers containing it collapsing. "Hendrik's after us, not them! Leaving the village was the best thing we could've done for those people. It was the only way to help them. Once Hendrik realizes we're gone, he'll have no reason to stay. He'll come after us!"

"Yeah," Nigel replied, his tone sullen. "That's if he even notices we've left. By then, he might have slaughtered half the village."

Annabelle's face contorted with rage, but she bit back further retorts, turning away in frustration. The air between them crackled with tension, their simmering resentment palpable.

Annabelle couldn't fathom why Nigel refused to see things from her perspective.

Must he always have to save the day? she asked herself. *It's just ridiculous! He can't keep doing this forever. One day, he has to realise that he can't always be there to save the day.*

Their anger and hurt weighed heavily upon them. Their affection for each other made the heated exchange even more unbearable. For the moment, they opted to keep their distance, wary of igniting the volatile emotions that lingered in the air.

After what felt like an eternity, Nigel pursed his lips and decided to break the silence. Someone had to be the first to speak, and he preferred it to be him.

"Where are we going?" he asked. "What did Tui tell you?"

Annabelle sighed, eyes fixed on the road. *The Protector of the Great Cloak of Tia holds your final clue. Follow the Koru.*

"What does that mean?"

"She's referring to a famous Māori rock in Lake Taupo."

"Lake Taupo," Nigel echoed, scrutinising the name as if searching for flaws. "I've heard of that place before."

"Yeah, it's one of the most beautiful places you'll see here."

Nigel pulled up a map of Lake Taupo on his phone. "We're about half an hour away. It's an hour's journey in total. Wow."

"Thank goodness we have a head start."

Annabelle braced for Nigel's disagreement, but it never came. Instead, she focused on reaching Lake Taupo as quickly as possible.

Nigel broke the silence once more. "Now that Mikey's phone is destroyed, I think we might have lost Hendrik and his men."

"Not unless they know where to go next. I hope Tui is safe."

Upon arriving at Lake Taupo, they rented a speedboat with twin turbines, large enough to carry around ten people. They raced across the turquoise water, skimming the surface and leaving a frothy wake in their path. Annabelle leaned against the starboard railing, her gaze sweeping across the lake. The sky was a brilliant blue, marred only by scattered clouds. The afternoon sun danced on the water's surface, refracting into dazzling shards of light. The scene was breath-taking, but she couldn't fully appreciate it under the pressure of time. The boat's spray rose around her, misting her with cool air and droplets of moisture.

"I wish we were having a picnic or doing something much less life-threatening," Annabelle said. "What a waste of scenery."

"What?" Nigel yelled from the steering wheel. He could barely hear her over the roar of the engines.

"Don't worry," Annabelle replied. "Look, we're almost there."

She pointed ahead, and Nigel spotted it: a massive rock adorned with shrubbery. He slowed the boat as they approached, eventually stopping near an alcove on the rock. The alcove resembled an arched gateway, as if someone had tried to carve an entrance into the rock long ago. Instead of a doorway, it now showcased intricate engravings alongside several animal statues chiselled from existing boulders.

Nigel and Annabelle gazed at the rock face, captivated by the unique sight. The idea that someone had chosen to sculpt nature in the middle of the lake was awe-inspiring.

Annabelle took out her notepad and sketched the scene before her.

"Is this it?" Nigel asked, breaking the silence.

"Yes."

The water around them had a greenish hue, with a smattering of rocks visible on the sandy lakebed below.

The pair scanned the rock, searching for any sign of a clue.

"Tui mentioned the Protector of the Great Cloak of Tia, right?" Nigel inquired.

"Yeah." Annabelle continued looking.

"All I see here are animal carvings, elaborate lines, and curves," Nigel observed, frowning. "Do you think any of these could be protectors?"

Annabelle shrugged.

"Look at this.," Nigel said as he gestured to the imposing face etched into the alcove. "See how the animals are arranged around it? It's like they're protecting it. Maybe they're the protectors."

Annabelle sighed. "It's just too simple. Can't you see? If there's one thing this quest has taught me, it's that nothing is ever that straightforward. Darwin and his friends love puzzles and cryptic messages. So far, they've stuck to that pattern. It's something they've maintained diligently."

"Alright, we'll keep looking. But remember, this isn't Darwin or his friends' work anymore. This is the Māori's puzzle now," Nigel reminded her.

Annabelle nodded. "Fair point." They continued examining the rock.

Annabelle's attention was drawn to the base of the rock, where it disappeared into the translucent green water. The area seemed shallow, but something caught her eye. There was a section of the water that appeared to be deeper than the rest.

Nigel noticed her expression. "Did you find something?" he asked.

"Wait here. Make sure the boat doesn't drift away," Annabelle instructed before diving into the water without hesitation.

"Annabelle," Nigel warned, "be careful."

Annabelle swam towards the foot of the rock, while Nigel watched from the boat. Although she might not have appeared to be the daring type, Annabelle had proven time and again that she had nerves of steel.

"Yes," she exhaled in relief, discovering a small tunnel at the spot she had noticed. Taking a deep breath, she dove into the tunnel and followed it for half a minute until it led her to a small cave on the other side of the rock. Gasping for air, she surfaced; the tunnel had been longer than she'd anticipated. Her previous experience in swimming and scuba diving during her marine biology studies had prepared her for holding her breath that long.

She looked around as she tried to get a glimpse of her new surroundings. The ambient lighting was poor, not revealing much, but she was able to make out a few things. The cave was really small, but it had four tunnels leading down a dark pathway. Above each tunnel, Annabelle noticed that there were symbols carved into the stone wall.

"Follow the Koru," she said softly to herself, recounting what Tui had said to her.

She climbed out of the water and stared at the symbols once more. She knew from her expertise as an environmental scientist, the many different species of plants. She had come across a Koru before, which was a spiral shaped fern. *The second tunnel*, she thought to herself and felt her way down the pathway in the darkness. Her clothes were dripping wet, and she could hear her footsteps squelching on the stony ground.

After a few minutes of squeezing through the narrow tunnel, there was light at the end. The light was coming from above, through a small opening that was guarded by the growing vines. Before her, was a small dead end with an interesting presentation.

The walls were lined with several vials, sitting inside the cracks, like Mother Nature's own shelf. She walked over, picked one of them up and held it up to her eye. There was clear fluid inside. Some of the vials were full to the brim with this fluid, and other half-full. She couldn't place the identity of the fluid, but she was certain it wasn't water.

This place must be a storage room of sorts, she thought. *But for what exactly?*

She followed the vials until her eyes fell on a bigger bottle at the centre. It looked empty - emphasis on *looked*, because when Annabelle got closer, she saw that it carried something. A piece of paper.

I wish Nigel was down here, she thought. *I bet a huge sum of money that what I'm looking at here is the third piece of the map.*

She lifted the bottle. It gave a loud pop as she pulled out its wooden cork. The sound reverberated across the walls, creating a hollow musical quality that ebbed slowly.

She pulled the piece of paper out, and gently dropped the bottle on the ground. Then she rolled out the piece of paper and let out a gasp with excitement.

"*Paradisus,*" she said.

She couldn't believe she was finally holding the third piece of the map in her hands. *We've got all three of them. Take that, Hendrik. You cheating, lying, conniving filth.*

Annabelle shut her eyes as she tried to fit it in mentally with the rest of the map. She grinned. The remaining two parts had been cut into rough right-angled triangles. The third piece was a perfect fit.

She rolled the piece of paper and tried to put it in her pocket. But she froze mid-motion. Her clothes were dripping wet. And the only way back to the boat was to swim in the water again. She couldn't risk the map getting wet and torn, at least, not until she had shown it to Nigel.

She picked up the big bottle and slipped the paper back in. Then she recorked it and clutched it at the crook of her elbow. She trotted back down the narrow tunnel until she reached the water. Slowly, she got back in, dragged in air, and plunged into the depths. This time, she had a bit of a problem. When she entered earlier, she had all her limbs to herself. Now, she was one short as she held onto the bottle. Swimming was going to be less comfortable than before, slower, and longer. It also meant she could run up to oxygen problems much quicker. Her heart began to race. But she continued, trying to move as fast as she could.

As she moved, she could feel her lungs already begin to protest. Her air was thinning out. Annabelle clutched the bottle tighter, and she looked desperately ahead.

There it is, she thought. The entrance to the tunnel: it was a bright spot ahead.

Now, all she had to do was beat the crushing urge inside her to breathe. Every second, she felt her endurance give, like water chewing at a thin plate of ice from the edges. Annabelle pushed harder. Her face had grown tight, forming an unpleasant grimace. She strained, trying to beat the urge clawing at her brain. *Breathe. Breathe. Breathe.*

The ring of light ahead seemed to be stagnant, like it was teasing her.

Annabelle's mouth flew open instinctively and she gulped water.

The rush of water in her nose and down her air pipe hit her like a flair of pain in her brain. She almost threw her mouth open, the instinct to breathe becoming an overbearing influence. But she held on to herself by a thread. Bubbles flew out of her mouth as she gazed ahead, and continued swimming.

But she was losing it, and she knew.

Finally, she burst out of the surface, and into the light.

Annabelle gasped, coughing out water, and pulling in air. It was a hurried trade, but she began to feel the returns. Her head was getting clearer.

"I've got it," she yelled at Nigel as she thrusted the bottle into the air.

The smile on her face vanished instantly.

There were three black boats surrounding hers – empty boats. While hers carried much more than one person.

Nigel, she thought. Desperation clawed its way into her eyes as she scoured through the mass of bodies. They all wore black uniforms, armed with scowls, daggers, and guns.

"Annabelle," a familiar voice said as it emerged from the mix.

A steely expression crept into Annabelle's face.

"Hendrik," she growled.

Hendrik beckoned on someone, and one of the men stepped forward, pushing Nigel in front of him with a gun to his back. She and Nigel exchanged glances, and he shook his head at her.

Immediately, the man behind him, drove the butt of his gun into Nigel's back. Nigel grimaced in pain and collapsed to the ground.

"Stop!" Annabelle yelled. "Don't hurt him."

Hendrik giggled and looked down at Nigel. Then he smoothed his hair backwards.

"You do like him quite a lot," he said. "Good, because that means you're going to do exactly what I want if you want to save your friend here."

"What do you want?" Annabelle asked. She could plead with him, but the one thing she couldn't do was hide her anger and revulsion for him, and her voice carried mighty quantities of it.

"Why?" Hendrik laughed and clapped. "Isn't it obvious? I need that thing in your hand." He pointed at the bottle.

"What exactly do you think this is, Hendrik?"

"You think I'm a fool? I'll give it to you. You're faster than I was. Somehow, the universe seemed to put you on the better side of this quest. But it's over now, you hear me. This is where this all ends. I'm going to find that island and nothing's going to stop me. Give me the final piece of the map, and none of you have to die. Otherwise—" He pulled out a pistol from his jacket, cocked it, and aimed it at Nigel's head "—I'll pop one into your boyfriend here, and still get the map."

"Fine," she growled.

She waded slowly back to the boat. As soon as she climbed aboard, Hendrik grabbed her. He chuckled.

"It's so good to see the look on your face. Somehow, it sends an electrifying thrill through my body. First she had felt betrayal and hurt back at the Art Gallery. Now, it's" he bobbed his head from side to side, "hate, anger, revulsion, and frustration. Own up to it, Annabelle. You can't beat me. I'm smarter, faster, and I've got more resources."

He pulled the bottle from her arm.

Annabelle looked at Nigel. He was on his knees now, with his fingers linked around the back of his head. Hendrik's henchman hadn't let the muzzle of his gun off Nigel's head.

Nigel seemed to have gleamed the question in Annabelle's eyes, and he nodded imperceptibly. The remaining parts of the map were gone. Hendrik had it all.

Hendrik walked over to the countertop next to the wheel and pieced the pieces of the map together.

He gasped as his eyes shone with delight.

"Excellent," he whispered. *"Paradisus."*

He turned it back, and noticed the co-ordinates written at the back. It was divided into three sections along with the pieces of paper. Now, they were all together. *12°36'39.0"S 115°05'02.7"W*

Hendrik guffawed with utter delight. The sound of his laughter floated across the surface of the lake, until it dissipated with the breeze combing the surface.

"You know..." he said, turning to face Nigel and Annabelle, "you two have been quite the nuisance, interfering with my plans and taking out my hunter. But, you've also saved me a lot of trouble. I do appreciate your efforts, despite appearances. I'm not known for my ingratitude. Annabelle, how was the rest of your tour in the Art Gallery?"

There was taunting streak on his smile, and a plentiful glimmer in his eyes.

Annabelle smiled and tilted her head. "Screw you."

Hendrik tutted and shook his head. "That's not a very lady-like way to speak. Where are your manners? I'm pretty sure your father tried to inculcate that in you growing up. How're we supposed to work together if you keep speaking to me like this?"

"There's no way I'd ever work with someone like you," Annabelle said with disgust.

Hendrik looked disappointed.

"Shame," he said. Then he sighed and his demeanour became lighter. "Doesn't matter, I have everything I need right here. I have no need for you anymore. Let's eliminate them."

Annabelle gasped. "You said you'd let us go."

Hendrik chuckled. He stared straight-faced at her. "I lied."

In that moment, Nigel ducked, grabbed the henchman's gun by the muzzle and wrested it out of his grip. He thrust his elbow upwards, catching the man in his jaw. Then he spun around and pushed him into the counter.

Quickly, Hendrik cocked his gun and placed it against the side of Nigel's head, stopping him cold in motion.

"One more move," Hendrik seethed, "and your brains will be all over this boat."

Nigel panted as he rose his arms up. His opponent was having a more difficult time pulling himself together. A streak of blood ran down a cut on his head and his crooked nose.

"I wouldn't do that if I were you," Annabelle said.

Hendrik turned and his eyes grew wide with shock.

Annabelle was holding a piece of the map above the flame of a lighter. During the scuffle, the map had fallen off the counter. Annabelle had used the ensuing chaos to her advantage, reaching out for bag, and the lighter inside it.

She stared into Hendrik's eyes and held his gaze like an instrument of choice.

"Release us," she demanded. "Otherwise, this piece goes up in flames, and your precious co-ordinates will be gone for good."

Hendrick chuckled nervously. He looked like someone who was right at the precipice of insanity.

"Quite brave, aren't you?" he asked. "Don't be stupid now." He signalled his men to lower their guns.

Annabelle smiled and shook her head. In that moment, her eyes took on a dangerous glint. She dipped the piece of paper into the tongue of flame, and it started to burn.

Hendrik's face transformed into an expression of utter horror.

"No," he screamed maniacally. He barrelled towards her, swinging the butt of his gun in a full arc. It came crashing down the side of her head.

Annabelle hit the ground. She was out cold.

CHAPTER 13

OVERBOARD

ANNABELLE CRUMPLED HER FACE and groaned. Then her eyes fluttered open.

"Welcome back," Nigel said.

Annabelle tried to move, but her limbs didn't budge. She looked down to see most of her torso wrapped in a massive coil of ropes. She felt a slight rocking motion around, and then she looked up.

"I'm right behind you."

She turned and saw Nigel and breathed a sigh of relief. He was alive, and so was she. Both of them had been tied back-to-back to the same beam. He reached out with his fingertips and grazed hers. It was a small gesture, but one laden with meaning. None of them were alone in this. They had each other.

He gave her a little smile. Annabelle blinked hard and threw her face away. She felt a light spell of dizziness, and her thoughts hadn't gained clarity just yet. But the fog was clearing. At least she could recognise Nigel. Plus, she knew she wasn't going anywhere just yet. She felt that if their kidnappers had just tightened the bonds around them by an inch, they could have been confronted with the threat of suffocation.

"How're you doing?" Nigel asked.

Annabelle grimaced and groaned. "My head."

"Oh, yeah. That. You kind of took a beating."

"Yeah. Tell me about it."

"Do you remember any of what happened?"

Annabelle stared at him through narrowed eyes. "Yeah, I think so. It's all beginning to come back little by little."

"It's good to see you're finally awake. I began to fear at some point that you never would."

"How long have I been out?"

"You've been drifting in and out consciousness for a few days. Mumbled a few times."

"A few days!" Annabelle's eyes shot wide open. "Damn!"

"Yeah, but you were able to drink. Hendrik's men found it challenging feeding you. He really hit you hard."

"Where are we, anyway?" Annabelle surveyed her surroundings.

"We're in the hold of a fishing boat. It's been moving for days now."

"Wow..." Annabelle shook her head. "I can't believe I've been out that long."

Suddenly, Nigel's face grew taut, eyes bulged, and veins began to pop around his forehead. Annabelle drew her head back in shock. The vessels on his neck bulged like underground pipes bursting out.

"Nigel?" Annabelle asked, her face and voice peppered with uncertainty. "You're scaring me. What's going on?"

Nigel let out an audible gasp, and relaxed. "Yep. It's still no good."

Annabelle blinked rapidly for some seconds, still caught on the precipice between shock and the ebbing of it. Then it dawned on her. Nigel had been straining against his bonds.

"Christ, Nigel!"

"Shhh," Nigel whispered. "They could hear you."

Annabelle lowered her voice, but her face couldn't do much for the fury on it. "You had me scared."

"Scared?"

"I thought you were having a convulsion or something."

Nigel chuckled. "It's nothing of the sort. I've been trying to get out of these restraints ever since I woke up. I haven't met any luck."

"Jeez. I wonder why that is." The sarcasm in Annabelle's voice was inescapable. But Nigel chose to chew it down like a bitter pill.

"Hey, while you've been busy making snide remarks and sleeping, I've been devising a plan to get us out of here."

"Oh, really?"

Nigel nodded. "Look over there." He jerked his head toward a crate near her foot. Annabelle followed his gesture, her gaze settling on the crate.

"What am I supposed to do with this?" she asked. "Is there something inside?"

"What's inside is definitely going to be of little importance to us. But look. Look by the side." He jutted his chin forward. "At the corner of the crate close to your feet, there is a splinter that's almost off."

Annabelle sat up and swiped her eyes around the room. The room's mostly empty except for a few boxes strewn about. However, at the end of the room, there were very large objects arranged together. She couldn't tell what they were because they were covered by a black tarp and strapped to the ground with belts. Her eyes fell on the splinter on the crate by her foot, and she got to work. She began kicking, but not too fiercely. The last thing she wanted was the splinter skidding across the ground and getting out of reach. Besides, silence was of the utmost importance.

"Come on," Nigel egged her on with a whisper. "You can do this."

Annabelle continued to kick, wincing with pain every time. The ropes binding her torso to the beam didn't afford any movement for her hands, and little for her legs. Still, she would do anything if there was a chance that they could be looking at an opportunity for escape.

The splinter widened with a soft crack, and Annabelle and Nigel exchanged hopeful glances. A faint smile crossed their faces—it was nearly over. She nudged the splinter, which clattered to the ground. Breathing a sigh of relief, she stretched her legs to bring the splinter within reach. Nigel deftly picked it up and began sawing at their bonds. Although using wood on ropes wasn't ideal, they had no alternative. Despite his cramped wrists, Nigel persevered, praying the splinter would prove effective. Suddenly, the tension around them eased, and Annabelle gasped.

"It's working!" she exclaimed. "It's working, Nigel."

"Quiet," he hissed. "You'll alert them."

"Sorry." Annabelle tucked her lips in. She hadn't really thought that getting out of their bonds would have been so easy. Not that Nigel was making mincemeat of it, but the process was just straightforward.

It's funny to think that if I'd been awake a day or two ago, we'd have been out of this mess, she thought.

The ropes laxed progressively as cord after cord was cut through. Eventually, they fell off. Annabelle sighed audibly and wrung her arms, enjoying the feel of blood rushing back in like an aroma. Her little bag was still dangled from her neck. She figured Hendrik's men had gone through it and left it to her. The only really important thing there was her notebook. Nigel got to his feet, cracked his bones and stretched.

"We need to get off this boat now."

"Yep. I totally agree with you. I feel like Hendrik's been waiting for this moment."

"He seemed concerned about getting you back to consciousness these past few days. And I don't think he still intends on handing out a dinner invitation."

"I don't expect him to do so either."

"Okay." Nigel looked around. "I say we make the best of this opportunity and move now."

"Aye aye, captain."

Nigel chuckled softly. It was good to have Annabelle back. The two of them made their way up the stairs to the trapdoor above and winced every time their footsteps made the slightest sound. At the trapdoor, Nigel nudged it tentatively, and when he felt it budge, he pushed all the way. He poked his head out and felt a cold draft brush past his face. It was dark and quiet outside. The night sky was littered with stars, and some of them sheathed underneath wispy clouds. Nigel turned his head around and scouted the area. It was all quiet on the boat, not a single soul in sight; just the sound of the water lapping at the sides of the boat.

"Hey," Annabelle whispered from below. "What's going on out there?"

"Nothing." Nigel looked down at her. Then he took one more peek outside. "It's all clear."

Nigel climbed out and helped Annabelle onto the deck. They moved quickly, hugging the wheelhouse and avoiding the windows. When he stepped onto the starboard side, a soft creak caught his attention. Looking up, his eyes widened. An inflatable lifeboat hovered above the water, suspended from a crane.

"See that, Belle?" He pointed and grinned. "That's our ticket out of here."

Annabelle's eyes held a different resolve. "There's something I need to do first," she said.

Nigel frowned. "Not now, Belle. We have to leave immediately. You know we're as good as dead if we're caught, right?"

Annabelle cast a wary look around, then she tucked an errant lock of hair behind her ear. She looked at Nigel, imploring. "Please, Nigel. This is something that I must do. You have to trust me on this."

"A-alright." He sighed." I'll stay here and get the dinghy ready, but don't take too long. I don't know how long I can go without being spotted."

"Yeah, I got that."

Annabelle slipped away, and Nigel watched her vanish around the wheelhouse corner. He exhaled deeply, shook his head, and began working on his part of the plan. A nagging feeling told him their escape would likely be far from quiet, contrary to their original intentions.

Annabelle froze in her tracks. *I thought Nigel said it was all clear out here.* She tilted her face upwards and casted a wary eye at one of Hendrik's men who had just walked out to the port. Annabelle's heart pounded. All that stood between her and being discovered was sheer probability, the slight chance that the man would turn in her direction. She stuck close to the body of the wheelhouse, hoping that it would just assimilate her in like a membrane. But the man didn't look in her direction, she continued moving when he left. Finally, she came around to where the steering wheel was located. There was someone manning it. However, Annabelle's eyes were on something else – a parchment of paper taped to the window right in front of the wheel.

The map! Exactly what she came for.

"Jacob!"

Annabelle jumped, startled by the sudden call. But she collected herself immediately and squeezed her face. She knew that voice. It belonged to Hendrik, and it was coming from the next room.

"Easy on the steering," he continued. "We don't want to damage the tanks down below. If any of them snap because you can't keep the boat steady, then we're wasting our time."

Jacob, apparently the man manning the wheel replied,
"Yes, boss."

Now the scowl on her face had transitioned into folds of worry resting just above her brow. *Tanks? Why on earth is he transporting tanks? Does he plan to go to war? And with whom?* Her mind travelled back to the large hidden mass she had seen below deck. *Was that what they were? Tanks?*

Her train of thoughts were leading her towards an interesting prospect, she had no doubt about that. But the map was right in her line of sight. That wasn't something she could let go for the promise of another lead. She needed to get that map. So, she looked around.

There was a fire extinguisher mounted on the wall next to her. *Hm...* She raised her brows and unhooked the extinguisher from its holder. *These are fortuitous circumstances indeed.* Keeping her eyes on the man, she inched forward gingerly. Her heart raced, and she seemed to be swallowing more than normal. She was aware that one wrong move could send everything to hell. But she could save the day or make an attempt at the least, if she succeeded. At every step, the man drew closer. Annabelle prayed hard that he would keep his eyes trained on the sea in front of him. She got within close distance of the man, and she brought the extinguisher down hard. Jacob crumbled to the ground like a heap of potatoes and laid still. Squatting and pushing her index and middle finger into his neck, she exhaled deeply as her face became saturated with relief.

I thought I killed him, I'm glad I didn't.

She straightened herself, walked to the window, and snatched the map off the window. She turned immediately and began to head outside. As soon as Annabelle crossed the threshold, the boat rocked violently and pitched her violently to the side. She caught herself just in time. She would have created one hell of a crash if she hadn't reacted quickly. The weather outside started to change a bit.

There were more clouds in the sky now, and the wind blew more frequently in strong gusts.

"Jacob! What the hell are you doing out there!" Hendrik's voice came again.

Annabelle collected herself immediately and half-jogged back to the back of the ship where Nigel waited. He straightened as she approached. He was glad she made it back. He already began brainstorming the possibilities of him facing a ship full of armed men just to get to Annabelle.

"Let's go," Nigel said, steadying Annabelle as she got into the rocking dinghy. "We need to move quickly."

No sooner had she gone in than chaos ensued. It first started from shouting, more shouting, and then an alarm tearing the silence of the night like a piece of paper.

"Crap." Nigel started the engine and steered the dinghy away. After a while he shook his head and turned to Annabelle. "What happened back there?"

Silently, Annabelle retrieved the map from her pocket, and showed it to him. She tore the map pieces into smaller bits and scattered them like seeds into the water. She stared at Nigel until he straightened his lips and bobbed his head repeatedly.

"Wow," he said. "I didn't think you were going to do that."

"Why?"

"Given your interest in this quest and all. I was thought you probably would want to see what the big deal was about this island."

"I made a promise that I would destroy it. This island isn't worth getting ourselves killed for. Besides, my father said that Darwin must have kept this place hidden for a reason. Maybe it should be kept that way."

Annabelle smiled and stared out into the massive sheet of ocean before them. Nigel gunned the engine and put more distance between them and Hendrik's ship. But they were far from the fire.

The further along they went, the more agitated the waves became. It started from gentle perturbations in the water. Then they became little turbulent crests that tossed the boat around. Now, the wind rushed through like it was running a marathon as it whipped Annabelle's hair into her face and sprayed some of the ocean all over her and into the dinghy. The dinghy danced atop the waves, buffeted like a feather, directly at the mercy of the ocean. Annabelle and Nigel exchanged looks as the wind whipped at them. They couldn't see each other clearly, but they knew the other was thinking the same thing. They might go under at any moment.

Nigel kept a tight grip on the rudder and turned the boat whenever he felt the crest of a wave had too much on them. Annabelle kept her eyes trained on an armament of angry clouds brimming inwardly with threads of lightning. She could feel its wrath, its lust for destruction. It was a tang that rode the crest of the wind like an experience surfer. Her heart banged against their chest. She knew that if they were still at sea by the time those clouds reached them, they would be in trouble. The armament moved quickly like a businessman working in the stocks industry.

There was a sudden flash of lightning, throwing the entire effervescent sea into clarity, if only for a moment. The darkness returned immediately and filled the air with its daunting mystery. However, in the flash of the moment, Nigel had spotted a mass of land in the distance. He was sandwiched between two options, and he didn't think making a decision was a difficult one. Anything that required them to stay in the ocean any longer than they already had was a no-no.

"Hold on, Belle," he yelled so his voice could carry above the wind. "We need to get over there." He pointed in the direction of the land.

"What's there?!"

"Land!"

"Are you sure it's land?"

"Positive! It's our best chance!"

A ripple of thunder rolled through the sky. Annabelle cowered. It felt like the sky was about to be ripped apart, and it may have well been ripped because the next moment, it began to bucket down on them. Nigel narrowed his eyes, constantly spitting water out of his mouth. His visibility was mired in drifts of rain, high crests, the darkness in the sky, and the dinghy's constant tossing. His muscles were taut from trying to keep the dinghy going in the right position despite the force of the elements.

Gradually, the silhouette in the distance grew larger. The glimmer of hope in their hearts grew.

And then without warning, Nigel yelled.

A large rock, sticking out of the water like a tooth, had come out of the dark at them, and they crashed, unhindered, into its side. There was a loud ripping sound as the rock's jagged edge tore through the dinghy's side. Nigel and Annabelle were thrown into the air, and into the waiting waves.

The cold water stunned Annabelle the moment she went in. She had been getting hit by spindrifts and the rain all the while. But this was different. The rain had a certain gentleness to its cold. The cold in the water was hard, harsh. It felt like getting bit. She broke out of the surface, gasped for air, and struggled to keep herself above the waves. They tossed her about, wrestling, grappling, trying to get her back within its bowels, but she held out.

"Annabelle!"

She whipped her face around. *Thank God he's still alive.*

"I'm here, Nigel," she yelled back. "I'm coming to you."

She paddled with her arms and kicked out with her legs, intending to go over to Nigel's position using his voice as an anchor. However, it felt like she was pushing against a solid brick wall. The ocean's current gave stronger resistance, and she felt herself petering out. She stopped trying to swim and turned around, searching, scouring the ocean for the lifeline. She saw it in the eye of that pandemonium. The shoreline. It was much closer than she had expected. She kicked her legs from under her and moved towards the shoreline. Then she turned and yelled at the top of her voice.

"Shoreline, Nigel! Swim over there!"

The ocean's current moved in the direction of the shoreline, so it propelled Annabelle forward.

Finally, she thought. *Some part of nature that works in our favour.* As soon as she said that, a flash of lightning illuminated another piece of rock that she was gradually speeding towards. The current already had her by the feet and was rapidly pushing her forward. Even if she wanted to do something, it was too late. Annabelle thrusted out her arms immediately and braced for impact. But she misjudged the position and shape of the rock. The current carried her just past it, though it was not entirely successful. She cut her arm on it as she sped past. The saltwater from the waves stung the wound immediately, throwing Annabelle's face up in a grimace of pain.

Quite auspiciously, the wave vomited her out on the beach, leaving her, helpless, cold, and too petered out to do anything. Her nostrils flared as she breathed rapidly. She felt the waves lap at the lower part of her body, felt the solidity of the beach sand below her, but her limbs just wouldn't obey the commands in her head.

Suddenly an arm wrapped around her and pulled her in close. That touch, the arm, the gentility in the way it pulled her, and the body she lay against – it was familiar. It belonged to Nigel. Annabelle felt a flush of relief. They had both made it out of the nasty storm alive.

"It's okay," Nigel panted. 'We're safe now."

He collapsed to the ground. Both of them lay there until morning, unmoved by the roiling in the sky or the crashing waves. They were beyond exhausted. But most of all, they skirted death by the whiskers. Yet again.

CHAPTER 14

PARADISUS

THE FIRST THING ANNABELLE experienced, suspended between full consciousness and unconsciousness, was the damp sensation of water persistently lapping at her face. Tentatively parting her lips, a wave splashed in, carrying a gritty mixture of sand and sea. Her eyes snapped open as she expelled the briny water and sand. Coated in a sandy layer, Annabelle inhaled deeply and pushed herself upright. Nigel's faint groan alerted her to his presence, and she glanced over to see him stirring.

Welcome back to the land of the living, she thought.

Before her, the sea extended toward the horizon, its turquoise surface gently rippling—a stark contrast to the tempestuous waves from hours prior. To the left, a cluster of rocks protruded from the water, likely the same ones that had threatened them during the storm. The island's coastline remained obscured to her left and right, its landmass extending further seaward, causing the beach to curve inward like a sheltered bay. The sun had yet to fully rise, its golden crown peeking just above the horizon, gradually infusing the sky with its radiant hues.

Nigel sat up and stretched his jaw. Then he stretched his hand upwards until they popped at his shoulder joints.

"We had quite the nap, didn't we?" he yawned.

Annabelle tittered. "I guess you could say that."

"How do you feel?"

Her arm throbbed from the impact with the rock. The bleeding had ceased, but her sleeve was stained with blood. She pursed her lips and then relaxed them. "I've felt worse."

"Yeah. I mean, we were just in a storm. But I didn't think it would turn out this way."

"You expected us to be at the bottom of the sea, twitching and struggling as the water snuffed out our last breaths, right?"

"That's a bit too graphic for my taste, but yeah. Something like that."

They exchanged glances, and then they erupted into gentle laughter. The sentiment went unspoken, but it shone in their eyes like the rays of the morning sun: they were grateful for many things, but above all, they were glad to be alive. Their shared history contained countless adventures, but nothing had been as intense as their recent experiences. The past few weeks had been a relentless roller coaster of events, and it was miraculous they remained unscathed.

"You know what?" Nigel mused. "We could stay here and let the sun complete its arc while our backsides remain nestled in the sand."

"Or?"

"Or we could stand up and try finding a way off this island. See if anyone else is living here."

"The latter sounds like the better option."

Nigel rose to his feet, then walked over to Annabelle and offered her a hand. She grasped his arm and hoisted herself up. Miraculously, her bag had remained strapped to her despite ample opportunity to slip off. She reached in and sighed with relief upon finding her water bottle still sealed. She took a sip and passed it to Nigel.

"Don't drink too much, we may need it later if we're stuck for water."

Nigel agreed, took a sip, and handed it back. Annabelle cringed as her wet, sandy clothes chafed against her skin. A shudder rippled through her, and she nearly tried to tear the garments from her body.

"Why can't storms just wash people onto shores with a spare change of clothes?" she asked rhetorically.

"Because they're not swimming pools," Nigel retorted.

Annabelle shot him a glare, and he chuckled. "Besides, if you really need a change of clothes, I'm sure we can find something for you on this island."

They turned around, faced the rest of the island for the first time, and froze. It wasn't the kind of freezing where a chill ran through their veins freezing their blood over. It was the kind where someone felt patches of goosebumps on the skin because of the jolts of awe that traversed the entire length of their bodies. Annabelle and Nigel's eyes said it all. They had never seen something as breath-taking as this before.

The entire island stretched out before them. Though it didn't stretch like the islands they had been to. This one was unusual. Its verdancy was opulent – too opulent. In a way in which it was almost intoxicating. The sand on the beach wasn't completely white. It looked brown, almost like there were particles of gold right between the sand. There were rocks of different shapes, sizes, and colours littered further up the beach. However, the beach only covered a tiny fraction of the entire island. From where Nigel and Annabelle stood it ran on a for a couple of miles, then it transitioned into a flush of exotic flora.

There was a burst of varying colours among the green, including different shades of green. It was like looking at a circus – an organised one where different plants could flourish. As unavoidable as the island's flora was from the outside, its hills were one of its self-delineating features. They were dressed in full green plants and along in varying sizes, creating an undulating mountain range that spanned the island's entire length.

Nigel and Annabelle exchanged glances, like explorers on the cusp of venturing into the unknown. They returned their gazes to the island, strode away from the shoreline, and delved into the heart of the island's greenery.

The moment they stepped in, it felt as if they had passed through a portal into a different realm. The island was unmistakably the same, but it appeared far larger from within.

"Woah!" Nigel exclaimed as he looked around. "Are you seeing what I'm seeing, Belle."

"Yeah. The flora is more opulent from inside here. I've never seen such a burst of exotic, colourful flowers and shrubbery before. They're so robust, so lively, it's like they're breathing."

"Plants breathe, Belle," Nigel replied sarcastically.

"Yeah, I know that." She rolled her eyes. "Just get the point. You know what I'm saying."

"Yeah, yeah," Nigel replied slightly absentminded. He was still taking looks around; his eyes, the flash of a camera, and his mind the production room for the pictures. "But that's not what I'm showing you. The island looks way bigger in here than from the outside. Don't you see?"

"Yeah, actually" Annabelle exclaimed with surprise. "I see that now."

They continued to walk, their eyes pouring out wonder in exuberant volumes. It was like someone had left the tap on in their minds, and it was gushing effusively – gushing admiration and surprise.

After walking for what seemed like hours, panting and slowing, Nigel looked at Annabelle. She stooped, placed her hands on her knees, and met his eyes.

"This isn't a walk in the park after all," she said.

"Yeah." Nigel tittered. "No kidding."

Breathing heavily, he took a quick scan of the area. The island grew wooded the further inland they moved. So, there were more trees here than there were when they first started. The entire floor was layered by varying expanses of shrubbery. But there were few empty pockets between them where the island's floor was evident. It was as though the island was reserving space to grow something else.

Suddenly, there was a flash of yellow within the trees. Nigel took a double look but saw nothing. *Did I really see that? Maybe my eyes are playing with me.*

Nigel spotted a rise in the terrain slightly to the left. He stepped out to the left a little, coming out from behind a tall coconut tree. And then he saw it, another hill on the island, one he didn't think he had seen from outside. Nigel shook his head. *This place is just amazing.*

"Belle," he called. "I think this is the path we should take."

"Why?" Annabelle asked as she approached him. "Suddenly, you've got a compass and a map in your head?"

Nigel laughed. "Don't be silly. If we got to higher ground, we'd be able to get a better view of the place. We'll be able to properly weigh our chances there. Maybe see if there are any inhabitants here."

"Okay," Annabelle shrugged. "I still feel I should have taken up running, even if it was just in school. Right now, my lungs feel like they want to give out."

"I'm so sorry. You know, you could stay down here and collect your breath while I go up."

"You're kidding me, right? I leave you to go up alone, and miss out on all the beauty that's to see from up there? Not a chance in the world."

"I thought as much."

Both of them carried on along the steep terrain. Their progress slowed at some point. The incline had risen sharply, costing them much more effort. Flower stalks jutted out of from the surrounding greenery as they walked. Colours that they never knew flowers could have before. At one point, they came across a flower that had multiple petals, but each of them had different colours. Annabelle took proper mental documentation of the flower. She intended to recreate it later on paper.

Upon reaching the summit, Nigel and Annabelle surveyed the island in every direction, taking in as much as they could. From their vantage point, the island unveiled itself like a willing offering. They beheld a vast array of diverse exotic plants, an island fostering unrestrained growth, an island brimming with vitality. It bore life like a banner held high in the wind, and they felt its charge like a whisper carried on the gentle breeze. As they observed, the pair realized something: there was no evidence of human activity, not even the slightest trace. The paths they had used were hardly trails, merely areas where the shrub population was sparser than in other places.

"I think it's uninhabited here," Annabelle said.

"Yeah. I think so too," Nigel replied.

Annabelle turned and took in a panoramic view of the island. Her eyes settled on a mountain in the distance, and she frowned. She felt that tug inside her – that tug one feels whenever they're staring at something they feel they've seen once but can't place.

She narrowed her eyes. *Come on, come on, come on. I know I've seen you somewhere. But where? And I've never been here.* Then it came it to her like a bullet.

Annabelle gasped audibly as her eyes spread wide open.

"What's the matter?" Nigel asked as he looked a little confused.

She jabbed her finger repeatedly in the direction of the mountain. It took a second before she could find her tongue.

"That's it, Nigel," she enthused. "That's it."

Nigel looked at the direction of her finger. Then he squinted. "A mountain?"

"Yes! Can't you remember? The map! That mountain looks very much like the one drawn on the map. The mountain called *Altare.*

Nigel's forehead wrinkled slightly as his brows arched. "Are you sure?

"Yes! The mountain had a flat top on the map. Just like this one. It really is *Altare.*"

Nigel turned around, taking in the environment with newfound understanding. Annabelle followed suit. It all made sense now—the vibrant colours, the ethereal beauty, and the incredible diversity of flora. They had washed up on Darwin's secret island, *Paradisus,* without even intending to do so. It was almost as if destroying the map had been the final requirement to gain entry to the island. Nigel and Annabelle laughed as they gazed upon the island, astounded by their incredible fortune.

"And here I was thinking we crashed into the unknown, into oblivion," Annabelle wondered out loud.

"I guess there really is a silver lining to mishaps."

"Oh my God." Annabelle felt goosebumps crawling across her skin. "Just look at it, Nigel. Look at it all. I've never seen beauty so untarnished. So pure."

The sun emerged triumphantly from the horizon, casting a warm, golden embrace over the island, as if awakening it from a peaceful slumber. Flower petals spread open, welcoming in the softness of the sun's rays. The island took on a slight sheen, glowing even better. If they hadn't been on the island before the break of the sun, this change would have gone unnoticed. The sun's rays broke off on the ocean in a million sparkles. The turquoise blue of the ocean took on a lighter hue, becoming more translucent, revealing the sparkling ocean bed, and the rocks lying on it.

Annabelle's eyes roved impatiently, as though they were conscious of what little time they had and wanted to swallow as much as possible within the present. Nigel stared at her. His eyes held the same awe and admiration, the sheer joy, in Annabelle's eyes, but they were different. They weren't just for *Paradisus.*

"You probably didn't think you were going to lead us here, did you?" he asked.

Annabelle looked at him and laughed. The sound of her laughter was like a song floating in the air. Nigel thought it was a perfect extra to the stunning aesthetics in the island.

"I mean, I did dream of it..." she tossed her head from side to side. "But, you know, there were many setbacks along the way, and I just gave up on it. At first, I was carrying my father's enthusiasm to unearth Darwin's secret island. All I had from the start was mere curiosity. Then little by little that enthusiasm became mine. So, it hurt whenever I hit a brick wall."

"Yeah, I understand."

Annabelle inhaled shakily. Then she threw her eyes back to the island. "Honestly, I can't believe our luck. It's just like a dream. Especially after I tore up the map." She giggled. "I'd kissed the idea goodbye that we'd confirm the truth of the secret island."

"Yeah. Giving up did seem like an option so many times in this journey. But here we are."

"Here we are." Annabelle's eyes darkened by a fraction. "I only wish my dad could see this now. He'd devoted most of his life to this, and he couldn't even see it."

"Well, he let you see it."

The meaning of Nigel's words hit Annabelle like a sudden change of weather and sank like a rock in water. His words could be as simple as that. But it had a different impact on her. All this while, she thought that her father had been negligent towards his family, especially during the early parts of their life. Still, he had done everything in his power, including getting involved in a heist, just to make sure she got here. Her lips spread and formed a small smile.

Thank you, Dad.

"Uhm," Nigel said as he looked down at his hands. "I guess apologies are in order." He raised his head and looked Annabelle in the eyes. "Look, I know that I can be an ass sometimes, and I'm apologising for that. I'm sorry for getting mad back at *Whakarewarewa*."

Annabelle stayed silent and locked eyes with him. Nigel continued.

"I shouldn't have reacted like that. I should've just trusted you. I'm also sorry for not trusting you on the boat. I should know, by now, that you always have a plan hatched in that head of yours. I should know that you're determined and strong-willed, and that you can accomplish whatever you set your heart to do." Annabelle giggled. "I'm serious."

"No, I'm not doubting that. It's just that these words are a bit too sweet."

"I mean every bit of it though."

"Hey," she held his wrists, and looked into his eyes. "I don't doubt that. Not even for one second." She smacked her lips. "You aren't the only person who owes an apology. I've got to apologise for dragging you into this whole mess."

"Are you kidding? Please." Nigel waved dismissively. "This journey was dynamite. Every bit of it. This is the kind of adventure story one tells their grandkids around a fire."

Annabelle laughed. "So, you are looking towards that life."

"What other life did you think I'd be looking towards?"

"I always figured you for a wanderer." Then she added quickly. "Don't take that the wrong way."

Nigel smiled. "Of course. You see," he sighed, "I do like wandering. Being in one place for a long time really does bore me. But if I find someone who can make me stay, someone who makes every day of my life feel like an adventure, I don't see why I wouldn't embrace that person."

Nigel let his eyes linger on Annabelle's. She thought there was a meaning behind his stare, and that drew her in further. Both of them stared for a while, lost in thought, immersed in the emotion welling in their eyes, the silence of the moment, and the beating of their hearts. Then a bird fluttered nearby and squawked. Both of them blinked simultaneously, smiled and turned back to the island.

Annabelle's chest rose and fell as she drew in a shaky breath. She felt electrified. Her heart raced. Nigel kept stealing glances at her from the corner of his eyes.

"If my recollection of the map is correct, that should be *Litus Scopulosum* on the map." She pointed back at the beach where they had washed up on.

"Um, ok." Nigel bobbed his head. "Any other place you recognise?"

Annabelle tutted and shook her head. "I wish I had photographic memory, but I can only remember glimpses of the map."

He laughed. "Come on. Don't you think we should be doing more than standing around here?"

"Yeah. We've still got lots of sightseeing to do."

They turned back and walked down the hillside. Going down was easier – too easy they had to take extreme care otherwise they would tumble down to the bottom.

"Wouldn't that make quite the nursery rhyme," Annabelle joked. "Us both rolling down this hill."

Nigel chuckled. "Instead of Jack and Jill, it'd be Nigel and Belle."

"Well, let's hope you don't break your head like Jack."

"Let's hope we don't fall at all."

They carried on further into the island as soon as they got down from the hill. As they walked, they kept looking around like an excursion of children in a museum. Everything was new. Strange. Refreshing. Just curious. Even the ones they were used to seeing looked different here. However, they could only find familiarities within the plant life. They found none in the fauna. Everywhere they looked they were seeing birds, the kind they had never seen before. One bird in particular, a blue bird that looked like a finch, but slightly larger, landed on a tiny branch in front of Annabelle. Red streaks ran from both its eyes to the tail. Annabelle smiled and sat down gently. She didn't want to scare the bird away. It chirped in the sweetest voice she had ever heard, and then a few clicks north, there was a response. Another chirp, just like this one.

"It must be a mating call," Nigel said.

"Or just two birds having fun," Annabelle replied.

"Yeah. That too."

Annabelle unzipped her bag and dug out her notebook and pencil. Thankfully, while it was still damp inside, the leather bag had protected the contents from damage in the storm. She looked at Nigel and chuckled gleefully.

"Talk about stuff that serves its purpose."

"Tell me about it."

He sat silently and watched as she sketched an accurate depiction of the bird right in her damp notebook.

Then as if it had been posing for her all along, the bird took off as soon as she was done. Annabelle exchanged a surprised look with Nigel, and they burst out laughing.

"This place is simply amazing," Nigel said. "In just hours of being here, I can understand the appeal. I totally get it now. I totally get why Darwin and his people would want to keep this place hidden from the world. I mean look at the species of fauna and flora here. Almost everything here is new, never seen before."

"I get the feeling that we've only skimmed the surface."

"Right?"

Another flash of yellow whipped past Annabelle. She looked up. *Did I see something or was that just me? It must have been the sunlight.*

They carried on some more through the forest. At some point, Nigel stopped, and bowed his head.

Annabelle turned. "Is something wrong?"

Nigel stared at her from the top of his eyes. Annabelle could tell that he was thinking about something. His eyes said that much. He sighed and lifted his head. Then he walked up to her.

"I need to get something of my chest, Belle," Nigel said. He looked around at their surroundings. "And I don't think there's a moment more perfect than now."

Annabelle swallowed as her heart beat faster. She couldn't take her eyes off Nigel. She felt expectant, like Nigel was meant to do something, and it had been a long time coming.

"Yeah? What is it?"

Nigel swallowed. He stared into her eyes. *Such beautiful eyes.* "We've had quite the rollercoaster ride throughout our reunion. And now that I feel it's all coming to an end, I find myself not wanting it to end." He narrowed his eyes a little. "Do you understand?"

Annabelle let out a shaky breath. "Yeah." She nearly stuttered.

"There's something I don't think I've said enough of all this time we've been together. You're an intelligent and beautiful woman, Belle. I don't call you that for no reason. You know that. But this moment we've spent together has impressed on me just how incredible you are."

Annabelle's heart picked up speed like a plane on the runway.

Nigel chuckled nervously. "But anyone who's been with you and doesn't pick out all these things at first is a real idiot."

Annabelle chuckled. It sounded even more nervous than Nigel's had.

"You can be wild, Belle."

She laughed.

"Yeah." Nigel bobbed his head. "You can be stubborn too. And very infuriating. But that comes with the whole package. Since our, uhm, break up, I've missed you. I've never stopped missing you. It's like I carried you with me everywhere, my little figurine in a special place in my heart. But then I could explain how much I missed you. Now, I can't. I just know that I've missed you so much, and I still do.

So much that going our separate ways after this will feel like tearing my heart in two."

Annabelle watched Nigel continue on, and she shuddered. Beads of tears slipped out the side of her eyes and rolled down the sides of her face. Without thinking, she obliged the swelling push in her chest. She cradled his face in her hands and mashed her lips against his, stopping him midsentence. Nigel was stunned at first, but he eased into the kiss, trying to make her feel what he felt just like she was doing.

More tears poured down Annabelle's eyes. Deep within her, she felt a bubbling lake of joy. It spilled over, finding its way to every nerve, every synapse, electrifying her, keeping her floating above the wind. She was in the arms of the man she had always loved, and that to her was a reality that superseded the discovery of *Paradisus*.

CHAPTER 15

THE TREE OF LIFE

ANNABELLE AND NIGEL CONTINUED their hike, hands interlocked, their smiles stretching from ear to ear. They came to a halt before an unusually tall tree. Nigel, having travelled to Africa, was familiar with the towering stature of iroko trees, but this one surpassed them all.

"I've never seen this type of tree before," Annabelle said.

"Me neither."

Drawn to the tree, they approached it and ran their hands along the bark, taking in its texture. The surface was smooth, but not entirely so. The colossal trunk would require ten men, arms linked, to encircle it. As it reached skyward, the trunk tapered into slender branches, adorned with dense foliage. Scars and stumps marked the spots where weaker limbs had fallen away. Though unfamiliar, the tree's strength and beauty were undeniable.

"I can recall this from the map," Annabelle said. "This was the tree labelled *Lignum Vitae.* It's Latin for 'the tree of life'."

"Wow. You speak Latin?" Nigel asked.

Annabelle grinned, shaking her head modestly. "No, but as an environmental scientist, I've encountered countless Latin terms. I've picked up a few along the way."

Nigel stared up at the treetop. Then he narrowed his eyes. "Hm. The Tree of Life. That's such a peculiar name. I wonder why they called it that. You know, now that I think of it—" he looked at Annabelle, "—I keep wondering how Darwin and his friends were able to keep everyone on board the *HMS Beagle* quiet about this place. Someone, surely, would have said something."

"Yeah. You're not entirely wrong." Annabelle eyes wandered off from the tree. She looked around at its huge roots, at the surrounding earth, and then she paused. She squinted. *Yep. It's not a mistake.* She had seen the top part of a cork sticking out of the dark brown earth. She stooped and tried to pick it up. But it didn't budge. She tried again, but it didn't budge. Then she got on her knees and pried off some of the dirt surrounding the cork, revealing the throat of the bottle attached.

"Nigel," she called, her voice laced with excitement. "Come take a look at this. I think I've found something."

Annabelle resumed digging as Nigel made his way over. Once she had unearthed the object, she held a dirt-covered green bottle in her hand. She pulled the cork off and tipped the bottle, allowing a rolled-up piece of paper to slide out.

Nigel looked on quizzically. "Don't tell me that's another map or clue. We're here already."

"Well, we won't know until we open it." Annabelle unfolded the paper. "Nope. This isn't a map. It's a letter."

Nigel stooped. "What does it say?"

Annabelle cleared her throat and read out loud:

IF YOU ARE READING THIS, I HOPE THAT YOU TOO WILL FOLLOW MY PATH. THE LOVE FOR ALL LIVING CREATURES IS THE MOST NOBLE ATTRIBUTE OF MAN. TO PROTECT THESE

ANIMALS AND THE ISLAND'S SECRET, A SECRET THAT THE CAPTAIN AND I HAVE NOT REVEALED TO THE CREW, I HAVE FORMULATED A MESSAGE OF FALSEHOODS.

ACROSS THE GLOBE, I HAVE WITNESSED MANY DIFFERENT CULTURES AND TRIBES, WHOM ALL SHARE A SIMILAR CHARACTERISTIC. AN UNSPOKEN TRAIT. THE STRENGTH OF MANKIND'S BOND WITH THEIR OWN DEITY. WITH THIS KNOWLEDGE, THE PERSUASION TO DO GOOD IS EASIER. WE REMEMBER THE SINS OF THOSE IN THE PAST, SELDOM DO WE REMEMBER THEIR GOOD DEEDS. MANKIND'S FIRST SIN SAVED THIS NEW PARADISE AND WILL KEEP ALL MOUTHS SEALED.

CHARLES DARWIN - 16TH NOVEMBER 1835.

Annabelle and Nigel continued to stare at the letter in silence, waiting, perhaps, for its content to settle properly. Annabelle's eyes widened.

"Of course!" she exclaimed. "Darwin was a genius. That's how he kept everyone quiet."

Nigel grimaced a little. "I don't know why I'm the one that keeps getting confused when you go on these private journeys of revelation."

Annabelle sighed. "Everyone aboard Darwin's ship was religious. He used that to his advantage. He warned them that if they told anyone about this place, they would repeat mankind's first sin."

Nigel's brows knitted together. "Like, Adam and Eve?"

"Exactly. Remember how in the story of the Garden of Eden, they disobeyed God and ate from the Tree of Knowledge?" Nigel nodded. "Darwin suggested that history would repeat itself if word of this place got out. This was the test. He adapted the biblical narrative, shaping it to fit his purposes, and presented it to his ship's crew as though it were divine truth. He even named this place *Paradisus,* which means 'paradise.' Now, it was a matter of whether he could trust them to do what was right to protect this place. This tree represents the temptation described in the biblical story. This is it, Nigel."

Annabelle was animated. Once again, her mind swirled with the excitement of yet another epiphany. But the expression on Nigel's face was more contemplative. He folded his arms across his chest and used a crooked finger to hold up his chin.

"I don't know, Belle," he shook his head. "What you're saying has some pretty huge ramifications. So, you're saying he tricked his crew into thinking that this place was the real Garden of Eden? Wow." He clicked his tongue and nodded repeatedly. "That's a lot to take in. A whole lot."

Nigel lapsed into silence, and Annabelle observed him, aware of the thoughts churning in his mind. If she focused, she could almost hear the gears turning. Nigel had always been the more sceptical of the two. She was quick to embrace ideas like this, while Nigel typically approached them with a discerning eye.

I guess some things don't really change, she mused. After everything they'd experienced on this journey, she had half-expected him to readily accept each new discovery. But this situation was unlike any they had encountered before. Believing in an undiscovered island with unknown species was one thing, but attributing mystical, mythical qualities to it was another matter entirely. So, she simply watched and waited. She knew he'd come to his own conclusions in time.

"What about the tree?" Nigel asked after a while. "He named it incorrectly. You said it yourself, the original temptation to man, this first sin that Adam and Eve had indulged in, was the Tree of Knowledge - not the Tree of Life."

"True." Annabelle nodded. "But come to think of it. Perhaps, the tree was named after its purpose. This representation is what saved this place from external influence from the world outside."

"Well." A small smile spread across Nigel's face. "I wouldn't say it did a particularly good job keeping foreign interference out. We're here, aren't we?"

Annabelle smiled and rolled her eyes. "Anyway, as I was saying, this representation gave the animal life here a chance to survive the grasp of human greed and avarice. It gave them a chance of life. That's probably why he called it the Tree of Life. Do you understand?"

"Yeah." Nigel bobbed his head. "I think I get everything you're saying. But there's still one issue though. Something else that I haven't been able to get an answer to. He said that he and Captain FitzRoy were protecting the island's secret. What secret were they keeping from the crew?"

Annabelle stared into the open, quiet and puzzled. "Hmm." She pursed her lips. "I can't quite say. Even Tui said that it wasn't the animals they were protecting. It was something much more. And if you ask me, this entire island is so much more. I mean, this isn't the kind of stuff you let the world see. It's just too beautiful. Too untouched. The world will destroy it in a matter of years."

"Besides..." Nigel scratched his temple. "I haven't seen that many animals around in need of protecting. It's just the birds. I'm beginning to think that at this point, we should keep our minds open to certain possibilities."

"Like what?"

"Well, for one, the possibility that whatever was around when they arrived here could be long gone by now. Extinct."

Annabelle remained still for a while, pondering on Nigel's words. Then her eyes fell on something else behind Nigel. She smiled.

"What is it?" Nigel asked, thrown into confusion once more.

"I don't think they went extinct," she said. "Look." She pointed.

Nigel turned as he followed the direction of her finger and he stepped back a little.

"Woah," he mouthed.

Annabelle got to her feet slowly, and they both looked at it. A large primate, a mix between a monkey and an ape, sat on the branch of a tree a few meters ahead of them. Its black face stood out contrastingly with its full yellow-golden fur. It watched them quietly as its long tail dangled below it. Nigel compressed his lips and stared in wonderment. He was clearly impressed by the primate's muscular build. He didn't know anything besides its similarity with other primate species outside the island, but he knew one thing. He wouldn't want to pick a fight with this creature. Not even if he had been pumped with adrenaline. *This is one monkey that will beat the living hell out of me.*

"How long do you think it's been there?" Nigel asked. "You think it's been watching us this whole time?"

"I'm not sure. But it's just as exotic as this place. There's just so much colour for it to camouflage. We could have seen it and mistaken its fur for some kind of flower or something."

"Do you think it alerted others that are like it about our presence?"

"The great Nigel, strong and fearless."

Nigel picked the sarcasm in Annabelle's voice, and he glared jokingly at her. She chuckled.

"Don't tell me you're scared?" she asked.

"I'm not scared, no. But I also don't want to have come all this way, past the mad *striking* lunatic, only to be pummelled by monkeys."

Annabelle sighed and rolled her eyes. "I don't think he's striking anymore."

"I know. I just like to see your reaction. Besides, he could never compete with me."

Annabelle smiled. She didn't say anything, but the glow in her eyes did. Nigel hadn't lied. Hendrik would never have been able to compete with him. He had that hot guy pizzazz, sure, but Nigel was equally tall, standing over six feet. And though his looks weren't as striking and in-your-face like Hendrik's, Nigel was a good-looking man. It wouldn't take long to see. Plus, he was extremely resourceful.

They stared back at the monkey, who hadn't moved a muscle. It was like staring at a lifelike statue of something. But its tail, and the ripples that formed on its fur as the breeze cruised through, gave it away.

"You know what," Annabelle said as she gently pulled out her notebook and pencil. "I've got to get this. I'm not leaving here with only an image of that bird in my notebook. I just wish I had a phone. I'd have taken pictures as well."

"No," Nigel shook his head slightly. "I don't think that would have been a good idea. The flash and the sound of the shutter would have agitated that primate. I can imagine it barrelling towards us now, screeching with rage, fangs bared, eyes malicious. Our only hope would be to outrun it. One blow from that thing would floor one of us instantly."

"Why has it been staring at us silently then? It hasn't done anything."

"It's probably watching, studying to see if we are threats. Primates are intelligent, you know this. Besides, it's probably used to seeing other animals drone on in their own language. So, while we're foreign animals to him, we're also droning on."

"Alright. I shouldn't be questioning you. You've got more experience handling this."

Annabelle sat down, crossed her legs and started sketching the monkey.

Nigel shook his head. "I think Mikey would have loved this place. He'd have loved this place a great deal. An opportunity like this isn't something he'd be willing to pass on."

"What about the storm? I presume it's one of the island's defence mechanisms?"

"Yeah. It could be. But we didn't die. As long as that variable exists, people like Mikey would continue to take that chance just to get here. This place is a goldmine."

Annabelle ran the sketch quickly and spent a little more time drawing its mane. She had to excise a little effort and precision here to get a life-like representation.

"Gibbaki," Nigel said suddenly.

Annabelle looked up. "What?"

"I just remembered that back at Whakarewarewa, Tui had said the name Gibbaki when she was talking about the animals. She said they could protect themselves. Look at that guy. He can hold off against a squad that's for sure."

"Yeah, no kiddi—"

Suddenly, something whooshed past them, landing just behind Annabelle. They jumped and looked around. Their hearts were thumping hard against their chests now.

"What the hell was that?" Annabelle asked, casting wide eyes around. She slipped her notebook and pencil back into her leather bag, and zipped it shut.

Nigel looked around until finally he stopped and stared at the tree behind them with consternation. He gulped hard. "Belle, we've got a problem."

"What?" she turned.

"Look." He nodded towards the tree trunk.

Annabelle saw it and her eyes grew full circle. "Crap crappity crap."

The shaft of spear protruded towards them, it's tip heavily buried within the tree trunk. As if on cue, rocks and stones began to bucket down from the tree lines. And then it was followed by a chaotic chorus of howling. Annabelle and Nigel exchanged looks, and in that split second, they knew what to do.

"Run!" Nigel shouted, and they took off.

More and more stones rained on them, and occasionally a spear.

"I thought you said they weren't going to attack!"

"No," Nigel replied. "I never said that. I said he was studying us."

"Studying what?"

"Studying how to attack! Run!"

CHAPTER 16

THE SECRET

ANNABELLE'S HEART POUNDED FURIOUSLY, her legs straining to keep up with its frantic tempo. She had never experienced such terror, not even when Hendrik held her and Nigel at gunpoint on the boat. This was far worse, with the Gibbakis' primal fury like an inferno raging behind her. As she stumbled over an outstretched limb and careened toward the jungle floor, someone snatched her by the scruff of her neck. Nigel. Her collar bit into her skin, but it was a small price to pay compared to the potential wrath of a stone or spear.

Just in time, she thought.

Before she could thank him, a rock grazed her face, leaving a searing scratch. Nigel shoved her onward, and their desperate race continued.

In his line of work, Nigel had faced his fair share of wild creatures, but the Gibbakis were different. Their movements were coordinated, their attacks organized. It was as if they were being pursued by a human community bent on expelling them from their land. Spears and rocks rained down, one nearly clipping Nigel. Spotting a divergence in the path, he shouted.

"Left!"

He veered onto another animal-made trail, momentarily disappearing between the trees. A fatal mistake.

A spear whisked past his ear, embedding itself into the tree ahead with a resonant thud. He froze, staring wide-eyed at the quivering weapon. Annabelle's shriek jolted him back to reality.

"Nigel!"

He resumed running, realizing that the Gibbakis were more than just an annoyance. The pair hurdled over a fallen log, and then Nigel glanced up. The onslaught of spears and rocks intensified, pelting them like a hailstorm from the treetops. Despite the cacophony of Gibbaki shrieks and the relentless barrage, they couldn't see their assailants through the dense foliage. The ability to remain hidden while mounting such a ferocious attack was an impressive feat. Perhaps, once they were safe and far away, they would discuss it.

Nigel's foot caught on a protruding root, nearly tripping him, but he managed to regain his balance just in time. As he left the spot, two spears landed where he had stood mere moments ago, their shafts crossed menacingly.

Come on, he thought. He turned and carried on through the path. Their faces, arms, torso, and feet were whipped by errant wild branches leaning into the torso. Little by little, small tears began to appear on their clothes, but it didn't matter, unless they wanted something far larger and lethal tearing through.

Nigel spoke through gasps. "This is what Tui meant when she said that the Gibbaki can defend themselves."

"This is more than defending," Annabelle retorted, struggling to catch her breath. "Scared rats defend themselves; snakes defend themselves. This is a coordinated onslaught from a frenzied battalion."

"Tell me about it."

A couple of rocks ricocheted of the surrounding trees, flying into their path. Annabelle winced as one came especially close.

"We need to get away from the trees," she yelled.

"Yeah. Good idea!"

She cast frantic glances around, and then she caught a hidden path cutting upwards through dense foliage.

"Hey, hey!" She stabbed her finger repeatedly in the direction of the hidden track. "Let's keep going up this way!"

She and Nigel turned into the track, narrowing their eyes, and using their arms to keep the shrubbery off their faces. They ran on, their feet hurting from the effort, but their minds intent on getting them away from death.

Suddenly, they spilled out of the dense foliage into an opening. They were hit by a blast of liquid cool air and a rushing sound. Annabelle must have gone into overdrive because she kept on running as though she didn't see the lagoon in front. Nigel skidded to a stop, and stretched his arms, grabbed her by the arm, and yanked her backwards.

"Sorry," he gasped. "Had to do that."

"It's okay."

Nigel and Annabelle turned around and glanced at the foliage of trees they just escaped from. The treetops rustled endlessly, but there were no spears or rocks flying at them. The attack had stopped. Just as abruptly as it had begun. Nigel sighed with relief and stooped, placing his hands on his knees. Annabelle shook her head repeatedly and stared out into the lagoon. She couldn't believe she hadn't seen it earlier.

I guess when there's a lot of adrenaline and panic pumping through your veins, she thought, *it's easier to oversee certain things. Like how we fell in love with the Gibbaki because of their colourful fur.*

Silence followed. The Gibbakis had apparently retreated. Nigel and Annabelle were struggling to catch their breath. If anything, they were relieved that the chaos was over. At least for now.

The lagoon behind them was a sparkling deep turquoise green. It sat, a rough circle at the bottom of a drop. At the other edge, there was a waterfall, falling from different spots on the rock. The rock itself was covered by lush green plants. With her shoulders heaving from every breath she took; Annabelle stuck her fingers deep into her hair and scratched.

"I really thought we'd have all day to admire this spectacle," she wondered out loud.

Nigel flicked his head up. "I don't doubt that Annabelle, but didn't you see what just happened? That was insane. We're definitely not safe here."

"I know. I was just commending the wonder of this place."

"Yeah, and that's fine." He stood and shrugged. "Just like the Gibbaki when we first saw them, remember? Yellow-golden full fur, black face, serene appearance, and then boom, all hell let loose. I won't be surprised if this spot—" he gestured at their surroundings "—suddenly began sprouting man-eating flytraps."

Annabelle chuckled. "Come on, Nigel. Even if those existed, we'd see them."

"I'm just saying." Nigel spread his arms in self-justification. "I still wouldn't be surprised if I saw them. This place is a home for new species after all."

"I'm not ruling that out, but that back there—" she pointed in the direction of the trees "—escalated so fast. In here, at least, there's peace. Let's just settle here first, and then we can go back to the shoreline. We'll try and see if our boat hasn't been torn beyond repair."

"And if it has?" Nigel folded his arms across his chest.

"Well, we do the obvious." She shrugged. "We signal for help."

Suddenly, Annabelle's brows arched in surprise. "Nigel! You're hurt!"

"Serious?" He cocked his brow. Then, he felt a slight, ticklish sensation just above his right brow. He touched it and came back with bloodied tips. "Woah." He drew his head back a little. "I thought it was all sweat. I must have cut it during the chase. It's what these kinds of stuff can do. You're too busy trying not go get impaled by a local crude spear or struck by a rock that you don't even feel your own wounds." He tittered and shook his head.

"How painful is it?" Annabelle asked as she neared him with concern welling up in her eyes.

"Come on, Belle. It's ok. It's nothing. Really. It's just a scratch."

"It's not nothing, Nigel."

"It barely even hurts."

"No," she shook her head vigorously. "I'm not taking that. Come on," she beckoned to him as if he was a child scared of being hurt, "we need to clean it before it gets infected. Look at this place. We don't know when we're getting out of here, but we're hoping it's soon. If it's not soon, this isn't the time to have an infected wound. Please, I'm begging you. We'll just wrap it up and be assured that we're at our best strengths for when we need to do stuff that requires strength."

"Alright, alright," Nigel said and let out a dramatic sigh.

"Go and clean the blood off your face. Just do it by the lagoon. The water looks clean enough."

"Alright." A thoughtful smile played on his lips as he walked past her. He slowed down, leaned in, and gently kissed her forehead. "Thanks for caring." Then, he peppered her face with multiple quick kisses.

Annabelle playfully swatted at him, and he ran off, laughing. She shook her head, a smile on her face, and watched him approach the edge of the water. Suddenly, she remembered something.

"Nigel."

He looked back.

"You need this." She tore of a piece of cloth from her sleeve.

"Come on," Nigel grimaced. "You should have just told me to do that. Why'd you have to tear your cloth off?"

"Well, because I think mine's the cleanest of the two of ours."

He grinned as he stood up and laughed.

Nigel walked towards her and took the piece of cloth. She blew him a kiss, and he smiled. He mimicked catching the kiss and blew it back to her. She caught it and placed it on her chest. He laughed, shook his head, and walked back to the lagoon. He never doubted his feelings for Annabelle, but now that they were back together, it felt as if their love had grown fiercer. It was as though they needed that time apart to figure themselves out, to test other waters, and know just what they wanted from each other as much as from themselves. Nothing much had changed. They were still the same couple that had disbanded a couple of years back, but they understood each other better now.

Look at me, Nigel thought, *swooning over a woman like a child. But I'd be damned if she's not the only thing in the whole wide world that makes me feel this way.*

Nigel bent down, cupped his hands, scooped the water and began to splash it on his face. At first, he felt nothing. It was when he splashed water the third time that he let out a horrifying scream. Annabelle wheeled around immediately. Her heart had skipped a beat, and when she saw Nigel screaming at the top of his voice, it skipped another beat.

"Nigel. No."

She ran to his side.

Nigel fell on his back as he clutched his face and screamed through his fingers. He rolled away from the lagoon and began to daub the water off his face with the piece of cloth Annabelle had torn from her sleeve. In the blink of an eye, the screaming stopped. Nigel quit daubing at his face and stared at a confused Annabelle. The pain had just stopped as abruptly as it had begun.

He stared at his palms as though they had been the source of his pain.

"What happened, Nigel?" Annabelle asked. "What's wrong?"

Nigel stared back at the water. "That burned!" He got to his feet. "Is the water acidic or is it just really salty?" The piece of cloth Annabelle gave him had got wet, so he lifted the bottom of his t-shirt and used it on his face.

"What are you talking about?" Annabelle asked.

"I'm serious? I wouldn't have screamed for nothing now, would I? The water. It just started burning my face all of a sudden. And now, the pain's gone. It is as if it never happened."

Annabelle stared quizzically at the lagoon. It was beautiful, but it didn't look like anything out of the ordinary. There were no indications that it was more than what was apparent. Annabelle walked towards the water.

"What're you doing?" Nigel asked. "Where are you going?"

"To see exactly what you're talking about."

Annabelle walked towards the water, squatted, and dipped her fingertips in. She paused for a while, turning her eyes to her fingertips to see any reaction. She frowned. There was no burning sensation. Nigel stared at her, quite confused himself.

Nothing's happening, he thought. *Why's nothing happening?* He started to conjure a scenario where he would have to swear to Annabelle and tell her that he hadn't made the pain up, and the water really did burn him. Annabelle pulled her fingers out of the water and dabbed them on the tip of her tongue. Then she shook her head. It didn't taste salty either. *What was Nigel talking about?*

She faced him.

Here we go, I'm going to look insane Nigel thought.

"I don't understand what happened Nigel," she said. "Did you—"

She froze, staring at Nigel like she had just seen a ghost. Nigel put his hands mid-air and walked towards her, and started launching an apology when Annabelle asked: "Where is it?"

He paused and knitted his brow. "What?"

Annabelle's eyes spread wider. Almost like she was worming deeper into a big reveal.

"Uh, Belle, you're frightening me now," Nigel said as he gave her a wary look. "Is there something behind me that'll maul me to bits if I make any sudden movement?"

"Your cut," she pointed at his forehead, "it's gone."

"What?" The frown on his face deepened. "What're you talking about? What do you mean it's gone? It's still here."

He placed his finger on the spot was, and he felt nothing. Just smooth skin like the rest of his face. He paused, tethering between confusion and uncertainty. It was probably a slight miscalculation. He moved his finger further. And he still felt nothing. The search became more frantic. This time around, his fingers groped all over his face as though the wound had changed location. He felt nothing still. It was as if the wound was never there.

He gasped in confusion. "I don't understand. I was bleeding. You saw it right?" He pointed at Annabelle. "You saw it." She nodded frantically. "It was right here." He touched the corner of his forehead.

Annabelle turned back slowly and stared at the lagoon, a musing expression on her face. The waterfall crashed mildly into the main body of water, creating ripples that spread towards the edge of the land where she stood.

"It's the water," she wondered out loud. "It has to be."

"How sure are you about that?" Nigel asked. "I knew this place would be weird, but the weirdness is just going beyond expectations."

"Well, there's only one way to know..."

"What do you plan on doing?"

She stared at her bloodied sleeve on her arm. The cut was still there from when she had smashed against the rock. That event felt like a week ago when it only occurred last night. She carefully rolled her sleeve up, revealing the sore and red skin around the cut. Then she walked towards the water.

"Belle," Nigel stepped forward, and held out his hand, "that's not the very best of ideas."

"It doesn't have to be," she replied under her breath.

She stuck her arm into the water. And waited.

Annabelle didn't have to wait long. Within seconds, a searing pain spread through her arm, arresting it like jolts of electricity and eating through her arm like a brutal armada of ants. It was as though she had immersed her arm in a pool of boiling water. Her face burned crimson as she grimaced in pain. Then the scream rolled out of her mouth. She pulled her arm out of the water immediately, heaving herself backwards with the effort. She landed on her haunches and clutched her arm like she could lose it at any moment.

Nigel dashed towards her, and got to his knees; his face, masked with concern.

Annabelle looked at the cut in her arm, and her eyes nearly popped out of her eyes. Though the pain was jarring, she couldn't keep out the shock of the bizarre occurrence. The cut on her arm was fading rapidly like a sketch on a notepad being erased. As it faded, it was being replaced with immaculate healthy skin. She could feel the torn tissue and skin reknitting themselves. It was like a restless tingle at that part of her arm. Nigel gasped. His entire face was bedecked in awe. He had never seen something like this before. Annabelle could only stare with her lips half-open as her skin worked itself back together. Then the pain disappeared, and with it, the cut.

She and Nigel stared at each other.

"Did you see that?" Annabelle asked.

Nigel bobbed his head repeatedly. "How on Earth is that possible?" He looked around. "I mean I know this place is mysterious and all, but water that heals you? That's just out of this world."

Annabelle stared at the water. "I can't tell you the mechanics of it, but there must be something in the water. Something that speeds up the body's healing process."

"If only there was a way to test the water and make out its properties. Obviously, there's no lab on the island, and we don't have the apparatus to take a sample with us."

"I'm not even sure if science would be able to find anything here. This place is just straight out of a fairy-tale."

"Tell me about it." Nigel stared at the water. "Something that speeds up the healing process. How does this even sound real?" He lifted his arm up. It was littered with cuts and grazes he had racked up during the run from the Gibbaki horde. His eyes sparkled with the birth of an idea. He moved towards the edge of the water, and dipped the arm with the bruises in. It stung immediately, and he stiffened his arm. There was a slight grimace on his face. The water didn't hurt as much before. And then he watched with brilliant fascination as the cuts and grazes disappeared, much in the same fashion as Annabelle's cut. He gasped.

"This is simply amazing, I'm telling you," he said.

Annabelle shook her head and exhaled with excitement. "You know, this could be it." She stared at the lagoon. "This could be the secret that Darwin and FitzRoy were trying to hide from the world. Now that I think about it, it all makes perfect sense."

"Why would he hide something like this? Water that accelerates the body's healing process a hundredfold! This is ground-breaking, a discovery that trumps whatever part of his voyage he decided to let the world in on. And I can bet you all the money in my life that healing nips and grazes isn't the only thing this water is good for. I bet it can cure some terminal illnesses too. This is lifechanging, you know. It could keep a lot of people from dying, save families and friends the heartache of losing a loved one. People could kill for this."

"Exactly." Annabelle looked at him pointedly. "I believe that was Darwin's point exactly." She sighed and walked up to Nigel. "Imagine what would happen to this island if the world got wind that it had water that could heal all external wounds in a matter of seconds? You've interacted with society. You know a thing or two about how people behave, and you can estimate their behaviour based on past events. I want you to think about this honestly, and let this scenario unfold as you know it would. What person wouldn't want a piece of this water? What government? What organisation? Can you imagine the political strife this would unlock? Governments claiming that it's their territory. People invoking the law of founder's keepers because they found it first. Companies trying to make a quick profit.

"Darwin knew this phenomenon would cause a potential massacre. A fight for a limited supply. People would spend even the last drop of blood for a resource like this. It holds so much promise. Ask yourself, Nigel," she shook her head and flung her hair away from her face, "how much attention do you think this place would curry before others started looking at it for its financial value alone? I know you're looking at this from the amount of help it could offer the world. But you and I know that it isn't those who want to use this to genuinely help the world that'll finally gain access to it. It's those with power, and they're the real villains. I think Darwin and FitzRoy knew this. That's why they kept that secret from the crew."

"You're exactly right," a voice called out.

Nigel and Annabelle spun around immediately and stared intently at the trees. For a while, there was nothing. Nigel and Annabelle exchanged a slightly confused glance.

"You heard that too, right?" Annabelle asked.

"Yeah." Nigel nodded. "You're not hearing things."

Annabelle stared at the trees again. "Whoever you are," she called out, "come out! We mean you no harm."

"Is that true?" The voice came again. "In that case..."

A young man stepped out of the trees and into the open area leading to the lagoon. Annabelle's expression became flinty.

"Hendrik."

He smiled broadly and raised his hands in the air as though he was issuing his surrender. "Guilty as charged."

As he walked further away from the trees, a company of armed men emerged, all dressed in black with their rifles aimed at Nigel and Annabelle. He looked around, unable to keep the awe from shining on his face. Then he looked at Annabelle.

"It's impressive, isn't it?" he asked. "This place" He crossed his arms and exhaled with pleasure. "And to think that it's finally mine."

"How did you find this place?" Annabelle growled.

"Woah!" He leaned backwards, staring at Annabelle with mock-consternation. "Easy there. You don't want to be yapping at the hand that has the power to keep you alive just yet." Then the smile on his face broadened. "You, of all people, should know me by now, Annabelle. I'm a resourceful man. A man of many talents, and I'm always keen on getting my way regardless of what's happened. I'm surprised that you can't still see that, after all we've been through. Come on, you're smarter than this."

"Go to hell, Hendrik. This place isn't yours or anybody's. And it's going to remain that way."

Hendrik's laughter died away, replaced by a chilling gravity. "You think you can stop me? Just the two of you?" He gestured toward them, his eyes icy with certainty. "The sheer audacity is almost commendable. You can't even complete a basic quest without fumbling at every turn, always a step behind the curve, outclassed by better players in the game." He paused, letting his words hang in the air as he adjusted his jacket. "Perhaps the allure of this place has blinded you, so allow me to clarify your situation: You're hopelessly outgunned. With a mere flick of my wrist, I could have you riddled with bullets before you even think to move. You would be torn apart."

"Yeah, Hendrik," Annabelle spat sarcastically. "You know, it's not the first time you've had us at gunpoint. Isn't that quite interesting? That for a piece of megalomaniac trash like you, you and all your armed men were outwitted by just two people."

Hendrik chuckled.

"Like I told you, this place isn't yours."

"It almost wasn't," he replied. "You and your boyfriend here," he stabbed a finger in Nigel's direction "almost caused my boat to tip over due to your recklessness. You know," he clicked his tongue, and stared musingly at the air. "You do have a knack for being a bloody pain. It's just pain, pain, and utter destruction wherever you go. Aren't you tired?"

Annabelle shrugged. "As long as you feel the pain and destruction, that's good enough for me."

Hendrik clapped and laughed. "Isn't it amazing? That your hatred for me has burned this long, and there isn't even hope of it diminishing sometime in the future. Tell me, Annabelle, is there really no chance that we can work together? We did have great chemistry when you and I first saw each other, don't you think? Where'd all that go to?"

"I wonder, you lying, conniving prick."

Hendrik signalled at his men. A couple of them pulled their rifles down, stepped out of the company and pulled Nigel and Annabelle away from each other.

"Nigel," Annabelle cried, panicking.

Nigel struggled. "Belle." His voice was strong, but there was a hint of fear in there. "You let her go. Now." He turned to Hendrik. "If you hurt one hair from her head, I swear to God—"

"Oh please," Hendrik cut him off. "You've got too much drama in you, man. Don't think you're the first man to fall in love. We've all been there. But I wonder how far you're willing to go to protect this woman of yours." Hendrik appeared to be contemplating.

"Is that it then?" Annabelle asked. "You're going to just kill us now, aren't you? After all, you've got what you wanted from the start." She scoffed. She couldn't believe how she hadn't seen through Hendrik's friendly mannerisms the first time she saw him. Now, that she looked at him, his selfishness and avarice was as plain as day. He wore it like cloth and didn't bother to hide it. *Unless he wants to snivel up to you like the groveller he is and ingrain himself,* she thought. *How did I ever feel attracted to him?* Those moments popped into her head like seeds, and they made her shudder with disgust.

Hendrik's expression darkened, and he pointed a finger in Annabelle's direction, nodding his head in agreement. "You're exactly right, Annabelle." She shuddered, and then exchanged a look with Nigel. Both of their eyes conveyed the same emotion - they were teetering on the edge of helplessness. Escaping as they had done on the ship seemed impossible here.

"See?" Hendrik continued, his voice smooth and dangerous. "I always knew you were smart. But first, I'm going to have my men move you elsewhere and kill you there. I can't have any parts of you and your boyfriend contaminating this pristine water." Nigel and Annabelle couldn't help but glance at the water. "It's so beautiful.

So gorgeous. One of the most enchanting sights I've ever seen, and I've seen a lot. Now, imagine your guts swimming in this beauty, marring it with your blood and whatever else you've got in those intestines. I won't have it."

Suddenly, there was a shuffle behind him. He turned and his face lit up. "Look, here they are! My tanks."

The men wheeled in black giant ellipsoidal tanks on moving platforms and parked them right at the edge of the water.

Suddenly, it dawned on Annabelle.

That's it, she thought. *That's what he meant by tanks. Not war tanks. Wait! How did he even know about the water if he came prepared?*

Nigel grimaced with anger, then he strained against the men holding him. They tightened their grip, matching his strength with theirs. There was no room for slippage here. It was as if they had learned a lesson after the incident on the boat.

"You're a coward, you know," Nigel yelled at Hendrik.

Hendrik stared at him, unfazed. Nigel continued, his voice dripping with disdain. "For a man your size, you are a despicable coward. You're trying to claim this place for yourself, huh? Why not do the hard work? You claim to be industrious, strong, intelligent. But you never do any of the dirty work. You cower like a frightened puppy, letting others do the heavy lifting, then you stroll in and claim all the glory. Now, you want your men to kill us because you don't have the nerve, the guts, to do it yourself. You know what's funny? You can work all you want, but when people see you outside, they'll only see one thing: a pampered, spoiled brat living off his father's money. A pampered brat who can't do a single thing for himself, even if his life depended on it. You can claim to be the discoverer of this place, but you'll see the disbelief for yourself. It'll hang like portraits on people's faces."

Hendrik whistled a short tune. Then he burst into laughter and turned to face Nigel. "You." He paused and stared into the open. He looked at Nigel with narrowed eyes. "You're one to talk, aren't you? You killed Mikey and you fled that stupid little village instead facing me. If you're so brave, why did you run? Huh? You heard my presence and you scurried off like the scared little mouse that you are. You want to talk to me about cowardice? You're the real coward here, my man." Hendrik walked up to Nigel, whipped out a pistol from his waistline and aimed it at the man's head.

"No!" Annabelle yelled, and tried to go for him, but thick hands gripped her arms and kept her in place. Her eyes beaded over with tears.

"I'd happily blow your brains out right here," Hendrik said.

"Hendrik!" Annabelle called. "Please, don't kill him. You don't want to do this, trust me. He's not the one you want. You don't have anything to do with him. I've been the one in this from the onset. You know this. I just brought him in to help so we could make the discovery faster." Annabelle whimpered and tried to strain against her captors, but it was futile. Her desperation clawed at her insides, wailing to be let out. The man she loved was at the end of a muzzle. The more she realised that it could all be over with a gentle squeeze on the trigger, the faster her heart ran.

"I'd do anything, Hendrik," she continued. "Anything at all. Just let him go."

Hendrik didn't budge. He maintained a cynical grin and locked eyes with Nigel.

Suddenly, a rock flew out of nowhere and struck Hendrik's outstretched arm.

"Ah!" He jerked, and there was an instantaneous roar from his gun. Nigel hit the ground and lay still.

Annabelle felt her heart melt. "No!" She screamed. Her face crumpled up in pain, and she wept. "Nigel! Nigel!"

He didn't move a muscle.

Hendrik flexed his arm. It hurt like the devil. "What the—"

The words vanished from his tongue when a spear went right through one of his men, impaling him against the trunk of the nearest tree. Hendrik spun around, flashing surprised and panicked looks around.

"Fire!" he yelled.

There was a return of rapid gunfire. He and his henchmen turned to the trees, firing at the tops and at the foot. They shot sporadically, unaware of the source of the attack.

Abandoned in the heated exchange, Annabelle got to her feet, and stared at the direction of Nigel's body. Her heart ached to run to his side, to check if he was really dead, but she stood, rooted to the ground. Her heart burned immensely. Tears dropped down the sides of her face. Nigel's body was surrounded by Hendrik and his men, and they were busy engaging the attack from the trees. She had to leave in order to survive. There was no other option. If Nigel was alive, that's what he would have wanted. He wouldn't want her to get caught up in the fray. She shook her head, turned and ran. She ran as far away as she could.

CHAPTER 17

TRAPPED

TRAPPED. THAT WAS THE sensation that engulfed Annabelle as she stumbled through tangled underbrush, snapping twigs, and gnarled roots on the forest floor. Her surroundings blurred, melding into a chaotic whirlwind, while her mind surrendered to the overwhelming heat of her grief. Hot tears cascaded down her cheeks, inconsequential droplets against the earth, yet she didn't pause for respite. Desperate to distance herself from the past, she soon realized it was impossible to escape, especially one so significant and haunting. The scar of her past seared her heart, a relentless pain refusing to release its grip.

Annabelle thought she detected the murmur of voices behind her, spurring her to coax her legs for more strength, to propel her further. Tree branches encroached the path, lashing her skin as she sprinted, leaving welts that stung but paled in comparison to the anguish in her heart. Eventually, the pain grew too burdensome, and she crumbled into sobs. Her shoulders heaved, her knees wavered, and she tripped, crashing to the ground with a force that stole her breath. Her lungs screamed for air, but the agony remained unrelenting. Once her breath returned, the sobs resumed, echoing through the forest, carried on the whims of the breeze.

Surrounded by the verdant embrace of shrubs and trees, Annabelle hauled herself up and resumed her flight. She resembled a faltering robot, doggedly adhering to its original programming. Yet Annabelle's destination remained elusive, driven solely by the tempest of emotions and hormones coursing through her veins. In that moment, her own wellbeing and sense of direction held no significance.

All that consumed her thoughts played like a disjointed reel from a damaged movie clip. Nigel. The scene unfolded on an endless loop, each vivid detail painfully intact. She saw Hendrik aim the gun at Nigel's head and the unwavering defiance in Nigel's eyes. She recalled believing this wasn't his first brush with death and that they'd somehow escape unscathed, as they had before. But this time, they were marooned on a hidden island, facing the Gibbakis and their lethal rain of rocks and spears.

Annabelle relived the moment the rock soared from nowhere, striking the gun in Hendrik's hand, the single gunshot that shattered her dreams and happiness. Nigel crumpled to the ground, motionless as a fallen tree.

I can't believe it, Annabelle thought. *It's not true! No. It's not possible. Nigel can't be dead.*

She remembered seeing him lying on the grassy floor, face down. She had screamed his name. *Yes, I screamed his name. He can't be dead? But Nigel would have answered me if he was still alive. He wouldn't hear my voice and not come running. Nigel, oh Nigel!*

She cast frantic eyes at the foliage surrounding her, as though Nigel would jump out at any moment with a huge smile on his face. He would laugh and tell her that it was all an elaborate ruse to get themselves out of harm's way. She would laugh and cry with relief, get angry for the turmoil and anguish, but he'll be by her side. She would feel his huge arms around her waist, feel the solidity of his warmth and the certainty of his presence. It would seep deep into her – her own personal bit of reality. But it wasn't an elaborate ruse. It just wasn't in Nigel's character. Everything that had happened was unplanned. She had seen it unfold right in front of her, and it made her heart burn all the more. The fact that Nigel was gone beyond redemption. That there was nothing else she could do for him.

Annabelle continued her desperate flight, but her body began to falter under the strain. She stumbled through the forest, limbs flailing without purpose, her tear-streaked face locked in a frozen gaze. Suddenly, the ground beneath her vanished.

A gaping hole, unnoticed until it was too late, swallowed her whole. She plummeted through the air, unable to scream before splashing into the icy water below. The jarring impact and the water's cold embrace shocked her, as if a mild electric current coursed through her veins, jolting her from her melancholic stupor.

Gasping for air, she dragged herself to the bank of soft, wet sand. She found herself in a cavernous chamber, its ceiling punctuated by the largest naturally-formed skylight she'd ever seen. At the far end of the pool, a small opening hinted at a connection to a larger body of water outside. She surmised that the exposed land in the cave owed its existence to the low tide, and that a high tide would submerge this sandy refuge beneath the waves. The cave's towering walls were etched with tiered, concentric circles—evidence of nature's persistent carving hand.

Annabelle crawled out of the water and settled at its edge, drawing her knees up to her chin. She wrapped her arms around herself and dug her toes into the soft sand. The crushing weight of her grief returned like an avalanche, contorting her face as a fresh torrent of tears erupted. Her shoulders convulsed with sobs, releasing the unbearable pain.

Never before had she felt so utterly alone. She recalled the hollow ache that consumed her when she lost her mother, the haunting sense of absence that lingered for weeks after the burial, akin to the phantom sensation of a missing limb. But with time, she had grown accustomed to her mother's absence—life goes on.

The last time she had felt such loneliness was after her breakup with Nigel. The decision to part ways had been mutual, as their long-distance relationship and demanding careers had hindered any progress. Rather than growing or even remaining stable, their bond had fractured, splintering when it should have been steadfast. Trying to repair the damage only led them to watch the cracks widen before their eyes. They cared for each other too deeply to end on a bitter note, and so they agreed to separate. Annabelle remembered that fateful evening in Amsterdam when they had shared a final coffee at a cosy café, baring their souls, their pain, and their thoughts. The loneliness had washed over her as Nigel stood up, offered a friendly smile, and vanished into the wistful winter evening.

But this time, the loneliness was different. Before, there had been hope—Nigel was alive, and if they both failed to find someone else to fill the void, they might reunite. Now, all hope had been extinguished, the flame snuffed out, irretrievably lost.

"Nigel," she whispered. "Oh, Nigel."

The sound of his name felt hollow, like it lost its meaning. He was supposed to be present. He was supposed to respond to his name. But the ensuing absence was stinging. She stared into the open air, feeling Nigel's absence as though it had taken concrete structure, as though it breathed and lived like a sentient being.

"Oh no," she tilted her head up until she faced the sky. "What have I done? What did I do? This is all my fault. It's all my fault!"

She lapsed into another bout of weeping. *I shouldn't have got him* involved, she thought. *If I hadn't, he'd still be here. I should have told him off after Sydney.*

Annabelle wrapped her arms around herself, squeezing tightly as tears streamed down her face. She sniffed hard and shook her head with regret. She should never have dragged Nigel into this mess. He hadn't been there when her father and Hendrik's discussions about Darwin's mysterious island had piqued her interest. She had initially embarked on this journey alone, believing she'd found a partner in Hendrik. After his betrayal, she had turned to Nigel for help, thinking she was in over her head. Now, she realized there must have been other ways to resolve the situation.

I've been in worse situations, she thought. I could have just talked myself out of it. I should have stood my ground and maintained my innocence. I had to pull the poor man in and now he's dead.

Maybe, you just missed him.

She did miss him. She missed his suave. His gentility. She ached for that charismatic thing about him that allowed him to worm his tall frame through the most heated situations. Most of all, he was the only one she could turn to, the only one she could trust. He had been there for her, every inch of the way, even when he didn't understand her motives; even when she gave him cause to second-guess the motive of their mission. Nigel didn't waver. He had her back, just like he promised he would. And what did she give him in return? A shocking and untimely death.

I should have handled my business myself. I should have kept it together. You're a grown woman for God's sake, Annabelle.

Every moment she had spent with Nigel from Sydney had been perfect, their reconciliation, even more heavenly. He had done everything she needed him to, and more. The more she thought about him, the more she realised that she needed him. And the more she needed him, the more his death burned. She sniffed and wiped the tears off her face with the back of her hand.

"I'm sorry, Nigel," she whispered. "I'm so sorry."

At that moment, she wished that the concept of an afterlife was true. Then, Nigel wouldn't really be dead, and there would be hope for her to see him again. *Maybe it is real,* she thought. *If an island like this can exist, safely tucked away from human eye, then who's to say that all the stories aren't true. They may not be exactly how they've been portrayed, but at least, there's some truth in them.*

Annabelle looked at the cave again. A fresh wave of emotions washed upon her. The initial wave had been for Nigel, now this one, though not as heavy, belonged to her. She hadn't even the slightest idea of her bearing or location. She sighed.

I wish I hadn't destroyed the map after all.

She felt that she could have kept it safe on her person. In that moment, it would have been the perfect guide out. Now, she was stuck, without any idea how to untangle herself from the island's bowel. She suspected the water would lead out to a larger body, but she didn't know exactly what to expect outside that opening. If she went out there half-prepared, the repercussions could be dire.

What if the currents out there are stronger? she thought. *What if it sweeps me off the moment I swim out of the cave? What if there are sharks out there in the ocean? I don't know what to expect of this place anymore.*

Her mind went back to Hendrik, the source of her loss and sorrow. He could still be alive. The last time she had seen him, he joined his men in returning fire, an unlimited reply of bullets for every rock or spear thrown from the treetops. But she knew that having the superiority of armed power didn't guarantee survival. The Gibbaki were natives of the island. They had spent decades, no, generations getting acclimatised to every single contour, every edge on the island. They already demonstrated an amazing command of attack tactics by keeping themselves hidden, while releasing lethal projectiles on who they deemed a threat. Annabelle wished they were intelligent enough to tell enemy from friend.

Annabelle scratched at her hair and let her head loll between her knees. She knew that she couldn't stay here for too long. Soon, she would have to find her way out of here and begin the search for a way off the island. It wasn't wise to assume that Hendrik and his goons had fallen to the Gibbakis' onslaught. She could be practical and assume that their force had been dealt a tremendous blow, and thus couldn't operate at full strength anymore. But that still left them with the guns and her with nothing but smarts and the swiftness of feet. That was just cutting it close. She still had to bother about other animal life on the island that would be hostile to her presence. They were the worst because she didn't know them yet and couldn't tell when one would spring a surprise on her.

I'm going to die here, aren't I?

She didn't have much of a life besides Nigel, and her family. Nigel would have been one more person to mourn her demise. But now he was gone, leaving only her father, sister, and Charlie. *At least, I know I'd be sorely missed.* She chuckled sadly.

Suddenly, she heard a growl bounce off the walls of the cave, and a chill shot through her veins. Annabelle froze, unable to command her limbs to move as willingly as she wanted. But her mind was spinning fast. *What was that?*

She heard the growl again. This time, it was more intense by a bit. She turned and looked at a recess to her left. She peered intently, she could make out the form of something moving underneath the row of twigs and vines running along the cave's walls.

Annabelle craned her neck forward and stepped gingerly towards the recess. She made a mental note to make a mad dash for the water if something unexpected were to happen. She didn't know anything about her odds of survival yet, but she would be damned if she gave up trying. Nigel hadn't died for her to throw up her life so willingly.

As she stepped closer, the visibility within the recess improved. She straightened with a start. It was a Gibbaki. Its eyes were sunken and pale; the bottom lids, drooping like pouches. The limbs were thin like the withered branches that littered the forest floor, but that did nothing to stop the fury dancing in its eyes, or the menace in its body language. It wanted the new visitor to know that it was very much a danger, much like the rest of the clan. Even though it did everything but look the part, it's arms, legs, and much of its torso had been entangled hopelessly in the vines. It was as though they had grown around it.

Annabelle inched closer, and it snarled, pulling back thin lips and revealing gleaming teeth and long canines. She paused, went into a half-crouch and held up both hands in a placating manner.

"Easy now," she said. "I mean you no harm. I'm just trying to help you out."

She took one foot forward, and it snapped as it lurched forward violently. Annabelle retreated in an instant, grateful that the vines were strong enough. Her heart pulsated heavily, agitating like an animal aching to be let out of its confines.

"Yeah," she replied wryly. "What was I thinking, talking to you like you understand English."

She placed her hands akimbo and sighed. *What can I do to help you out here?* She looked at the Gibbaki. It quietened considerably.

"Look, I'm trying to help you out of there," Annabelle continued. "By the look of things, you've been stuck here for quite some time. I want to help you. I really do. But you've got to help me out here too."

She stared at the Gibbaki, and it stared back as it made feeble lip movements.

Annabelle sighed and shook her head. "If I didn't know better, I'd say you were trying to speak. But that's not a trait your kind share with mine. Otherwise, you'd want to think a little first before you spring into action." She wished Nigel was present. He was the expert with animals. *What would Nigel do?* she asked herself.

She scratched her scalp and took a studious look around the cave. *There's got to be something in here that can help me gain its trust,* she thought.

She narrowed her eyes as she walked around the bank, looking at the walls, the sand, the plants running across the walls, anything. There was nothing but wet leaves all around. Suddenly, her brows arched. *That gives me an idea.* She opened her leather bag. The small water bottle she sipped from earlier was still there. It was almost empty. She took it out and hurried over to the wet leaves. With difficulty, she tried to drain as much of the water into the bottle. The water she fell into was too salty and undrinkable.

After a few minutes, the bottle was almost full.

"This should do."

Then she took small, cautious steps towards the Gibbaki, stretched one arm sideways as if to maintain her balance, and held the bottle forward with the other. The Gibbaki grew alert, and leaned against its bonds, but rather than snarl like before. It licked its lips and stared greedily at the bottle.

Annabelle followed the direction of its gaze and felt a small twinge of triumph. *Aha! I've got you.*

"Easy now," she cooed. "I don't mean you any harm. I just want to help."

The Gibbaki's breath became quick and hurried, growing into a pant. It tried to stretch out its arms, but the twigs held it back.

"Sorry," Annabelle said. "You'd have to let me handle this one."

As she got close enough, she stopped moving. She wanted to have enough room to run should the Gibbaki try something funny. She held the bottle by the bottom, and then tipped the top towards the Gibbaki's mouth. Its lips curled as the bottle got nearer. It opened its mouth, let the top of the bottle in, and wrapped its lips around it. The gurgling sound that rose from its throat was a hair's breadth away from all out violence.

"Wow," Annabelle said. "You must have been trapped here for longer than I thought."

The Gibbaki stretched one of its hands out through the vine and managed to grab the bottle. Now, it could control the flow of the water itself.

"Time to get myself busy," Annabelle said to herself. "Alright," she moved closer, "I'm going to try and set you free now. I'd ask that you don't make any sudden movements as that could hamper the freedom effort." The Gibbaki continued to drink, oblivious of her constant gibberish.

Annabelle tugged at a vine and paused, waiting for the Gibbaki to growl or snarl or lurch for throat. It did neither. For now, it was fixated on the bottle of water. Nothing else mattered.

Annabelle continued pulling, twisting and stretching. Sometimes, she would have to bend a vine both sides to break it off. The more she worked, the freer the Gibbaki became. All the while, Annabelle was conscious of how much her heart beat. She could feel her pulse like a throbbing in her ears, and her breathing was quite pacy, as if she was on the run. In her mind, she kept expecting the Gibbaki to toss the bottle aside and make her the new attraction. But she worked nonetheless, keeping a third eye out.

As soon as she's disentangled the Gibbaki from the last vine, she took careful steps backwards, keeping her eye on the Gibbaki the whole time. She stole a momentary glance at the opening. It was the only exit she spotted, and it was on the other side of the water. That and the opening in the roof. She began to calculate the possibility of getting to the water opening before the Gibbaki could inflict any serious harm on her.

She watched the Gibbaki empty the last contents of the bottle, and then it tossed the bottle aside. Already, there was a freshness of vigour to its movements. Suddenly, it flicked its eyes towards Annabelle. Her heart lurched. The time had come. There was no way she could stand and fight. The Gibbaki looked emaciated, but she was no fool. She knew she was no match for its fury and rage, and that alone could tip the balances in its favour. It was better to run, and she was already prepping herself to do so.

The Gibbaki's eyes never left hers, even when it tilted its head to the left and right. Annabelle got this feeling that she was being studied, crafted into the Gibbaki's memory. She thought she caught a glint of amusement and curiosity in the Gibbaki's eyes before it turned and scurried up the vines, and out the huge hole in the roof.

Annabelle shut her eyes and sighed with relief. She walked close to the edge of the water and looked up at the hole.

"Bye, Gibbaki," she said. "You didn't even say thank you, but I understand. That's far better than throwing rocks and spears at me or trying to strip my flesh from my bones with your teeth and claws."

She thought she heard a shuffle up by the hole. She paused and listened, but she didn't get anything else.

Annabelle shook her head and decided to sit down by the water. The flush of relief she experienced drew an audible gasp from her. She had been so intent on trying to rescue the Gibbaki and to stay alive that she hadn't noticed she had been working at the tip of her toes.

Look at me, she thought. *I've become a lot of things on this voyage. I've had to improvise at the spur of the moment, when it looked like there was no other way out. Who would have known that I'd detest my father's interest in Darwin and his scientific escapades, only to be embarking on a solo animal rescue mission sometime in the future? Reminds me so much of Nigel. Oh, Nigel.*

Annabelle rubbed her hands against her arms as a cold draft from the water brushed against her skin. She felt the waves lick at her toes, and she listened. For a long time, the sound of the waves would be her only accompaniment in the silence.

CHAPTER 18

GUNPOINT

ANNABELLE HAD LOST COUNT of the time spent in the cave. Her bottom hurt from sitting for too long. She turned her face upward to the sky. It was still bright, though she couldn't see the sun. *Who knows how much time has passed?* She thought. *It could be minutes, hours. Hell, it could even be a new day.*

She looked around the cave as though she was seeing it for the first time. Her eyes lingered on the recess where she rescued the Gibbaki from. She wondered where the animal was now. *Probably back with his murderous pack,* she thought. *Or roaming the island. It was theirs anyways.*

Rising to her feet, Annabelle brushed layers of damp sand from her clothing. Her gaze shifted between the cave's mouth that led to the sea and the gaping hole in the ceiling through which she had fallen. The Gibbaki had clambered out through the hole, but she was no animal. The water seemed her only escape. With a resigned sigh, Annabelle waded toward the opening, praying it wouldn't lead her to an even worse fate.

As she progressed, the water deepened until she floated

effortlessly. Annabelle dove in and swam for the exit. The current surged near the mouth of the cave, carrying her into the open sea. Gasping for air, she scanned the horizon and spotted the nearest landmass. Drained from the effort, she hauled herself ashore.

I thought I rested enough, she thought. *Clearly, I was wrong.*

Annabelle ventured into the trees, acutely aware of the unsettling silence. The hush seemed to have swallowed every sound, leaving even the leaves on the trees motionless. In this eerie quiet, she could have detected an exhale from a mile away. The forest seemed to hold its breath in anticipation. Alert, Annabelle scanned her surroundings, her instincts warning her not to focus on any one point for too long.

What if something jumps out at me from nowhere?

Once, she stepped on a twig and the ensuing snap had nearly set her heart on fire. It had taken a couple of seconds for her thumping heart to final settle.

The sun in the sky was trailing ever so closely to the edge of the sky. The light of day was beginning to seep out silently, like a mourning procession. Suddenly, she felt a change in the atmosphere. The air was filled with a soothing cool, a freshness that she wanted to soak up if she had all the time in the world.

Her nostrils narrowed as she inhaled deeply. She looked around. A water source was close. She couldn't tell how close, but she knew it was within the vicinity. She forged on, convinced that she was headed in the right direction. She heard the crashing sound a few minutes later, and some of the gloom on her face lifted. She knew what to expect even before she broke out from the cover of the trees.

After walking in silence for about thirty minutes, the sound of the waterfall felt like an abrasive violation.

The waterfall, even with all the elements of destruction on its banks, was still gorgeous. If anything, the light from the fading sun gave it a different shine. The water wasn't sparkly and turquoise green like before. It had taken a slightly darker hue now, but it was a sight to behold, nonetheless. However, Annabelle wasn't about to be fooled. She faced enough already on the island to know that the most beautiful things had the most dangerous bite.

She moved further, walking gingerly to avoid announcing her presence to whatever lurked behind the crashing sound created by the waterfall. Some of the tanks Hendrik had wheeled in were damaged. Most of them had spears jutting out of them, others had been pulverized until they turned into hunks of ugly plastic. Then she saw it and she cringed. A bloodied corpse, with its neck twisted in an unnatural angle.

Annabelle walked out from behind the tree, and the rest of the ground opened out before her, uncovering a spread of corpses, Gibbaki and men alike. Most of the Gibbaki had several small holes staining their fur. Hendrik's henchmen looked like they had the ugly side of death. They had spears jutting out from different parts of their bodies, others had their heads caved in with giant rocks, and some were just mutilated and mauled.

Annabelle felt a churning within her stomach. It grew rapidly, a wave of revulsion that wanted out. It rose up through her throat and she puked. She placed her arm over her mouth, turned her eyes away and continued to walk. But she didn't look away entirely. She had her eyes out for someone else. The first casualty of the unfortunate exchange. Nigel.

She could recall the exact spot where he had fallen, which is why she had a frown on her face the moment she had to look twice. Annabelle stopped abruptly. *What the hell?*

Nigel's body was nowhere to be found. She scanned the gruesome tableau, noting the dominant colours—black for Hendrik's henchmen and gold for the Gibbaki. Nigel had worn neither, so he should have stood out among the sea of dead bodies, but he simply wasn't there.

She stepped back, her gait, a bit shaky. *What is going on?* She walked around in circles, searching for Nigel's corpse. She just wanted to hold him one last time. Her heart burned, and her mind spun. She wanted Nigel. She needed to feel his cold body before she left the shores of this island.

Suddenly, there was a rustling from the trees. She gasped and flung her eyes towards the tree line. Her heart thumped relentlessly like a mad animal. She could think of only one thing good enough at remaining unseen within trees. The Gibbaki.

Oh no! I didn't come up all the way here, just to die now.

Taking one last desperate glance around for Nigel, she found her luck had not changed. She turned and sprinted toward the shoreline, intent on finding a boat and escaping before it was too late.

Back in the forest, she darted through trees and clusters of shrubs. The flora in this part of the island was sparser, hinting that she was nearing the shore.

Suddenly, a gun clicked, and someone yelled.

"Stop right there!"

Annabelle came to a halt; her face froze with terror.

"I swear to God if you make one more move, I'll shoot you without a moment's thought."

Disappointment clouded Annabelle's face, and she groaned inaudibly. She knew that voice anywhere. The voice of the person that killed the man she loved. *How the hell is he not dead?*

"Turn around," Hendrik said. "Slowly."

Annabelle obeyed and stared directly into the muzzle of his handgun.

Though Hendrik had survived, he hadn't escaped unscathed. Numerous bloody cuts marred his body, with a large gash on the side of his forehead. A dried stream of blood stained his face, originating from the wound. His once-impeccable shirt and trousers hung loosely, tattered and torn. His eyes were sunken, and he breathed heavily.

"I see you've gotten your fair share of the battle," Annabelle remarked.

"Shut your mouth!" Hendrik growled. "You had to go and make this whole venture difficult, didn't you? Most of my men have been killed or have deserted. But it's not over yet. I'm not done. I'm not leaving here until I get what I came for."

Annabelle sighed, feeling a profound weariness envelop her bones. It settled within her like a pool of stagnant water. She just wanted out.

"Hendrik, please," she began, but he cut her off immediately.

"Shut your mouth! I'm not done yet! You hear me! And nothing's going to change my mind about that. You're going back there with me, and you're going to get as much water as you can. I don't get to lose. Especially not with this."

Annabelle stared out into the distance, a look of hesitance on her face. Then she felt something hard and cold press against the back of her head.

"Move," Hendrik seethed. "Or I swear to God, I'm going to blow your brains out."

Annabelle shook her head. There was no way out of this one. She had slipped out of tough situations like this before. Maybe, if she had Nigel—

I got him killed, she thought. *I got him killed by roping him into situations like this and thinking we could face the whole world with one by the other's side.*

A thought nagged at the back of her mind. She ruminated, weighing it, like a biscuit in her mouth. Then she decided to let it out.

"I don't understand," she said. Hendrik jabbed the muzzle of the gun into her back, and she increased her pace. "How did you know about the water? You've never been to the island before now. This place was essentially a mystery; shrouded from the rest of the world with unknown animals, unknown plants, and unknown phenomena. How could you possibly have known?"

Hendrik chuckled. "Making small talk now, are we?"

Annabelle rolled her eyes and looked straight ahead. Her arms were already beginning to ache from holding them up.

"Alright," he said. "I'll tell you. It's going to be a long walk back to the waterfall anyway. I might as well occupy the time while I'm at it." Then he cleared his throat. "Where to start?"

"The beginning?"

He laughed. "Yes, the beginning. I like you. How did we end up at opposite sides of each other?"

Annabelle turned her head to glare at him, unable to hide the accusation in her eyes.

"Alright," he said, "How I did know about the water? I was at this discrete event where they were auctioning off really pricey stuff belonging to credible historical names. That was the same auction where I saw the original *On the Origin of Species*, written by Charles Darwin himself. I couldn't buy it, because I didn't think I should have been spending my money on a silly book. I mean, he discovered evolution and all, but what was I supposed to gain from that book that I couldn't gleam from the internet. Someone else bought it. I don't know who, but they splurged a lot of money to do so. Another item for sale was Captain Robert FitzRoy's suicide letter. In the letter, the old man rambled on about how he'd discovered the Garden of Eden and tried to keep the "Lord's Garden" a secret. The man was disgusted by people who didn't believe in God, so he left the only piece of evidence he'd taken away from the Garden. He called it the "holy water imbued with Christ's healing powers." He said he hid this under a cross in a cathedral in New Zealand. Now, that I think of it, it's funny how I almost moved over the letter. But on second thought, I realised that was the only thing I'd be buying after thirty minutes of watching them auction one thing after the other."

Annabelle started to slow, and Hendrik shoved the muzzle of his gun into her back. "Don't even think about it," he warned. "After reading the letter I was curious and thought I would go investigate it. I enlisted Mikey's help with the promise of a fortune if he found what we were after. And he did find the vial of holy water FitzRoy mentioned. But nothing else, no other clues. It seems FitzRoy was a man of his word, even from beyond the grave. He wasn't just going to hand this place over to us. But no door is ever truly closed. There'll always be another way in, you just have to know where to look." He shrugged. "So, I turned my interest over to Darwin's voyage. I needed to find out all about it. And what better person was there than Professor Young, your father. He's the only one who knows Darwin's journey inside out." Hendrik paused for a while. "Mikey's condition was that I'd leave the animals alone. He believed this place would be teeming with unique species. He thought they'd be worth far more than any near-extinct creature." He chuckled. "I think he should have been here to see one of his animals tear people apart like they were made out of straw." He sighed and shook his head. "There were moments when I thought I'd hit a dead end. I had someone follow you when you went to the museum to take the compass looking thing from there. I must commend you and your family's efforts. That was mighty sleek getting that object away from the museum. You know what else was impressive? Replacing it with a fake one, right under everyone's noses. You guys are the real deal. It's a pity we couldn't come up with anything good, you and I."

"That compass looking thing," Annabelle said, "it's called a sextant. You'd know if you did your research properly." Her words dripped with sarcasm.

Hendrik gave her a small knock with the butt of his gun. Annabelle grunted in pain and tried to touch the painful spot with her hand.

"Don't you dare," Hendrik warned as he kept the gun trained on her. "I won't hesitate to use this. You should know that by now."

Annabelle kept her hands up in the air, but it was an extremely difficult task, especially with the spot Hendrik had hit her burning with pain.

"I even tracked down the priest who'd bought Darwin's book," Hendrik continued. "I sent Mikey over there to go retrieve it. But your idiot of a boyfriend had to show up and kill my man."

Annabelle stiffened when he mentioned Nigel. She felt as if the layer of insulation she had built over her pain, had ruptured and everything was rushing back out. It hurt just as fresh as the moment she heard the gun go off, and saw his body hit the ground.

She picked up the sound of crashing ahead and lifted her head. She sniffed slightly as a tear rolled down the side of her face. They walked out of the trees, back into the array of collateral damage lying still before the waterfall. Annabelle felt the cold bite of the gun as Hendrik pushed it hard into her back.

"Move," he commanded.

Annabelle obeyed. They walked over dead bodies, and countless tufts of dried blood on the grass. He directed her towards the tanks, and then he stopped just before he got there. There was a cannister lying carelessly on the ground.

"Pick it up," he ordered. "Pick up the cannister. I'm going to bring back enough evidence. And after I'm done, I'll find my way back here, end every miserable semblance of life on this island, and make this water mine. It's going to make me trillions. I'd be the richest and most powerful man in the world. Can you imagine that? The power to heal residing right in my palms. That's some feat."

Annabelle stooped gently and picked up the cannister. "You won't get away with this, Hendrik."

Hendrik gasped in mockery. "Tell me that your plan is to deny people access to healing after everything you've seen here today. After seeing the wonders that water—" he pointed towards the lake, "—can do. If your father got ill, wouldn't you want him to get a taste of this? You'd do it with no questions asked, right?"

Anabelle's lips parted and then closed. She lacked the initial words to respond to Hendrik's claim. But that was only for the moment. She cleared her throat. "You claim to want this water to heal people, but at what cost? Destruction? Annihilation? Tainting something pure and perfect? Our existing medicines work just fine. Better to use them than let your greed ruin this place."

Hendrik laughed. "My greed? My greed!" He laughed some more, shaking his head. "It amazes me, Annabelle, you know. How you never cease to be the voice of morality even when your life hangs on the line. Ask your boyfriend how that worked out for him. Oh wait…"

Annabelle spun around and gave him a steely look. Hendrik took it in and gave her a smile in return. His smile was a statement, an act of suppression. The ball was right in his court, and there was nothing Annabelle could do to hamper that. He could deal with her however he wanted. Perhaps, that was why she didn't do any more than glare at him.

"You know," he continued. "I'm going to do you a favour and send you to your boyfriend real soon, wherever he is." He looked Annabelle in the eye and teased her with the smile on his lips. "You know what that means, right? You won't be leaving here alive."

Annabelle jutted her chin forward, and stared Hendrik straight in the eye. The last thing she wanted was to give him the satisfaction of being in total control. He would kill her, but she wasn't afraid of him. She knew, one way or the other, that her luck would eventually run out with Hendrik. Though her face was steely, she was a cauldron of pain inside. It just dawned on her that she would never be seeing her family again. Her father. Sarah. Little Charlie. She turned around and shut her eyes tight. Beads of tears slipped out, and she wiped them off quickly with the back of her hands.

"Enough chatter. I've had it with this wretched place. Just fill the canister already. I can't wait to—"

Suddenly, a raucous and chaotic chorus of growls burst out into the air, interfering with the gentle crashing sound of the waterfall. Annabelle's heart leapt as troops of Gibbakis flowed into the area, rounding them up in a circle. They were swift. Calculated. Purposeful. There was nothing she or Hendrik could do, they had been fully surrounded.

"Damn it!" Hendrik cussed. "Not these dastardly things again." He dashed forward, wrapped his arm around Annabelle's neck and pulled her right in front of him as a shield, while he turned around, pointing his gun at the Gibbakis.

The Gibbakis stared at them, a little agitated, but there was a sliver of curiosity dancing in their eyes. They were all tall, standing up to the human shoulder in height.

"Back off, you hear me!" Hendrik shouted as he turned around. "Take your sticks and stones and get the hell out of here, before I kill all of you! I mean it!"

One of the Gibbakis croaked. Another followed.

"Keep your voice down, Hendrik," Annabelle seethed covertly. "You're getting them jumpy. You're going to get us killed."

"Oh, yeah. Oh, yeah. How about now?" Hendrik shoved her towards the Gibbakis.

Annabelle whimpered as she fell on her knees. She bent down, buried her head in her arms, and waited for the pain to start. She saw what they had done to Hendrik's men. It wasn't going to be any different from what they would do to her. She didn't know how long she waited before she became aware of the ensuing silence.

What's going on? She opened her eyes but didn't lift her head out of her arms just yet. Suddenly, she felt a gentle touch on her arm. This one was different. It was rough and hard; inhuman. She lifted her head, and stared eye-to-eye at the skinny Gibbaki she had freed from the cave.

Without warning, the Gibbaki tightened its grip on her arm, and pulled her up from her knees. It grunted something indecipherable, and Annabelle frowned. She was lost. But she started to get the hang of things, when the Gibbaki started moving without letting go of her arm. Annabelle followed judiciously.

The Gibbaki walked her through the horde of his kin, and then out at the other side.

Hendrik's legs began to quiver. He stared at Annabelle who was already out of danger's way with shaky eyes.

"What did you do?" he asked, gently. Then his face contorted with rage. "What did you do!"

Annabelle turned to face him, and a sardonic smile formed on her lips. "Something you could never do, Hendrik," she replied.

The Gibbakis began to bare their teeth, closing in on Hendrik. He retreated, looking around frantically while pointing his gun. Their growls deepened – a guttural rumble emanating from within.

"Annabelle," Hendrik called, his voice quivering with fear. "Tell these creatures to back off. Tell them to leave me alone, or I swear I'll kill all of them." Annabelle didn't say a word. She simply watched him, as the circle of the Gibbaki tightened around him.

"Annabelle," he called, desperate for anything. "Tell these animals to move away. I won't hesitate. I'm warning you now."

He stopped moving. There was nowhere else to go. Everywhere he turned he faced a Gibbaki with fury in their eyes, and spittle dripping off bared teeth. He kept spinning in a circle, holding his gun out at them, and at nothing at the same time.

Then he looked at Annabelle, standing beside the lean Gibbaki that had walked her out. Hendrik's face suddenly crumpled up with disgust and fury. *No,* he thought. *I won't go out this way. I won't go out alone.* He aimed the gun at her and started to squeeze the trigger.

As soon as Annabelle saw Hendrik point the gun at her, her heart dropped, and everything slowed. She saw his index finger begin to apply pressure on the trigger, and realised with a start, that there was nothing she could do. She was already too late.

She closed her eyes and expected to hear the roar of the gun anytime soon.

The Gibbaki were quicker. They lunged towards him, jumping on top of him like two tributaries clashing. They swallowed him up in a flash of fur and screams of fury. The Gibbaki pummelled him relentlessly. Annabelle winced as Hendrik's screams pierced the air, threatening to splinter it into several pieces.

She was seeing first-hand what the Gibbaki had done to Hendrik's men. They rained down their fists on Hendrik.

The Gibbaki beside Annabelle grunted something, and she looked at him. There were tears in her eyes. She couldn't tell what emotions danced in those black eyes, but the fury she met in the cave was long gone.

The Gibbaki tugged at her arm, and they continued walking – walking away from Hendrik's judgement.

Annabelle had only walked a few steps when Hendrik's screaming stopped abruptly. She heaved a sigh, and continued walking. It was done.

CHAPTER 19

A NEW BEGINNING

ANNABELLE COULDN'T HELP BUT steal glances at the Gibbaki as they walked through the trees. Now that she saw him beyond the entwined vines, she noticed something she'd missed before. He emanated an intelligence, a level of civility that seemed to hover above him like a cloud. Aside from his size, he appeared distinct from the rest of the Gibbaki. An aura of authority enveloped him, as if he were their leader.

He must be their leader, Annabelle thought. She replayed the incident a couple of minutes ago in her head. There was no way he would have waded through a horde of his kin to single her out without opposition if he wasn't the leader. Whichever it was, Annabelle was glad she saved him back at the cave. *I guess one good turn deserves another.*

She longed to say something, anything. She knew the Gibbaki wouldn't understand, but she didn't want to risk ruining their delicate rapport. So, she kept her thoughts to herself and tried to become accustomed to the roughness of his palm encircling her wrist.

Annabelle couldn't help but imagine the Gibbaki tightening his grip and twisting his hand the other way. Snapping her wrist would be as effortless as breaking a dry twig. She shook her head, dismissing the thought.

The Gibbaki turned, and their eyes locked simultaneously. They both quickly averted their gazes, as though they'd committed some grave offense. Annabelle suppressed a nervous laugh as they pressed onward. A few minutes later, she perked up.

What was that?

She heard something. She knew what it sounded like, but she just wanted to be certain. She stared at the Gibbaki, who kept his face straight ahead as usual. *Was that—*

The sound of swashing interrupted her thoughts. Annabelle felt her heart soar with excitement. If the Gibbaki didn't have a grasp on her wrists, she would have lurched forward, and began a sprint out towards shoreline. She felt elated, and most of all relieved. Returning to shore had been the primary goal after their expedition into the island had hit a bad note. They had been assailed by all manner of ill fortune ever since.

And I've lost Nigel, she thought. She wished he was here with her so badly. Perhaps, they would have been walking out of the trees together instead of her alone with a helpful Gibbaki.

As they emerged from the trees, a cool ocean breeze caressed Annabelle's skin. She tilted her face upward, closing her eyes to savor the refreshing touch of the sea air. She couldn't help it. The past few days had been grueling, and this taste of freedom was a welcome respite. The promise of liberation seemed to hang tangibly in the air, and she relished it.

The Gibbaki released her wrist and nudged her forward. Annabelle nearly stumbled, her eyes flying open as she spun around to face him. He stared back at her, grunting and gesturing towards the ocean.

A smile spread across Annabelle's face, and her eyes misted with tears. *They're not so bad after all,* she thought. *We're just the strangers who, as usual, think that everything in this planet is meant to be for us.*

"Thank you," she said as she waved at the Gibbaki.

The Gibbaki watched her for a moment, then he turned and disappeared within the trees. Annabelle would never know how they were able to do that. No part of their body was green. Yet, they were able to meld with their surrounding so effortlessly. It was a skill unmatched by any adaptive feature she had ever seen or heard of in an organism.

The waves crashed against the surface of the sand. It was time to go home. She ran her eyes along the shoreline, looking for a boat. There had to be one somewhere. And then her eyes fell on something in the distance.

Annabelle leaned forward, almost stooping, and narrowed her eyes.

What's that? she thought. It looked like—

A body?

Annabelle straightened herself. Whatever that was, she was sure it wasn't a Gibbaki. She started walking towards the object. The closer she got, the clearer it became. It was a body.

Annabelle's heart jumped and her eyes widened. It wasn't just any body. It was Nigel.

What is his body doing here? she asked herself. She broke into a run.

The lower half of his body was in the water, while his torso lay on the beach sand. As she knelt down beside him, she saw the bloody graze on his forehead where the bullet had struck. Her face contorted as she broke into tears.

"Oh, Nigel," she cried.

Suddenly, his eyes fluttered, and he groaned.

Annabelle gasped and scrambled backwards. Her face was frozen in utter terror and shock. Her heart threatened to jump right out of her chest.

Nigel groaned again. "Be...Belle?"

The fear and shock dissipated in an instant, replaced by overwhelming joy. Her shoulders shook as she resumed crying, but now her tears were of relief and elation, unrestrained and uncontrolled.

Annabelle lunged forward, pulling Nigel into a tight embrace.

"Ugh," he groaned.

"I thought I lost you," Annabelle cried.

"No," he replied weakly. Then he winced and touched his temple. "Wha...what happened? My mind's still a bit fuzzy. Where's Hendrik? How did I get here?" He groaned and winced again, tightening his grip on his head this time. It ached immensely.

Annabelle still held on to him, scared that if she let him go, she might lose him. A part of her still thought that all this was a dream, a hallucination that the island had spun to keep her from leaving. Even if it was a hallucination, she wasn't willing to let go of him too quickly. His presence was like a salve, and it filled a gaping hole.

"It's over," Annabelle said. "You hear me? It's all over. Finally. You don't have to worry about anything else."

Nigel winced a little. He was about to tell Annabelle to ease up on the embrace until he spotted something in the ocean.

"Uhm, Belle," he called.

"Shhh," Annabelle replied. She sniffed. "I know. You don't have to say anything. You don't. It's all my fault. I never should have dragged you into this mess in the first place. I was selfish, and I'm sorry. Oh, Nigel, how could I ever make it up to—"

"Belle," Nigel called again and stopped her from delving deeper into her self-imposed apology speech. "Who's that?"

"What? What?" She pulled her head away. "Who's who?"

"Finally," Nigel said. "I thought I was never going to get your attention. Who are they? The ones coming towards the beach?"

Annabelle turned and saw several boats approaching the island. Her jaw dropped slightly. The mysterious and hidden island was now receiving a small armada of visitors. How quickly things change, she thought. She studied the boats with a mix of curiosity and wariness, unsure of their occupants. She didn't know how they had found the island; it could be a mistake, or it might not be. But she wasn't entirely comfortable with their presence, even though the boats meant a possible escape from the island.

One of the smaller boats separated from the group, heading towards the beach. Annabelle stayed close to Nigel, who was struggling to stand. He winced and groaned.

"Belle, a little help here?"

"Sorry," she apologised, and helped him up to his feet.

"Gently," Nigel winced. "Almost everything hurts."

"I'm sorry." She draped his arm over her shoulders and spread her feet a little so he could lean on her.

As soon as he was comfortable, she took her eyes straight back to the water. The little boat had reached the shore now. As soon as she saw the occupants of the boat, her worry abated like smoke in the wind. It was Tui and her Māori people.

"Hey," Nigel said. Then he chuckled weakly. "It's Tui. She's come to check up on us. If we're behaving or not."

Annabelle smiled and shook her head. It was definitely great having Nigel back again.

Annabelle's brows rose. Tui had just shouted something from the boat.

"What's she saying?" Nigel asked.

"I've got no idea," Annabelle replied. "I didn't hear her the first time."

"Why is she still standing in the boat though?" Nigel asked. "They can all come out to land. What're they so scared of. I'm not sure that the Gibbaki will attack us here."

"Quiet," Annabelle shushed Nigel. "She's saying something again."

"Come over!" Tui yelled. This time around, she gestured with her hands.

"She's asking us to go over to them," Annabelle told Nigel. Her eyes went to the boat. True to Nigel's words, the boat floated so close to land, but none of them disembarked. They just stood in and beckoned to Nigel and Annabelle.

Annabelle suspected their reluctance to set foot on the island was due to superstition. She shared a similar hesitance, not because of superstition, but because of her experiences on the island. She had lost Nigel there, and even though they were reunited, she didn't want to linger and risk encountering more dangers.

"Well, what are we waiting for?" Nigel asked Annabelle. "I don't know about you, but I want to leave this place so far behind it actually fades away from my memory."

Annabelle laughed. "You know that's not possible."

"Doesn't mean that I don't wish it."

Annabelle hooked her arm around Nigel's waist, and they moved towards Tui's boat. They struggled to hop on board, especially because Nigel wasn't strong enough to hold his own. But after he got on, Annabelle came on board without a fuss.

"Tui," she said and gave the village tribeswoman a smile of gratitude. "You came for us. How did you find us?"

Tui clucked her tongue and gave the order for the boat to withdraw from the island. "You outsiders are the only ones that believe that *Paradisus* is uninhabited, mysterious and undiscovered. The Māori people have known about *Paradisus'* existence since Captain FitzRoy told our tribe about it. We swore to protect it for generations and to never set foot on the island."

"Well, it's a good thing you found us," Nigel said weakly. Then he chuckled. "We would have spent days on the shore, looking for a way off that island. Thank you very much, Tui. You have my gratitude. Right now, all I need is rest."

"What about the map?" Tui asked.

She smiled. "It's at the bottom of the ocean, torn to shreds." Tui nodded in approval.

Annabelle turned and stared at the island as it receded. "I understand what you said about the island now," she said. "It should be left alone. Mankind's not ready for the things that are there."

Tui turned and smiled. "I'm glad you finally understand. Now, let's get you home so your man can get some rest and treatment. You two are extremely lucky."

"You really think so?"

"Yes. Most of my people believed that you were never coming back out."

"Why? There's nothing fundamentally wrong with the island."

Tui looked at her. "No, there's nothing. But ask yourself this. How many people went onto the island, and how many people are getting out?"

Annabelle paused as she delved into thought. She saw the tribeswoman's logic in a spark. Everyone who had set foot on *Paradisus* was dead, except for herself and Nigel.

"Remember what I told you about the Gibbaki?" Tui asked.

Annabelle nodded.

"Well," Tui continued, "people who step onto *Paradisus* with ulterior motives never get out. The island is that special. Why else do you think Darwin wasn't in a haste to put its flora and fauna on paper?"

Annabelle shrugged. The further they went out, it looked as if the island was being swallowed by clouds and mist. Annabelle watched the phenomenon until the island vanished from sight completely.

They found Darwin's mysterious island, and now they had lost it. Annabelle sighed with relief. *What am I go to tell Dad, Sarah and Charlie? Should I tell them?* The prospect of going home hung in the air like an aroma, and it settled into her skin like a hot whiff on a cold winter morning.

She and Nigel exchanged glances, and she smiled at him. Her one and only. They were finally safe.

The first thing Tiu did was to bring Annabelle and Nigel back to her village. Both of them stayed over at New Zealand for quite some time, recovering in both mind and body, for the ordeal at *Paradisus* had affected both.

London, UK

Annabelle stepped out of the car and winced as the light from the sun danced into her eyes. It felt like it had been years since she was last here, but it was only a couple of months at most. She stood by the stairs of her father's house and looked at the entire building, lost in thought. She thought of a time when things were so simple, and she had way less respect for her father's interests in Darwin. In retrospect, it was easy to see how much of her had changed since Hendrik's conversation with her father back at the university's auditorium had piqued her interest.

Suddenly, the door swung open, and Sarah's voice pulled Annabelle away from her thoughts.

"Are you going to keep standing there like a visitor? Or are you actually going to come in?"

Annabelle stared at her sister and smiled. "I was just wondering when one of you would show up."

Nothing had changed since she was last here. They entered the house and into the kitchen. Annabelle frowned.

"What's the matter?" Sarah asked.

"I don't know," Annabelle said. "I just thought some things would have changed around here, you know?"

Annabelle sensed Sarah's eyes on her, studying her. She felt different, so different from the woman who had flown in to watch her nephew's piano recital just six months ago. It was as if she wore a new layer of complexity, a calculated or guarded veneer that had not been there before. Though her eyes still sparkled with the same youthful energy, she felt an unspoken hardness beneath it now. She couldn't put her finger on it, but something profound had shifted inside her during her journey, and she wondered if Sarah could see that change too.

"So, are you here to tell us how it went?" Sarah asked.

"Yes, tell us how it went?" a new voice said.

Annabelle spun around; her brows, high up in her forehead. "Dad!"

She left the kitchen counter and walked into her father's embrace. He cackled excitedly, as he wrapped his arms around her. Annabelle stayed in the embrace for a few seconds longer. She inhaled deeply and stepped out. She had been without family for a long time, and she never really realised how much she missed them until now.

Professor Young narrowed his eyes and readjusted the glasses sitting on the bridge of his nose.

"You look different, Annabelle," he said.

"Oh good," Sarah exclaimed. "I'm glad I'm not the only one noticing that."

Annabelle laughed. "How different?"

"You've changed, but it suits you," Professor Young replied. "Different isn't always a bad thing."

"What about Charlie?" Annabelle asked and looked around. "The little bugger should have snuck up on me by now."

Sarah rolled her eyes. "While you're busy running around the globe, Charlie still has to go to school."

Annabelle chuckled. "I wouldn't be surprised if little Charlie wanted to be an explorer."

Professor Young laughed. "I'm not sure that's something we can take away from this family. He'd be a traveller at the least."

Sarah shook her head. 'Well, tell me. Did you find it? Darwin's island?"

Annabelle locked eyes with Sarah, her expression steady but tinged with a secret weight. "There is no island, Sarah. It was all an intricate ruse Darwin and Marten concocted, perhaps to amuse themselves or test their children's wits."

Sarah's face registered disbelief. "But the lengths Darwin went to in order to conceal this island's whereabouts... You're saying it's all for nothing? A joke? What about the clues, the map pieces, and the coordinates?"

Annabelle nodded, her resolve fortified by the lie she felt she must uphold to protect what should remain hidden. "We found the third piece, followed the coordinates, and they led us to an unremarkable patch of ocean. It turns out Darwin admitted as much in his final letter to Marten. We're just the latest in a line of fools who misinterpreted their elaborate game as the discovery quest of a lifetime."

Sarah scoffed in disappointment.

"I thought you had no interest in this thing?" Annabelle asked.

Sarah rolled her eyes. "I went on a heist for this," she said. "Does that answer your question?"

"Yeah," Annabelle laughed, holding her arms up in surrender. "Guilty as charged."

Sarah inhaled audibly. "I'm so glad you're back home anyway. It's nice to finally have you around. She checked her wristwatch. "Shoot. Charlie will be done from school within the hour. I should be there to bring him home."

"Alright, Sarah," Annabelle said. "Take care."

Professor Young had been watching Annabelle from under his glasses. The look on his face had been neutral the whole time. Now, he broke it with a smile.

"I'm so proud of you," he said, pulling her attention from the plate of muffins Sarah had served her before leaving to go pick Charlie. "You and Darwin have so much in common. You both understand the importance of protecting the island."

Annabelle's hand froze, dangling a piece of half-eaten muffin before her lips. She looked at her father, and then she dropped the cake.

"What do you mean?" she asked.

Professor Young chuckled. "Allow me to explain." He dug into his pocket and slipped out a brown piece of paper. "This, here—" he held the letter up "—was one of the last letters Darwin wrote to his children in his final days. He gave it to his son, Francis, who had kept it hidden from the public." Annabelle moved closer, unable to peel her eyes away from the letter.

MY DEAR CHILDREN,

AS MY OWN HEALTH IS DETERIORATING, I WISH TO SPEAK MY LAST THOUGHTS BEFORE MY MIND GOES. WHAT I SHARE WITH YOU SHOULD ONLY REMAIN WITHIN THIS FAMILY. I TRUST THAT YOU WILL RESPECT THAT.

DURING MY VOYAGE ON THE HMS BEAGLE, THE MEN AND I DISCOVERED A NEW LAND, PARADISUS. WORDS ALONE CANNOT BEGIN TO EXPRESS THE WONDERFULNESS OF THIS PLACE. THE LIFE GROWING THERE BELONGS TO A DIFFERENT WORLD. THIS ISLAND HOLDS UNUSUAL PROPERTIES THAT

I HAVE NEVER SEEN IN ANY PART OF THE GLOBE.

OVER THE PAST FEW YEARS, I HAVE LEFT CLUES FOR YOU TO FIND THIS PLACE. NOT FOR PLEASURE, BUT FOR HEALTH. THERE IS A LOCATION ON THIS ISLAND CALLED 'CATARACTA AETERNAM'. THE WATER THERE IS UNUSUAL. ITS STRANGE PROPERTIES HAVE INCREASED HEALING ABILITIES. OUR UNDERSTANDING OF SCIENCE IS STILL LIMITED, AND I CANNOT EXPLAIN HOW IT WORKS. FIND THIS PLACE AND USE IT WISELY, FOR THE BENEFIT OF YOUR OWN HEALTH. I MUST CAUTION, DO NOT CONSUME IT. ONLY USE IT SUPERFICIALLY. I HAVE MADE THE TERRIBLE MISTAKE IN DOING SO AND HAVE NEVER RECOVERED FROM IT SINCE.

PROTECT YOURSELVES. CERTAIN SPECIES ON THE ISLAND WILL ATTACK IF THEY FEEL THREATENED.

IF YOU WISH TO DISCOVER THIS PLACE, LOOK THROUGH MY COLLECTION OF NOTES. A 'MOON ART' WILL GET YOU STARTED.

YOUR LOVING FATHER,

CHARLES

Annabelle gave her father a shocked look. But there was way more than shock in those eyes. There was a boatload of accusation too. "You knew what he was hiding this whole time? You knew? You knew about the water and the island? Why didn't you say something?"

"I didn't say anything for two reasons. First, if you or anyone read about water that possessed healing properties like the one you experienced at the island, would you have believed me or him? You all would have thought that the father of evolution and modern biology had turned into a raving madman at the twilight of his days. There was already evidence of his losing memory. Such an extraordinary thing didn't exist. It could only be malady. That's why his son, Francis, kept it quiet. He passed it down to his children, who passed it down to theirs and so on. Many years ago, I was given the privilege to look after it by his great grandchildren. I vowed to keep it safe.

Secondly, I had the utmost faith in you that you'd find this place, and that when you did, you'd make the right decision."

"How were you so sure?" Annabelle asked. "The healing properties of the water were enticing. Too enticing. It would have been a great discovery to publish."

The Professor laughed. "You're my daughter, are you not? I know you. I can place a bet on the things you're capable of, and the things you're not. I also know that every fibre in you is good and wouldn't do a thing that wasn't supposed to be done. Besides, I needed a little confirmation myself. A Darwin faithful like me can also fall out of faith sometimes. Now, I know I can defend him with extra vigour. I won't be able to publish recent findings, of course. But there's just this extra bit of conviction that comes with knowing that all the stories you heard were true."

Annabelle nodded. "Yes. That's true enough. I met this woman, the leader of the Māori tribe en route to the island. She warned us, Nigel and I. But I didn't listen. I wanted to get there at all costs. I saw the outcome of her warning much later when I almost lost everything."

Professor Young shrugged. "Sometimes, it's important to dip your hand into the fire to truly learn. It may burn hotter, or give you a nasty scar, but it's your experience, and nothing pays better than that."

Annabelle smiled. "Look at you, speaking like a true hermit."

Her father laughed. "I'm old enough to be one, don't you think?"

Annabelle chuckled. "Throw wise enough into the mix."

"So, what are your plans now?" he asked after a while.

Annabelle stared at him, and then she smiled. He caught the

glint in her eyes. There was something there – something she wasn't telling him. But he knew, nonetheless.

"How about that Nigel?" he asked. "He's a good one. The kind of person you keep. Is he among these plans you have but aren't telling me about?"

The smile on Annabelle's face widened, and she burst into laughter.

Australia, Sydney.

Annabelle looked up from the book she was reading, the moment she heard the apartment door close. Nigel was back home. He walked into the living room with brown rucksack over his back and his jacket draped over his right arm.

"Belle, I'm home," he said in a sing song tone.

Annabelle smiled, uncrossed her legs, and rose to meet him.

"How was work at the conservation?" she asked, pulling him closer by the collar, and planting a quick kiss on his lips.

"It was great, as usual," he said.

"Like really great, or the I'll-settle-for-this kind of great."

"The latter, of course." He laughed.

"You're getting too old for the kind of things you used to do."

"Belle, I'm only a year older."

She pulled him in for another kiss.

"Yeah, I know," she said.

"And how's your research paper coming along?" he asked.

She turned and pointed at the small round table littered with books and paper. "You can see it for yourself. But I'm making tremendous progress anyways."

"That's the kind of thing I love to hear."

Nigel dropped his rucksack on the couch, and draped his jacket over the backrest, then he grabbed Annabelle gently from the back and pulled her close until her back pressed into his chest.

He planted kisses on her neck. Annabelle leaned back and rested her head on his shoulder.

"I've got exciting news, Belle," he said. "But you'd need to sit down for this."

Annabelle twisted her head a bit so she could see him. "What's that?"

"Sit."

"Urgh," she groaned.

Nigel laughed. He released her from his grip and sat on the couch next to her.

"Well?" She looked at him impatiently. "What's the news?"

Nigel couldn't restrain his smile. "It looks like you're going to be the newest member of The Sanctuary."

Annabelle gasped. "No way!" Her eyes were wide. "What! That's not possible. I've had about three job applications get turned down. You know how hard it is to get a job there?"

Nigel laughed. Then he shrugged. "Well, it's a bit easy when you have someone on the inside. An old friend of mine, Father Fernandes has some connections. I told him about you. He made a few phone calls, and he was able to come up with something. Belle, you've got a job with The Sanctuary!"

He took his jacket from the backrest and dug out a letter from one of the pockets. "This—" he handed the letter over to her "—is your letter of acceptance."

Annabelle squealed with delight and wrapped Nigel in a tight hug.

Nigel chuckled. "Okay. I think you're squeezing too tight."

She pulled away from the hug and kissed him. Deeply.

"I don't even know where to begin," she said as she stared at the letter in her hand. Her face shone like the moon on a dark night. "Do I need to research on something beforehand? Do I—"

"Okay," Nigel cut her off, laughing. "Take it easy. It's nothing you haven't done or seen before. You'll enjoy it. Trust me. Besides, the wildlife there wouldn't be throwing any spears at you."

Both of them burst into a fresh spell of laughter.

Then Annabelle stared into Nigel's eyes. "I've lost you a couple of times, Nigel," she said. "The last time was most fearful because I thought I lost you forever. But gaining you back again, was one of the best things that ever happened to me. You're one of the best things that ever happened to me. I love you."

Nigel held her closer and smiled.

"I love you too, Belle."